Interest level: Grades 4-8
AR points: 11.0
ATOS Book level: 5.6

The CLASSY Crooks CLUB

The CLASSY Crooks CLUB

Alison Cherry

Aladdin

NEW YORK · LONDON · TORONTO · SYDNEY · NEW DELHI

This book is a work of fiction. Any references to historical events, real people, or real places are used fictitiously. Other names, characters, places, and events are products of the author's imagination, and any resemblance to actual events or places or persons, living or dead, is entirely coincidental.

ALADDIN

An imprint of Simon & Schuster Children's Publishing Division
1230 Avenue of the Americas, New York, New York 10020
First Aladdin hardcover edition March 2016

For information about special discounts for bulk purchases, please contact Simon & Schuster Special Sales at 1-866-506-1949 or business@simonandschuster.com.
The Simon & Schuster Speakers Bureau can bring authors to your live event. For more information or to book an event contact the Simon & Schuster Speakers Bureau at 1-866-248-3049 or visit our website at www.simonspeakers.com.
Jacket designed by Karin Paprocki
Interior designed by Hilary Zarycky
The text of this book was set in Bembo.
Manufactured in the United States of America 0216 FFG
2 4 6 8 10 9 7 5 3 1
Library of Congress Cataloging-in-Publication Data
Cherry, Alison.
The classy crooks club / by Alison Cherry.—First Aladdin hardcover edition.
pages cm
Summary: "Twelve-year-old AJ is dreading spending the summer with her uber-strict grandmother—that is, until she's recruited to join Grandma Jo's madcap band of thieves"—Provided by publisher.
ISBN 978-1-4814-4637-2 (hc)—ISBN 978-1-4814-4639-6 (ebook)
[1. Grandmothers—Fiction. 2. Old age—Fiction
3. Robbers and outlaws—Fiction.] I. Title.
PZ7.C41987Cl 2016
[Fic]—dc23
2015029378

To all the ladies who know you're only as old as you act

The
CLASSY
Crooks
CLUB

1

Every single piece of furniture in my grand-mother's house has a name with too many syl-lables.

At home we have chairs. We have a couch. We have tables. But right now my grandmother is pointing at this hulking wooden thing in the corner of one of her guest bedrooms—my bedroom, for the next month—and calling it a "mission chifforobe." It looks like what might happen if a dresser and a closet had a really ugly baby. "I trust you'll be very careful with this chifforobe while you're here," Grandma Jo says, like it's some fragile, spin-dly thing I could possibly break by accident. "It was once owned by Buckminster Fuller, as was that ottoman."

My dad puts my suitcases down next to the bed, which is big enough for five of me and so high up I might need a stepladder, and makes a sound like he finds this piece of trivia interesting. I, for one, have no idea who Buckminster Fuller is supposed to be or why I should care that his butt once touched some padded stool.

All I know for sure is that I really, really want to go home.

I've been at Grandma Jo's house for all of five minutes, and I already miss my low, squishy single bed with the pillow top and my red duvet with the chocolate stain in the corner. I miss my giant corkboard covered in photos of me with Maddie and Amy and my soccer team and my parents and Ben. More than anything, I miss Snickers, but my dad's friend Martin gets to keep him for the summer because Grandma Jo "can't abide having a dog in the house." She's probably worried he'd provide too much joy or something. Grandma Jo's not big on joy.

"Annemarie," my grandmother says, "are you even listening to me?"

I realize I've kind of forgotten to pay attention for the last couple seconds, so I try to distract her by changing the subject. "You can call me AJ, Grandma Jo," I say. "Everyone else in the world does." I know it won't make a difference—I tell her this every single Thanksgiving and Christmas and Easter—but it's still worth a try.

Grandma Jo stares at me from behind her half-glasses in that squinty way she always does when she's offended by something, and her eyes almost disappear into the nests of wrinkles around them. There's something about that look that always makes me feel like my entire body is being pricked with pins. "Certainly not," she says, like I've suggested she dye her hair neon green. "Your parents gave you a perfectly lovely name, and you will use it while you're under my roof. Respectable young ladies do not have nicknames like AJ."

I almost point out what a double standard that is— we call her "Grandma Jo" because Ben couldn't say "Josephine" when he was little—but it doesn't seem worth it. Grandma Jo has always been way more tolerant of Ben than she is of me. Then again, he has it a lot easier, since she doesn't expect *him* to be a respectable young lady.

"Put down your things," my grandmother orders. I'm still holding my backpack and my skateboard, and I lay them down on the floor next to my suitcases. I immediately wish I could pick them back up. In this creepy old house it was nice to be holding on to something familiar.

Grandma Jo looks down at my stuff and wrinkles her nose. "Put that infernal plank in the closet," she says, pointing at my skateboard with a gnarled finger decked out in a giant diamond ring. "You're going to step on it in the dark and break your neck."

That infernal plank? What does that even *mean?* I shoot my dad a look like, *Seriously?* But he shrugs and shoots me one back like, *Please just do what she says.* I'm pretty sure Grandma Jo scares him even more than she scares me, even though she's his mom.

I let out a really obvious sigh, but I pick up the skateboard and take it into the empty closet, which smells overwhelmingly of dust and old ladies and something disgustingly chemical. Before I set the skateboard down, I run my fingers over the collage of stickers on the bottom—Ben put them there when it used to be his. There's an exploding fireball decal on one side and that blue woman from *Halo* on the other, and the middle is covered with stickers from bands he likes: the Flash Mob Llamas, the Accidental Umlauts, Gazpacho Trifecta. I've never even heard any of their music, but I like the way the names sound.

God, I wish Ben were here right now. He's great at charming Grandma Jo.

My grandmother gives a curt, satisfied nod once the skateboard is out of sight, and her chin dips down into the lace collar of her high-necked black dress, which looks like it came straight out of a museum. I've never seen her in anything else, and I wonder if she has a whole closet full of identical gowns or if she wears the same one every day.

"Now we'll go down to the parlor, Annemarie, and I will acquaint you with the daily household schedule," she says. "I'll have the cook prepare us some tea."

I hate the bitter "leaves and dirt" taste of tea. I hate that my grandmother refers to the cook like she doesn't even have a real name. (She does, and it's Debbie—I asked.) I hate that I have to go sit in the *parlor* when I could be at home in the family room, watching TV with Snickers curled up on my feet. I hate everything about this place, and I really, *really* hate that Mom and Dad are leaving me here for four entire weeks.

Dad must see the look on my face, 'cause he says, "Go ahead and get that tea started, Mother. We'll be right behind you."

"Don't be long," Grandma Jo says. Then she finally leaves, her crunchy skirts rustling behind her and her cane thumping on the floor. It takes her a long time to make her way down the stairs; she fractured her foot last week, and it's all Velcroed up in one of those puffy boot things.

On the other foot she's wearing a high, lace-up leather shoe like the ones I imagine people wore before there was running water. When I hear her moving across the entryway downstairs—*clomp-click-rustle, clomp-click-rustle*—I take what feels like my first full breath in ten minutes.

I turn to my dad. "I can't stay here with her," I whisper. "*Please* don't make me."

Dad puts an arm around me and squeezes. For a second I think he's going to agree that I can't possibly be expected to live in this weird, echoey tomb of a house where I'm not even allowed to leave my skateboard out in my *own room*. But then he says, "It's only four weeks, kiddo."

"How am I supposed to survive four entire weeks with someone who hates me?"

"AJ, that's ridiculous. Grandma Jo doesn't hate you. She's a stern person, but deep down she cares about you very much."

From what I can tell by looking at the family photo albums, Grandma Jo did use to care about me when I was really little. There are all these pictures of her holding me and setting up tea parties for me and dressing me in frilly pink outfits before I was old enough to do anything about it. My dad is her only kid, and since Ben is a boy, I was her first opportunity to do girly stuff. But by the time I was in preschool, I was done with all that and had moved on to fire trucks and Legos and soccer balls.

Grandma Jo wasn't interested in having *that* kind of granddaughter, so she kept buying dolls and pink tutus for the girly girl she wanted me to be. My parents always made me invite her to my big soccer games, but she never showed up, even though she came to all Ben's Scholastic Bowl championships. On my twelfth birthday this past February, she sent me an etiquette book called *Sister Sadie's Secrets to Being Sweet, Seemly, and Self-Sufficient.* Maddie and I spent about an hour howling over how ridiculous it was before I stuffed it in the back of my closet under a pile of old cleats. Every time Grandma Jo sees the real me with my untied sneakers and scabby knees and messy ponytail, it's like she's disappointed all over again.

"She thinks I'm a defective girl," I say.

"Sweetheart, there's absolutely nothing defective about you," my dad says. He seems sad that I'd even think it.

"*I* know that, but *she* doesn't. Plus, this house freaks me out. How am I supposed to sleep with *that* on the wall?" I gesture to the huge oil painting of a parrot hanging in an ornate gold frame across from my bed. It's staring straight at me with its chest all puffed up, like it's running for president or something. "You know how much I hate birds."

"Well, that's something we can fix, at least." My dad hefts the painting off the wall, grunting a little with the effort. I half expect an alarm to go off, like it would in a museum, but everything's quiet as he flips it around and leans it against the wall. "There," he says. "Better?"

"I guess." I sigh. "I don't get why I can't go to California and stay with Ben. He actually wants me around."

"AJ, we've talked about this. I'm not leaving you in an apartment with five nineteen-year-old boys. They'd never do your laundry, and they'd feed you nothing but Cheetos."

"I like Cheetos, and I don't care about laundry!"

"I know. But if we sent you out there, you'd have to quit soccer and you'd never see your friends. You don't want that, do you?"

"No," I grumble.

"If you feel homesick, give Ben a call. I'm sure he'll be happy to hear from you, just like always."

My shoulders slump. This is really happening, and I'm not going to be able to talk him out of it. I twist the bracelet Maddie made me around and around my wrist, something I always do when I'm worried. Mom says it's going to break if I don't stop.

"I wish I could at least have Snickers," I say quietly.

"I know, kiddo, and I'm sorry about that. But Martin will take good care of him. He even promised to take him camping. You know how much Snickers will love that."

I picture my little Border collie dashing around in the woods, barking up a storm as he chases squirrels. Dad's right; he *will* love that. But that doesn't mean I'll miss his weight on the end of my bed any less, or the way he licks my toes in the morning when I don't want to get up.

"It'll be nice for Grandma Jo to have some help around here," Dad continues. "This is a very big house for one old lady all by herself, especially one with an injured foot."

I'm about to point out that she's definitely rich enough to hire people to help her, but I suddenly hear a really strange noise. It's far away, but it kind of sounds like someone screaming. "Do you hear that?" I ask.

"What?"

"That screeching sound. Wait. Is this house *haunted*?"

Dad laughs. "Of course not. It's a very old house; sometimes it settles and makes weird noises. It was probably just the pipes banging or something."

It didn't sound anything like pipes banging, but before I can argue, Mom comes in, carrying my last suitcase and my mesh bag of soccer balls. "I think this is the last of it," she says, plunking them down next to the rest of my stuff. Her bright pink shirt looks totally out of place in this room, where everything is beige and gold and printed with old-lady upholstery patterns. "Give me a hug, sweetheart. I need enough AJ love to last me four weeks."

I hug her tight and breathe in her citrusy smell. "I wish I could come with you guys," I say, even though I know that's ridiculous. Mom and Dad are headed to the Amazon rain forest to do research on malaria. They won't even have access to phones. But if I can't have my normal life, I'd much rather be going on an adventure than sitting here waiting.

Mom rubs my back in that familiar pattern she always does when she's trying to comfort me. "You might get eaten by an anaconda," she says. "We can't risk it."

"I could totally handle an anaconda." When my parents got home from one of their rain forest training sessions at the hospital, Dad taught Maddie and me exactly what you're supposed to do in case of a snake attack. If you thrash around, it'll squeeze you to death, so you're supposed to grip your machete really tightly, lie down on the ground with your hands by your sides, and let the snake think you're dead. Then it'll start swallowing you from the feet up, and if you can believe this, you're supposed to *lie there and let it eat you* for a while. By the time it gets up to your waist, your machete hand will be all the way inside its body . . . and then *bam*, you slash your arm up really quickly and cut it right open. Totally disgusting in the most awesome way possible.

Honestly, a giant snake would probably be easier to deal with than Grandma Jo. At least it wouldn't complain about my skateboard or make me drink tea.

"We'll take you to the Amazon when you're older, and you can wrestle all the snakes you want." My mom hugs me one more time. "We'll miss you so much, but four weeks will be over before you know it. You'll hardly notice we're gone."

I'm pretty sure I'll spend the entire time counting down the minutes until I can go home, but nothing's going to make my parents change their minds, so I might as well be brave about it. "I'm sure it'll be fine," I say.

Dad heads downstairs to make sure Grandma Jo has their emergency contact information. Mom turns to follow him, but then she says, "Oh, one more thing. I almost forgot."

She reaches into her purse and pulls out Hector, the beaten-up stuffed armadillo I've had since I was born.

Even though I left him at home on purpose—what kind of twelve-year-old still needs a stuffed animal to sleep?—I'm embarrassingly glad to see him. I make myself roll my eyes anyway. "*Mom!* I would've been fine without him!"

"Of course you would," she says, "but I thought it wouldn't hurt to have him around, just in case. If you don't want him on the bed, he can guard your suitcases in the closet."

"Then he'll smell like old ladies. I guess I'll leave him out." I arrange Hector in the center of my pillow, and the bed suddenly *does* look a little homier. He's not as good as Snickers, but it's still a pretty big improvement.

Mom smiles like she knows what I'm thinking. "Good plan," she says. "We can't have him reeking of mothballs."

She heads for the stairs, and as soon as she's out of the room, I hear that weird shrieking sound again, a little more distant this time. It's definitely not *the house settling* or whatever my dad said, and it sounds like it's coming from the vent near the floorboards. I crouch down and press my ear to the grate, and the noise gets a little louder. It almost sounds like garbled words, but I can't make them out. After a few seconds it breaks off as suddenly as it started. The room is pretty warm, but goose bumps spring up on my arms anyway.

"AJ, are you coming?" my mom's voice calls from downstairs.

"Be right there," I call back. I tell myself the noise was probably coming from outside, or maybe from a TV downstairs. My dad would know if this place was haunted—he grew up here, after all. But I can't shake the feeling that something isn't quite right in this house.

I snatch Hector off the bed, bury my nose in his nubby fur, and give him a quick, tight squeeze for reassurance. Nobody sees me, so I figure it doesn't count.

2

I've always loved soccer, but I don't think I've ever been so excited to go to practice as I am today. Honestly, I think I'd be excited if I had a dentist appointment. I'd take any excuse to get out of my grandmother's house.

After my parents leave for the airport, Grandma Jo spends the rest of the morning drinking tiny cups of tea with her pinkie extended, patting her tight gray bun to make sure no unladylike wips have come free, and telling me about the "household staff" and the "household schedule" and the "household rules." (Sometimes when you say a word over and over and over, it totally stops making sense, and that's what happens to me with the word "household.") I sit there on the "chaise longue," which looks like a couch with half the back melted off, and pretend to sip from my teacup, trying to figure out how I'm going to survive the next month. And I have a lot of time to think about it—there are so many things that aren't allowed in Grandma Jo's house that I feel like it would be faster for her to tell me what I *can* do.

There's no running inside, no walking on the front lawn, and no poking around in the flower beds. I'm not allowed to shout, make long-distance calls, or bother the staff. (In addition to the chef, my grandmother has a gardener, who she calls "the boy," and a cleaning lady who comes a couple times a week, who she calls "the maid." Until her foot heals, she also has a driver, who gets to go by "Stanley" for some reason.) I can't use my cell phone at the table or in the parlor or basically anywhere Grandma Jo can see me. There's no computer in the house, and the only TV is in her bedroom, so I'm not allowed to watch it or use it to play video games. I'm not allowed to pick up the knickknacks in the living room or open the china cabinet—as if I'd actually want to. The hallway at the back of the house—which leads to my grandmother's study, the laundry room, and the storage room—is off-limits. I have to turn my lights off at 9:30 on the dot. Luckily, I brought my flashlight from last summer's camping trip, so at least I can read comic books under the covers.

The worst part is that I'm not allowed to have friends over. I hope Maddie's prepared for me to spend the rest of the summer at her house, because I'll probably die of boredom here.

When Grandma Jo is done listing all the things that aren't allowed, she tops it off by saying she'll be giving me *etiquette lessons* for two hours every day after soccer practice. I swear I'd rather shovel horse poop for two hours every day. I wonder if my parents knew this was what my grandmother had planned for me when she agreed to let me stay. I consider trying to call them before they get on their plane, but it's not like they can do anything about it now.

My summer soccer team practices at my middle school, which is about four blocks from my house. Normally, I'd walk there, swinging by Maddie's house to pick her up on the way, but Grandma Jo's house is half an hour from mine. So the second the little silver clock on the mantel chimes twelve fifteen, I cut her off by clearing my throat as politely as I can. "It's almost time for soccer, Grandma Jo," I tell her. "I better get my uniform on." I know how much she hates being interrupted, but she also hates it when people are late, so I'm hoping it'll cancel out.

Grandma Jo sighs heavily and shakes her head, and for a

second I'm terrified she's going to tell me I'm not allowed to go to soccer anymore. But then she says, "Stanley will take you in the town car. Meet him in the garage when you're dressed."

I dash up to my room before she can change her mind.

The whole chauffeur thing shouldn't really surprise me—it's not like I thought Grandma Jo was going to drive me herself with a broken foot—but I'm still a little weirded out by the thought of some guy I don't even know taking me to soccer. Is he going to be wearing a uniform? What the heck is a town car? Is that the normal black car Grandma Jo drives when she comes to our house for holidays, or is it like a limousine? I can't show up for soccer in a *limousine*.

My uniform is in one suitcase, and my cleats and shin guards are at the bottom of another, so by the time I'm done getting ready, it looks like my luggage threw up all over the floor. In case Grandma Jo checks my room, I shove everything under the bed and pull down the dust ruffle. There's not a single dust bunny under there to keep my stuff company.

I fill up my water bottle, stuff my cleats into my duffel, and pull my hair into a ponytail as I dash down the stairs. "Bye, Grandma Jo," I call as I slip past the parlor.

"No running in the house, Annemarie," she calls back. "And no *shouting!*"

The door to the garage is off the kitchen, and I throw it open, then jump back with a little squeak—there's a guy in a button-down shirt and dark jeans standing about two feet from me. But this can't possibly be Stanley. Guys named Stanley are my dad's age and have beer bellies and mustaches. This guy looks like he could've walked right off one of the movie posters my friend Amy has plastered all over her room. I imagine Grandma Jo visiting all the gyms in the area and picking out the cutest guy she could find to drive her around.

"Miss Annemarie?" he says.

"It's not—I mean—yeah, but—it's AJ," I stammer, and I feel my cheeks go pink. Oh my God, I have *got* to pull myself together.

Stanley smiles. "Pleasure to meet you, Miss AJ," he says. "I'm Stanley." He reaches for my hand, and for a second I'm worried he might kiss it or something, but he just gives it a firm shake. I hope my palm doesn't feel too sweaty.

"Fenton's Foxes, huh?" he says, nodding at the picture of the fox on the front of my orange and white soccer uniform.

"Uh-huh," I say, oh-so-articulately. When he seems to be waiting for more, I say, "Um, Fenton's is the name of this ice cream parlor near my house? They sponsor us, and they give us free sundaes after our games, so . . . yeah."

"Sweet deal," Stanley says. "When I was your age, my summer soccer league was sponsored by an auto repair shop."

"What'd they give you to eat after your games? Tires?"

For a second I'm mortified by my terrible joke, but then Stanley bursts out laughing. No way; he actually thinks I'm *funny*! "Rubber isn't quite as delicious as mint chocolate chip, as it turns out," he says.

"That's my favorite ice cream too," I tell him, and suddenly I'm not quite as nervous anymore. For a second I imagine inviting Stanley to share a Fenton's grasshopper sundae with me when he comes to pick me up after a game. Brianna from my team would *die*—she's always bragging about the eighth graders she dates. Maddie and I are pretty sure she makes it all up, though. Who would go on dates with someone as snotty as her?

"Ready to go?" Stanley asks. When I nod, he goes around and opens the car door for me like I'm one of those respectable ladies Grandma Jo is always going on about. The car is just the normal one I've seen her drive before, and a tiny little part of me is actually disappointed.

I slide into the passenger's seat and tuck my soccer bag under my feet, and Stanley shuts the door gently behind me. On the other side of the garage is a big black van with tinted windows, the kind of thing you might drive if you wanted to kidnap someone. I wonder what use my grandmother could possibly have for a car like that.

"So, how did you end up working for Grandma Jo?" I ask when Stanley gets in beside me.

"She's friends with my grandmother," Stanley explains. "I was looking to make some extra money, so when Mrs. Johansen hurt her foot, my grandma recommended that she hire me for a little while."

"Huh," I say. I never really considered that my grandmother might have friends. "Is your grandma, um, a lot like mine?" I mean prim and proper and stuck-up, but I'm afraid I might offend Stanley if I come out and say that.

He laughs. "Not really. She's a lot more eccentric. I'm sure you'll meet her, so you can judge for yourself."

I'm afraid Stanley and I are going to run out of things to say really quickly, but we get into a pretty lively discussion about pro soccer, and there's not one single awkward silence. Before I know it, we're pulling up to Benedict Middle School, right behind the blue minivan that belongs to Amy's family. Amy's butt is sticking out of the backseat as she rummages around, looking for something on the floor. I'm about to open my door when Stanley hops out of the car and opens it for me. Amy straightens up in time to catch him standing at attention like a soldier while I gather up my stuff, and her mouth drops open.

"Have a good practice, Miss AJ," Stanley says. "I'll see you at four." He's smiling like maybe it was more fun driving a twelve-year-old kid to practice than he expected, and I smile back.

"See you," I say. "Thanks for the ride."

Maddie comes around the corner as Stanley shuts the door behind me, and her eyes get huge, just like Amy's. The second he pulls away in the car, they both pounce on me. "Who was *that*?" Amy breathes without even saying hello. Her super curly hair is poking out in all directions from the humidity and trying to escape from her ponytail.

"That's Stanley," I say. "Remember how I told you I'm staying with my grandma this month? She broke her foot last week, and she hired that guy to drive her around until it heals."

"Whoa," Maddie says. "Like a chauffeur? *That's* an unexpected perk."

"He's foxy," Amy says, pointing to the fox on her uniform. Maddie groans and rolls her eyes, and all three of us crack up. When Maddie laughs, I notice she has new turquoise rubber bands on her braces.

"He's really nice," I tell them. "We talked about soccer the whole way here. He plays too."

"What position?" Maddie asks, suddenly a lot more interested. She doesn't care about boys at all, but she really cares about soccer. When I tell her he's a center forward, she nods, impressed.

As we walk through the gate and onto the field, I notice a couple of huge crows hanging out a few yards ahead of us. I divert our path so we make a wide arc around them, and Maddie automatically moves to my other side so she's between them and me. She really gets how much I hate birds, since she was with me when I had my Bird Incident in kindergarten. We were at the duck pond near our houses with my mom and Ben, and I spotted this giant white swan paddling around with all the ducks, exactly like the one in a picture book I loved. I ran over, all excited to feed it a piece of bread, but the swan chomped down on my fingers so hard that two of them broke. I started screaming, obviously, and I guess the swan thought I was going to fight back, because it reared up, hissed in my face, and karate-chopped me right in the stomach with its wing. My mom managed to chase it away before it could do any more damage, but it was still scary enough that I never went near a bird again. Luckily, Maddie ran away before it could get her, too.

"So, how are things going at your grandma's house?" Maddie asks as we plunk our stuff down near another group of girls from our team. "Is it as awful as you expected?"

"Not with *Staaaaan-leeeeey* around, it isn't," Amy says, giggling and batting her eyelashes. She watches a lot of sappy romantic movies.

"Except for him, it's pretty awful. The house is super creepy, and everything smells like old ladies, and Grandma Jo won't let me watch TV or play video games or have you guys over."

"Man, that's the worst," Maddie says. "You know you can come over whenever you want, right? My parents never care if you stay for meals or sleep over. They love you."

"I know," I say, and it feels really nice to hear that I'm wanted somewhere. "Thanks. I don't know if my grandma will even let me go to your house, though. She's making me do *etiquette training* every day after soccer."

Maddie looks horrified. "Really? Like that book she got you?"

"I think so, yeah."

"Isn't that, like, cruel and unusual punishment or something?"

"What even *is* etiquette training?" Amy asks.

"I don't know. Probably, like, learning to ballroom dance and do housework and sew."

"Sounds like a sneaky way of getting you to do chores for her," Amy says. "What if she makes you do her laundry and stuff? Oh my God, what if she makes you fold her old-lady underwear?"

I'm in the middle of taking a swig from my water bottle, and I spit my water all over the grass when she says that. "That is *so disgusting*." I gasp, and Maddie and Amy both double over laughing.

I'm just getting my breath back when snotty Brianna comes striding through the gate. When she tucks her hair behind her ears, I see that she's wearing huge diamond earrings to practice again, and I roll my eyes. Seriously, can't she go five seconds without reminding everyone how rich she is? She waves to her best friends, Sabrina and Elena—we call them the Bananas, since you can spell that word by shoving pieces of their names together—and then, weirdly enough, she heads straight toward us.

"Hey, Maddie," she says, much louder than necessary. "I've got something for you."

I don't think Brianna's ever said a single nice thing to any of us, and the smirky smile on her face makes my heart speed up. Elena's already giggling at whatever's about to happen, and Sabrina looks a little worried—she's actually pretty nice if you can get her on her own. Brianna looks both ways to make sure everyone on the team is watching, and then she unzips her duffel bag and pulls out a handful of fabric. I can't tell what she's holding at first, but then I see a strap and a zipper, and I realize it's a heap of dresses. Even though she has them all crammed in her bag like that, they're probably crazy expensive.

"I was cleaning out my closet yesterday, and I found all these old dresses I've already worn a couple times," she says to Maddie. "They're so out of style I was about to donate them to Goodwill, but then I realized I could give them straight to you instead. I figure that's where your family shops these days, since your mom got fired."

A ripple of whispers goes through the soccer team, and Maddie's face turns the reddest I've ever seen it. "My mom did not get *fired*," she snaps.

"Oh, does it make you feel better to say 'laid off'?" Brianna says, making air quotes with her fingers. "It's the same thing in the end, you know. No job, no money, no nice stuff."

"It's not the same at *all*," Maddie says.

Brianna shakes out one of the dresses and holds it up against her body. It's purple and covered in sparkles, totally the opposite of Maddie's style. "You should really take these. I mean, I know they're not new, but they're a lot closer than anything else your mom can buy you now. At least you'll *know* who wore them before you."

"Leave me alone, Brianna. I don't want your stupid castoffs." Maddie's trying to sound strong, but her voice is trembling a little.

"So touchy," Brianna says. "Well, I tried. If you want to look tacky, that's on you."

Coach Adrian strides onto the field with a big bag of soccer balls, and he claps a bunch of times to get our attention. "What is this, a fashion show?" he says. "Put the dresses away and get ready to work. Five laps around the field."

"I was just trying to be *charitable*," Brianna says. She drops the dresses on the ground as if she wants to prove how little they matter to her and takes off running, her long hair swishing back and forth. She always wears it down at practice even though the rest of us pull ours back; she must think it looks cool when it whips around in the wind. Her minions fall into formation behind her. Sabrina looks back over her shoulder for a second as though she wants to apologize, but Brianna grabs her arm and pulls her forward.

Amy starts fiddling with her shoelaces. "You guys go ahead," she says. "I think I've got something in my shoe. I'll catch up with you." It's obvious she's avoiding running with us because she doesn't know what to say to Maddie. I don't really know what to say either, but I take off running next to her anyway. When you've been best friends with someone your whole life, you can't avoid them just because you're uncomfortable.

Maddie and I run in silence for about ten seconds, and then she says, "I *hate* Brianna."

"Of course you do," I say. "She's literally the worst person in the entire world. Except for, like, Hitler."

"Hitler's dead."

"That's true. I guess she's the actual worst."

"How did she even know about my mom? I barely told anyone. You didn't say anything, did you?"

"Of *course* not. I'd never do that. She probably has spies. Evil people always have evil henchmen."

"What is her problem with me?" Maddie says. "I never did anything to her. And it's not like we can't afford *clothes*. My dad still has a job. We just have to, like, cut back a little."

"I know," I say. "You don't have to explain it to me. Don't let her get to you, okay? You know how much she loves reminding people she has it better than everyone else."

Maddie glances over at me. "Not better than you."

"What are you talking about? We're not rich at all."

"Yeah, but your grandmother is. I know it's only for this month, but right now you have stuff even Brianna doesn't have, like a cute chauffeur. You should totally rub it in her face while you can."

I'm not usually a show-offy person, but Maddie's right—someone has to put Brianna in her place, and for the first time, I might actually be able to do that. Brianna has terrorized practically all of us at one time or another. In fourth grade, she told the whole class that my cleats were so smelly they made our coach puke when he accidentally got a whiff of them. Last year she made fun of Amy's new haircut so viciously that she cried in social studies. At the soccer barbecue last month, she told everyone how sorry she felt for our goalie, Chloe Savitsky, because she's adopted and doesn't have "real parents." She's a total menace, so if I have something I can use against her, it's pretty much my responsibility to take advantage of it.

"You're right," I say. "That's a great idea. I'm totally in." When Maddie gives me a weak smile, I know I've made the right choice. Nobody gets to make my friends feel like crap.

My first opportunity for revenge falls right into my lap

at the end of practice. We're all changing out of our cleats and gathering our stuff when I hear Sabrina say, "Hey, check out the cutie by the black car."

We all look up, and there's Stanley, standing by the town car. "Whoa," Brianna says. "Who *is* that?"

Right on cue he sees me looking and waves, and I wave back. "That's Stanley," I say, super casually. "He's my grandmother's driver; I'm staying with her right now. He's not bad, right?"

"Oh my gosh," Sabrina gushes. "He drives you around every day? You are so ridiculously lucky."

"I know, right?" I say. "He's *really* nice, too. So funny and smart and easy to talk to. We get along *so* well."

"Sabrina, are you coming out on the yacht with us on Sunday?" Brianna interrupts, obviously trying to draw her friend's attention back to herself. "If you want to go, you need to meet us at the dock at nine."

"Yeah, sure," Sabrina says, but she turns right back to me. "So, is he in high school or college?"

"College," I say. "He's nineteen."

"Wow," Sabrina says. "Doesn't hanging out with him make you super nervous? I'd have no idea what to say."

I give her a breezy shrug. "Not really. My brother's the same age, so I grew up talking to older boys. I'm sure it would be no big deal for you either, Brianna. You must be used to having long conversations with older guys, since you've dated all those *eighth graders*." Somewhere behind me I hear Amy giggle, and when I glance over at Maddie, she's smiling.

"Of course I am," Brianna snaps, but her cheeks are getting a little pinker. Stanley is so far from an eighth grader it's like they're not even the same species, and she knows it. She swallows hard, and when she speaks again, she sounds like her snotty old self. "It's too bad he doesn't have a cooler car—that town car is a serious snoozefest. I bet Stanley would have a *great* time driving one of my dad's Jags. Or maybe the Mustang."

"I mean, he always seems like he's having a pretty good time when he's driving me around," I say. "But maybe he just enjoys the company."

"Whatever," Brianna says. "I have to go." She gets up and slings her bag over her shoulder.

"Me too," I say. "Shouldn't keep Stanley waiting."

Maddie mouths *Nice* and gives me a sneaky thumbs-up, and I feel better than I have all day. As I gather the rest of my stuff, I make a promise to myself: If I have to spend a month living in my grandmother's stuffy house, I am *not* going to let it go to waste.

3

Stanley opens the car door for me, just like he did earlier. As I get in, I see Brianna glancing back at us as she walks toward a fancy red sports car. She's so busy staring, she almost crashes into a lamppost, and I snort out a laugh. It's not very ladylike, but I'm pretty sure Stanley doesn't care about stuff like that, unlike Grandma Jo.

"Friend of yours?" he asks as he slides into the driver's seat.

"Brianna? Ugh, no. She's the worst."

"You need me to take her down?"

Stanley's obviously kidding, but the image of him kicking Brianna's butt is kind of awesome anyway. "Don't worry, I can handle her," I say.

"I'm sure you can. Toughness obviously runs in your family."

For a second I wonder how Stanley knows anything about my parents and Ben, but then I realize he's talking about Grandma Jo. "What's it like driving my grandmother around all the time?" I ask. "Is it terrible?"

"No, not at all. She's not exactly warm and fuzzy, but she seems like a decent person. She does a lot of good work."

"Really?" I ask. "She *works*?"

"I mean, she doesn't have a day job, but she does a lot of charity stuff. She was even honored by this animal rescue league a couple months ago. My grandma went with her to the awards gala." It's hard to imagine Grandma Jo caring about rescuing animals, considering she won't even let me bring my well-trained dog into her house.

Stanley asks how soccer practice went, and we talk drills and strategy the rest of the way home. I'm feeling pretty happy and relaxed by the time we pull into the garage, but then I remember it's time for my etiquette lesson, and my stomach balls back up into a knot. Why is it impossible to appreciate feeling calm until you're suddenly not?

"Same place, same time tomorrow?" Stanley asks. He holds up his hand for a high five.

"Yup," I say, and I slap his palm. At least I've got one ally for the next four weeks.

The house is eerily quiet. I wonder if I can slip up to

my room unnoticed and avoid Grandma Jo, but it's not like I could hide from her for a very long in her own home. It's probably better to get whatever horrible thing she has planned for me over with. If I cooperate, maybe she'll let me go out and explore the neighborhood later.

I'm about to go look for her, but then I hear a muffled shriek from somewhere deep inside the house, and I freeze. It's that same noise I heard through the vents earlier, and now I'm positive I wasn't imagining things. I creep toward the sound, which seems to be coming from the direction of the forbidden hallway—maybe there's another TV down here after all, one Grandma Jo didn't tell me about. But as I pass the parlor door, my grandmother's voice makes me jump.

"I see you're back," she says, and she doesn't sound super happy about it. "Come here."

So much for my investigation.

I go into the parlor, and I'm surprised to find that there are three other old ladies sitting with Grandma Jo around a table. Each of them has a hand of cards, but they're all abandoned facedown, like they haven't really been playing. When they notice me, they all scramble to pick them up, looking a lot like Maddie does when a teacher catches her reading comics under her desk.

"This is my granddaughter," Grandma Jo says to the ladies. "Annemarie, this is my bridge club. You'll be seeing quite a lot of them this month, so you might as well get acquainted."

The ladies look me up and down, taking in my messy ponytail and my grass-stained soccer clothes. Two seconds ago I didn't care how I looked, but I suddenly feel incredibly self-conscious. If the rest of these women are anything like Grandma Jo, I'm about to get an earful about how I should make more of an effort with my appearance. But they all just stare at me, like I'm some sort of mythical creature they didn't know was real. Honestly, it's a little weird, but I smile and say hi since I have no idea what else to do. I realize I'm twisting Maddie's bracelet around and around my wrist, and I force myself to stop.

The lady closest to me reaches out to shake my hand, and there's a loud clanking sound because she's wearing about forty huge bracelets on her skinny wrist, wood and metal and ceramic all jumbled together. "Hello, dear," she says as she closes her knobby fingers over mine. "I'm Cookie. I've been *so* looking forward to meeting you." She's tiny and wiry, with dark gray hair cut almost as short as my dad's, and she's wearing bright red pants and a red blazer even though it's summer. Her giant, round, red-framed glasses make her look a little like a bug.

"It's nice to meet you, too," I say. "I'm AJ."

"Her name is *Annemarie*," Grandma Jo corrects, like I don't know my own name.

"I think my grandson Stanley already had the pleasure of spending some time with you," Cookie says.

"Yeah, he's really nice." I wasn't exactly sure what "eccentric" meant when Stanley used the word to describe his grandmother earlier, but now that I'm looking at Cookie and her outfit, I totally get it.

Cookie turns to the woman on the other side of her, who's wearing this weird flowy dress and a whole bunch of silk scarves with different patterns that don't match. "She's *perfect*. Isn't she perfect, Edna? So lithe and athletic."

"Come here, child," Edna says, holding out her hand to me. Her voice sounds super far away, like it's coming through a radio that's not quite picking up the signal. I drop my soccer bag, go around the table, and extend my hand to her, thinking I'm going to get another handshake. But instead she puts on the reading glasses that are hanging on a chain of glass beads around her neck, turns my palm faceup, and starts tracing the lines. It feels like someone is tickling my hand with dried leaves.

"Mmm-hmm . . . ," she hums to herself. "Ahhhh, yes.

Yes. Very good." She doesn't make eye contact or say anything directly to me, but she finally lets go of my hand and nods, obviously satisfied about something.

Cookie picks up her teacup, and as she turns to say something to Edna, she accidentally knocks the matching saucer off the table. I dive for it and manage to catch it before it hits the floor, and Cookie beams at me. "What *reflexes!*" she crows. "Such *dexterity!*" She peers at my hands as she takes the saucer back from me. "Such nice long fingers. Oh yes. This is very good."

"She's perfect through and through," says the last lady. The other two are so weird that I've barely noticed her until now. When she smiles at me, her face crinkles into a field of wrinkles and dimples, like a crumpled-up paper bag. Behind her glasses, her eyes are warm and brown, and her hair is short and curly and on the bluish side. There's a walker sitting next to her, each foot capped with a tennis ball. In her blue dress printed with flowers, she looks like a grandmother from a picture book, the kind who always has pies cooling on the windowsill.

"Hello, dear," she says. "I'm Betty. It's wonderful to meet you."

"You too," I say.

"So polite," Betty says, putting her blue-veined hand

over her heart. I notice she doesn't have any jewelry on, like the rest of the ladies do, not even a wedding ring. I wonder if her husband is dead or if she never got married.

All the ladies are staring at me again now, like they're expecting me to break into a song-and-dance routine, and the silence gets awkward pretty fast. "I guess I should go change out of these clothes," I finally say. "Respectable young ladies try to keep themselves neat and clean, right?" I glance at Grandma Jo, wondering if that got me any points.

Cookie snorts. "What are you *teaching* her, Jo? We have no use for respectable young ladies around here."

"Don't encourage her," Grandma Jo huffs. "She's wild enough already."

"I like a wild streak in a girl." Cookie pats my hand. "Be your wonderful self, AJ. We can't wait to see more of you."

"*Lots* more," Betty says. Edna makes a sound of agreement, but she's staring off over my left shoulder, like she's trying to crack a code painted on the fireplace.

"You guys too," I say.

I pick up my soccer bag and start backing away. I want to get out of this room while Grandma Jo is too distracted by her friends to remember that she's supposed to be giving me etiquette lessons. I'm nearly out the door when she calls out, "Come back down when you're finished changing, Annemarie, and you can get started on your sewing sampler."

Ugh, can she read my mind or something? And is she seriously going to make me *sew*? What is this, the Middle Ages? But I'm sure I'll get in trouble if I argue with her, so I say, "Okay. I'll be right back."

I change as slowly as I can, but I can drag out putting on clean shorts and a T-shirt for only so long. As I'm coming back down the stairs, I hear Cookie say, ". . . don't know why you didn't want to take her in, Jo. She's the perfect solution."

I freeze halfway down the steps. Are they talking about *me*? I'm suddenly hot with embarrassment. Even though I've made it clear that I don't want to be here at Grandma Jo's, it still feels like a punch to the stomach to hear outright that she doesn't want me, either. Isn't my own grandmother supposed to love me, even if she doesn't actually *like* me?

And what does Cookie think I'm the solution to?

"Having a child in the house makes it infinitely more difficult to stay under the radar," Grandma Jo says. "It puts us under increased scrutiny."

"But don't you see how much she could *help* us?"

"Absolutely not. Using her is not an option."

"Come on, Jo, are you kidding me? We have this invaluable resource right here at our fingertips, and you're going to ignore it?"

"She's not a *resource*, she's—" One of the steps creaks under my feet, and Grandma Jo breaks off. "Annemarie, is that you?"

I consider staying quiet so they'll keep talking. My grandmother and her friends are clearly hiding something, and I want to know what it is. But Grandma Jo seems like the type who might get up to check if I'm there, and if she finds me eavesdropping, she'll probably want me even less than she already does. So I call out a cheerful "Yes," paste a smile on my face, and go back into the room, pretending I haven't heard anything.

"Come with me," Grandma Jo says, and I follow her into the dining room.

On the table is a small wooden hoop with a square of white fabric stretched tight across its middle, a pincushion shaped like a tomato, a pencil, and some bundles of thick thread in blues and pinks and purples. There's also a slim hardback book called *My First Sewing Sampler*. "This should be basic enough that you can understand it," Grandma Jo says, tapping the book. That's when I notice that the smiley, happy kids on the cover are six years old, tops.

"I'm sure I can handle it," I mutter.

"Get started on your name sampler," Grandma Jo says, ignoring my tone. "I'll be back to check on your progress in a little while." Then, without telling me what a name sampler even *is*, she turns around and leaves the room, her long skirts rustling behind her.

I sigh and open the book. On the first page is a picture of a really overexcited little girl who's missing both front teeth. She's holding up a pillow that says KIMMY in neat pink stitches and beaming like it's a kitten that poops candy. In a cartoony speech bubble coming out of her mouth are the words *Sewing is fun! Sewing is fun! Sewing is fun for everyone!*

Oh my God, I think I might barf. I snap a photo of it and text it to Maddie, but she doesn't respond.

Trying my best to ignore the sappy rhymes and bug-eyed kids in pigtails, I read the instructions for sewing a name sampler. The fabric in my embroidery ring has a grid of little holes in it, and apparently I'm supposed to sew tiny *x*'s that make letters when you put them together, like pixels. The book suggests that beginners sketch their letters out with a pencil first—*Whoa there, partner, put on the brakes! If you sew with no guide, you will make more mistakes!*—so I get to work. I quickly discover that my name is too long to fit across the little circle of fabric, so I break it into two parts, ANNE on the top and MARIE on the bottom. I think about just doing AJ right in the middle, but I know how Grandma Jo would feel about that.

I'm finishing up my first *A*—*Crisscross, crisscross go the needle and thread! It's fun for your fingers and fun for your head!*—when Betty shuffles into the room with her walker. I assume she's on her way to the bathroom, but instead she comes up right behind me, so close I can smell her talcum-powdery scent, and peers over my shoulder. Has Grandma Jo sent her to spy on me? I try to look very busy and focused, just in case.

"Phenomenal," Betty whispers after about thirty seconds. "Such excellent fine motor skills. You're exactly what we need, AJ."

I'm doing okay with the sewing, but it certainly doesn't seem like anything to get excited about. "Um, thanks?" I say.

Betty nods to herself, pats my shoulder gently, and heads back toward the door. But when she's nearly out of the room, I hear her say, "Oh no . . . oh dear." She's looking around on the rug like my mom does when she drops a contact lens.

"What's the matter?" I ask.

"I seem to have lost one of my tennis balls. It's so difficult to walk when the feet are uneven like this." She gestures at the right front foot of her walker, which now ends in a bare plastic knob.

The ball can't possibly have gone very far, since she was going about a quarter of a mile per hour, but I don't see it anywhere. "Did you see which direction it rolled?"

"It went right under this gorgeous china cabinet." She pats the hulking piece of furniture next to the door. "Do you think you could help me get it?"

I crouch down in front of the china cabinet (seriously, who has a cabinet this big to display *dishes*?) and peek underneath. The ball is under there, way back against the wall. "I think I'm going to have to get something to fish it out," I say. "Do you know where the brooms are?"

"The legs on this cabinet are awfully tall, dear. Do you think you might be able to scoot underneath and grab it?"

"Yeah, okay. I can try." I lie down flat on my stomach and start pulling myself forward with my arms the way my baby cousin used to do before she learned to crawl. It's a little dusty under the cabinet, but Betty's right—there's enough room for me to worm my way all the way under.

"Got it!" I call as I grab the ball and start inching backward. I'm careful not to bang my head as I squeeze back out, and when I stand up, Betty's looking at me all misty-eyed, kind of like Maddie looked when she unwrapped her Xbox on her eleventh birthday.

"Oh, Annemarie," Betty breathes. "You're just perfect, aren't you."

Betty already seems to like me a lot more than my own grandmother does. "It's no big deal," I say as I squat down and reattach the ball to her walker. It fits pretty tightly, so I have no idea how it managed to fall off in the first place.

"It's a very big deal to me," she says. She gives me a watery-eyed smile, and then she shuffles back into the parlor.

When she's gone, I creep after her and lurk next to the doorway, eager to hear Betty tell Grandma Jo how wrong she was about me. "She squirmed right under there like a little eel, Jo," I hear her saying. "Cookie's right, she's the answer to our prayers."

"I said *no*," Grandma Jo snaps.

"Don't you think I should have a say in choosing my successor?"

"Betty, you've proven you are not to be trusted in matters like these."

"There's no need to bring that up, Jo," Betty says, and she sounds hurt. "I dealt with the consequences of my actions. Haven't I proven that kind of behavior is all in the past now?"

What kind of behavior could she possibly be talking about? I've only known Betty a few minutes, but she seems so sweet and wholesome. I can't imagine her doing anything worse than eating cookies in bed. Then again, according to my grandmother, almost *everything* counts as bad behavior. Betty probably walked in one of her flower beds or used her phone during a bridge game or something.

"This isn't about Betty," says Cookie's voice. "This is about AJ. Give us one good reason why she's not suitable."

"She's twelve years old! There's no way she can handle this level of responsibility. Do you honestly trust her to keep a secret of this magnitude? She hasn't been brought up to be decorous or discreet. She's even more unpredictable than Betty."

I bristle at that—I'm *great* at keeping secrets. When Ben planned a surprise party for my parents' twentieth anniversary, I didn't slip even once. But I *hate* it when people keep secrets from me, and if someone doesn't clue me in immediately about what my grandmother's friends want to use me for, I feel like my head might explode.

"I'm sure she can handle it," says Betty. "You never know until you try."

"All kids are a little unpredictable," says Cookie. "It doesn't mean she's immature."

"I was wild when I was young," says Edna's faraway voice.

"Betty's still wild," snorts Cookie.

"Cookie, be fair." Betty sounds super exasperated. "I *told* you that would never happen again."

"In all seriousness, Jo, we *have* to use AJ," Cookie says firmly. "We can't do it alone anymore, not with Betty's hip the way it is. We either include her or we're done. Is that what you want?"

Everyone's quiet for a minute, and I stand there motionless, holding my breath and dying of curiosity. "Of course that's not what I want," my grandmother finally says.

"Then it's decided," Betty says.

"We'll discuss it later," Grandma Jo says. "Now, quiet. Do you want her to hear you?" And to my dismay, their talk turns away from me and toward "trumps" and "redoubles," whatever those are.

I tiptoe back to the table and start working on sewing my first *N*, but my mind is spinning so much I can barely pay attention. Most of the ladies seem to want to share this mysterious secret with me, and that means my time living at Grandma Jo's house might not be as boring as I expected. Then again, if my grandmother gets her way, it sounds like I'll be sewing useless stuff all summer, totally clueless about what's happening on the other side of the wall. How dare she dismiss me without even giving me a chance, just because I'm not like *her*, obsessed with dresses and tea parties and bridge! Sure, I like to have actual fun once in a while, but that doesn't mean I should be kept in the dark.

Whatever they're hiding, I want in. It *has* to be more interesting than cross-stitch.

4

The moment the clock chimes six, there's a burst of rustling and creaking from the other room as the ladies push back their chairs and gather their things to go. I was hoping they'd stay for dinner so I wouldn't have to be alone with Grandma Jo, but it looks like I'm out of luck.

My grandmother comes in and watches me sew for a minute after they're gone. I'm less than halfway through my name—the thread got so tangled during the *E* that I had to totally undo it and start again—but I think I have the hang of it now. Grandma Jo peers down at the little fabric circle, making that horrible squinty face I hate, and for a second I'm sure she's going to tell me I have to start over. But instead she nods, and I almost fall over in a dead faint when she says, "You're making good progress, Annemarie."

"Thanks," I say. It's not exactly the over-the-top praise Betty gave me, but at least it's not a blatant insult.

"Of course, your stitching could be neater here and here," Grandma Jo says, pointing out a couple of mildly messy spots. She must catch the expression on my face, because she says, "Don't roll your eyes at me, Annemarie. A lady strives for perfection. What's the point of doing anything unless you do it as well as you possibly can?"

"I'll fix it tomorrow," I grumble, and she nods, satisfied.

"Go wash your hands," she says. "Dinner will be served in ten minutes."

Dinner is really awkward at first. At home, our meals are super casual—my parents and I are always laughing and teasing each other and making terrible jokes, and Snickers usually runs around under our chairs with his tongue hanging out, hoping for falling scraps. Not all of our forks and spoons match, and sometimes we use paper towels as napkins. But here everything is so quiet I can hear the clock ticking on the mantel in the next room. There are a whole bunch of forks next to my plate, and when I randomly choose one to eat my salad, Grandma Jo acts like I've mooned the queen of England and points out the "correct" one. I really don't see why it matters; all forks do the same thing. But I let her explain to me about salad forks and dinner forks and dessert forks, and it seems to make her happy. At least it's better than uncomfortable silence.

When Grandma Jo starts talking about how one of our future etiquette lessons will involve learning to set a proper table, I cut in and change the subject. "Hey, Grandma Jo, what do you like to do with your free time?" I figure if I catch her off guard, maybe she'll slip and tell me what she and her friends are really up to.

Grandma Jo pats the corners of her mouth with her napkin even though there's nothing there. "I do this and that," she says.

"Do you and your friends play cards every day, or do you do other stuff sometimes? Do you like to watch movies? Or go to baseball games? Or . . . I don't know, hike?"

She looks at me like I'm insane. "I certainly do not *hike*, Annemarie."

This is clearly going to get me nowhere. "What's your animal rescue league working on right now?" I ask.

My grandmother looks startled. "How do you know about the league?"

"Stanley mentioned it," I say, wondering if I've gotten my new friend into trouble. "He said you won some sort of award? That's really cool."

Grandma Jo relaxes when she hears that, and she spends the whole main course (steak and mashed potatoes) and dessert (*insanely* delicious chocolate cake) telling me about how tons of people buy exotic snakes and lizards and birds on a whim, even though they don't know how to care for them properly. I think about telling her I know how to kill an anaconda, but I decide against it.

Debbie comes in to clear the table, and my grandmother gets up, leaning heavily on her cane. "That steak was quite acceptable," she says. "I have things to attend to now, Annemarie. You are to stay out of the hallway at the back of the house so you don't distract me."

On a normal summer night, I'd run straight over to Maddie's after dinner for Xbox or bike riding or our complicated version of badminton. "Actually, I think I'll take my skateboard out for a while and explore the neighborhood," I tell Grandma Jo, hoping some exercise might distract me from how much I miss my best friend. "I'll come back in before it gets dark."

Grandma Jo's eyes bug out so much I think they might pop out of her head. "Absolutely not. I can't have my granddaughter hurtling around the neighborhood on that infernal plank. What would everyone think?"

They'd probably think, *Hey, there goes a perfectly normal*

THE CLASSY CROOKS CLUB

kid having a good time. "Come on, Grandma Jo, please?" I say. "Nobody cares anymore if skating is ladylike or whatever. Lots of girls do it."

She sniffs. "The fact that it's *popular* doesn't make it okay. Lots of girls put piercings in their faces and smoke cigarettes, too. Is that the kind of person you want to be, Annemarie?"

"That's not the same thing at *all*! And how do you expect me to entertain myself if I'm not allowed to watch TV *or* play video games *or* go outside?"

"You might consider exercising your brain," she says. "This house has a lovely library, and you're welcome to take all the books you want up to your room. Your parents may let you run around like a savage, but while you're under my roof, you will learn discipline and decorum." With that, she turns and leaves the room.

There's a pressure building in my chest, and for a second I'm sure I'm going to explode. I've been trying so hard to be polite and cooperative all day, and I've done everything she asked, including sewing that stupid sampler. But none of it matters at all, and she's still treating me like I'm a wad of chewed gum on the bottom of her shoe. What is her problem? Did she seriously call me a *savage*? Good behavior clearly isn't getting me anywhere, and I suddenly want to break every single one of her rules as fast as I can.

I push my chair back so it scrapes against the nice wood floor and sprint around the dining room table a couple times. Then I open and close the china cabinet with a loud *bang* and watch as all the plates rattle, but that doesn't make me feel any better. I go into the living room and move all the stupid china figurines around on the shelf my grandmother called a "credenza"; I even arrange a wolf figurine over a knocked-over shepherd girl so it looks like it's going to eat her face. I think about smashing a vase on the floor, but Grandma Jo would probably make me clean it up, and that's seriously all I need right now.

There's nothing else to mess with in the living room, so I go outside and walk through some of the flower beds, then make sure to track dirt across the floor as I stomp upstairs to my room. I grab my cell phone out of my soccer bag and send Maddie a bunch of angry texts.

i hate it here so so so SO much.

my grandmother is totally evil.

im so bored.

save me.

But she doesn't even reply. She's probably off riding her bike or playing Xbox without me. I slam my door and throw the phone at the bed, hoping it'll make me feel better, but it doesn't.

I don't know what Grandma Jo does for the next two and a half hours while I stew in my room, but at 9:25 on the dot, I hear her making her slow, stately way up the stairs—*clomp-click-rustle, clomp-click-rustle.* "Lights out in five minutes, Annemarie," she calls from outside my door. "I trust I won't have to remind you again."

"Whatever," I grumble.

"What was that?"

"I said *fine.*"

She's quiet for a minute, and I wonder if she's going to feed me some lie about how she's glad I'm here. But instead she sighs and says, "Good night, Annemarie."

"Good night."

I'm obviously not going to sleep this early, but in case Grandma Jo checks under my door for a stripe of light, I turn off the lamp and read one of Ben's old comic books by flashlight for a while. After about an hour, I tiptoe down the hall and press my ear against the door of the master bedroom. I'm not sure I'll be able to tell whether my grandmother is asleep, but then a snore that sounds like a chain saw rips through the air, and I have to clap my hand over my mouth to keep from laughing. My grandmother is *ridiculously* unladylike when she's sleeping. I like her so much better this way.

I go back to my room, switch my light on, and wonder what to do with my newfound freedom. I consider taking my skateboard out after all, but it doesn't seem smart to skate around in the dark in an unfamiliar neighborhood. Then again, that doesn't prevent me from skating *inside*. Thinking about how much Grandma Jo would hate that makes me smile. Maybe I can even figure out where those weird noises from earlier were coming from, now that everything's so quiet and still.

I put on my sneakers, grab my board and my flashlight, and tiptoe downstairs, testing each step before I put my full weight down to make sure it doesn't creak. I had thought Grandma Jo's house was creepy during the day, but it is *way* creepier in the dark. As I tiptoe across the foyer, I have this eerie feeling that someone is watching me, even though Stanley and Debbie are long gone by now. It's probably just all the portraits on the walls that are making me uneasy. About half of them are of people, but the other half are of birds, like the one in my bedroom. It figures that my grandmother would love the one animal I can't stand. I lower my flashlight and try to keep my eyes on the cold, smooth marble floor so

I won't feel their beady little painted eyes staring at me.

There's a small creaking noise to my right, and I whip the flashlight in that direction, half expecting to see my grandmother lurking in the shadows, her eyes glowing yellow like a raccoon's. But there's nothing there, only the long, empty hallway Grandma Jo told me was off-limits.

Perfect.

I switch on the light in my grandmother's study and leave the door open enough that I can see where I'm going. Then I hop onto my board, and having it under my feet makes me feel more like myself. The tension drains out of my shoulders as I glide up and down, humming softly to myself. Skating on a marble floor isn't the same as skating on the sidewalk—there are no gritty bits to help me get traction—but I get used to it pretty quickly. It becomes a problem only when I try to do an ollie and the board shoots out from under me and hits the door to the storage room with an earth-shattering bang.

I'm positive Grandma Jo is going to appear any second wearing a long black nightgown and toting a shotgun, but I don't hear any footsteps, just a slow, quiet creaking sound. I've probably knocked the storage room door ajar. I press myself into the shadows and hold very still until I'm sure nobody's coming, and then

I tiptoe toward the room to close the door back up.

But it's solidly shut. When I test the knob, I find that it's locked.

Okay. That's kind of weird. My heart's beating quickly now, but there are a bunch of doors in this hallway, and any one of them could've creaked. Maybe it was the house settling, like my dad said earlier. But now I've freaked myself out, and sneaking around in the dark is starting to seem more terrifying than fun. I decide to steal another piece of cake from the kitchen, take it back upstairs, and call it a night. Maybe I'll eat it in my bed. Grandma Jo would *hate* that.

I'm reaching for my board when I hear a girl scream.

I've heard lots of screams in my life. There's the happy kind; the frustrated "We lost the game by one point" kind; the creeped-out "There's a spider on my arm" kind. But this isn't any of those. This is the "There's a stranger hiding behind the shower curtain with an ax" kind. It sounds super close, like whoever's screaming is *in this hallway*. I grab the skateboard, hold it up like a weapon, and whip around. But there's nobody here but me.

Another scream echoes through the house, long and loud and terrified, and this time it sounds like it's coming from inside the storage room. This must be what I was hearing earlier. I can't believe my grandmother's sleeping through this. Should I wake her up or investigate the situation myself?

I still haven't made up my mind when I hear a totally normal, conversational woman's voice say, "Knock it off, Tommy." As I'm trying to make sense of this, I hear that creaking door sound again, followed by a third voice shrieking, "Let me out! Let me out!"

Oh wow, there are *lots* of people in there. My grandmother has *multiple people* locked inside her storage room. No wonder this hallway is off-limits. If *this* is the secret Grandma Jo told her friends I couldn't keep, she's 100 percent right. I'm going to do whatever I have to do to set them free.

Even though my heart is pounding so hard I can feel it in my fingertips, I reach out and knock softly on the door. There's no answer, so I knock again, louder this time. "Hello?" I call. "I'm here to help you. Can you open the door?"

I hear a rustle. "Knock it off, Tommy," a voice says again.

"It's not Tommy," I tell them. "My name is AJ. Tommy's not going to hurt you anymore." I have no idea who Tommy is, but it seems like the right thing to say.

"Let me introduce you to my trusty knife," a raspy

voice says, and a thrill of terror races up my spine. I jerk away from the door and stumble back a few steps. Is there a guard inside the room, watching my grandmother's prisoners to make sure they don't escape? Or was that one of the hostages talking? I know people in prison sometimes make knives out of things like toothbrushes if they're desperate to protect themselves. What has Grandma Jo been *doing* to these people?

"Please put your knife away," I say, trying to sound calm. "I'm unarmed. I'm just a kid. Can you tell me what's going on? Are you tied up? How many of you are there? Should I call the police?"

For a few seconds there's no answer. Then I hear the desperate woman's voice again. "Let me out, let me out!"

I wonder if I should call the cops right now and let them deal with this situation, but I doubt they'll take me seriously if I don't have any proof. "Okay," I say. "You don't have to tell me anything. I know you're scared. I'm going to get my phone and something to open the door, and then I'll come right back and get you out of there."

I fly upstairs, careful to avoid the creaky spots I discovered earlier, and grab my phone off the table next to my bed. Then I dig through my backpack until I find my library card—Maddie and I found an online video about how to open a locked door with one. I've only managed to do it once before, on her upstairs bathroom door (to the great annoyance of her oldest sister, Lindsay, who was getting out of the shower). Let's hope I can do it again, now that it really matters.

Back in the forbidden hallway, I knock gently on the door again. "I'm here," I say. "I'm going to try to open the door now, okay? Please stand back." Nobody argues with me, so I figure I'm welcome.

Just like in the video, I slip the library card between the doorjamb and the door, then slide it down so it's resting right on top of the bolt. Then—this is the tricky part—I tilt the edge of it toward the doorknob and jiggle it. It takes a little while, and my sweaty hands aren't helping, but I finally feel the card slide in a little farther. When I force it back the opposite way, the bolt pops open. I turn the knob and push against the door, and it gives.

I'm in.

I leave the door mostly closed for a second so I can grab my flashlight and skateboard from the floor; if someone in there really does have a knife, I don't want to face him without a weapon of my own. Then I call, "I'm coming in, okay? Please don't attack. I am *on your side*."

I take a deep breath, brace myself, and push the door open.

The first thing that hits me is the weird smell—sort of like wet cardboard and sawdust and rotting fruit. I feel around for a light switch, but I can't find it, so I do a quick sweep of the room with my flashlight to see what I'm dealing with. I'm expecting a cage full of terrified prisoners or maybe some ankle shackles like they used to have in medieval dungeons, but the only thing my light hits is a bunch of boxes, some stacks of newspapers, and a half-upholstered armchair. There are also some tall wooden stands with branches sticking out in all directions. Are those torture devices? And where are all the *people*?

"Hello?" I call quietly. "Can you say something so I know where you are? Don't be afraid."

And then a voice very, *very* close to my head says, "Ahoy, matey! Walk the plank!"

I gasp and flinch, whacking my elbow against the wall and dropping my flashlight, which winks out. I'm so startled by the nearness of the voice that it takes me a minute to register what it said. Did he just tell me to *walk the plank*? Was that the same voice that was talking about the knife? Is there more than one guard in here?

"Hang on," I say. My voice is trembling, but I try to keep it away from total hysteria. "Let me find the light switch, okay? Then we can talk this out."

"*Walk the plank! Walk the plank!*" the voice screeches again, followed by another irritated "Knock it off, Tommy," and a shrill, earsplitting scream.

I fumble desperately along the wall next to the door-frame with both hands, so scared and confused now that I feel like screaming myself. Finally my fingers land on a switch, hidden underneath some sort of wall hanging, and the room explodes into light. I blink quickly to help my eyes adjust to the brightness, and wheel around.

And then I blink a bunch more times, because what's in front of me makes absolutely no sense.

Scattered around the room, perched on the wooden stands and the backs of chairs, are about fifteen *parrots*. The light and the screaming must've disturbed them, because they're all rustling around, shaking out their feathers and looking at me with their glassy, unblinking eyes. They're all different colors—red and green and blue and gray and white—and they'd be superpretty if they were in a picture. But close up, they all have razor-sharp beaks and scaly dinosaur feet with claws that could easily gouge out my eyes. None of them are in cages. I stumble back until I'm pressed flat against the wall, and knowing there aren't any birds behind me makes me feel a little better, but not a lot. I hold my skateboard up in front of me so I can swat them away if they try to fly at my face.

But the weirdest thing is that I'm definitely the only person in the room. Where's the guard? Where's the screaming girl? As I struggle to calm down and make sense of everything, a big gray parrot with red tail feathers cocks its head, stares right at me, and opens its beak.

"Let me introduce you to my trusty knife," says a familiar raspy voice.

And then the bird next to it, which has a yellow front and blue wings with one yellow feather right at the tip, goes, "Walk the plank, matey!"

Oh my God. I am so stupid.

It's not like I didn't know parrots could talk—everyone knows that. But I guess I thought they all said stuff like *Polly want a cracker!* and *I'm a pretty bird!* Who the heck teaches their birds to threaten people?

My grandmother, apparently. This is *so twisted*.

"*Let me out, let me out!*" shrieks another voice near the back of the room. It sounds like a woman, but I trace it to a white bird with yellow feathers that stick up in a line on its head like a Mohawk. It stretches its wings a little, screams one more time for good measure, then hops down to a lower perch and starts nibbling on a toy. From the other side of the room, another large gray bird opens its beak, and the creaking door sound I keep hearing comes out.

Okay, I definitely did *not* know birds could do that.

There's clearly nobody here for me to rescue, so there's no reason for me to linger in this horrible, bird-filled room any longer. I'm about to go upstairs and have a good, long think about everything I saw, but then I notice a couple of terrariums in the corner. There aren't any birds over there, so I make my way toward them, skirting the edge of the room carefully and trying not to make any sudden movements. Inside are a couple of gigantic snakes, coiled back and forth on themselves like someone squeezed them out of a frozen yogurt machine. One of them is bright green and another has brown patches on a tan background. They both look super dangerous, and I wonder if either of them is an anaconda. A little farther back, there's another terrarium holding a lizard with a spiky ruff of skin around its neck. And in the very back, almost hidden behind a stack of cardboard boxes, there's a big metal cage with a large cat curled up in the corner. A *really* large cat . . . with spots.

That can't possibly be a baby *jaguar*, right?

A small gray bird across the room croons, "You'll be safe here with me, pretty. You'll be happy here with me."

It sounds exactly like my grandmother.

And that does it—I am officially too freaked out to spend one more second in here. I don't know *what* is going on, but I'm 150 percent sure I want nothing to do with it.

I turn off the light, shut the door behind me, and bolt.

5

'm nervous about going down for breakfast the next morning, sure I'm going to hear more screaming from Grandma Jo's personal zoo the second I hit the first floor. But the house is quiet and still, like last night never happened, and for a minute I wonder if I dreamed the whole thing. Grandma Jo is in the dining room, reading the *Wall Street Journal* and sipping tea (of course). She doesn't seem like the kind of person who would have a storage room full of exotic animals, especially considering how strict she is about following the rules. But I guess I don't really know my grandmother any better than she knows me.

There's a ton of food laid out on the table—a fruit plate, a basket of muffins and pastries, tiny pots of butter and jam, a dish of scrambled eggs, and a plate of bacon sitting on a doily. All of this can't possibly be for us. "Hi," I say. "Are there people coming over?"

Grandma Jo looks around like my question doesn't make any sense. "Not to my knowledge." She takes a tiny sip of tea. "Annemarie, you weren't by any chance in my study last night, were you?"

I open my eyes wide, which I've heard is supposed to make you look innocent. "No, of course not." Technically, I wasn't *in* the study—I just reached my hand in to turn on the light. Fortunately, she doesn't ask about the storage room. If she knew I was in there, who knows what she'd do to me. Probably chop me into pieces and feed me to her giant snakes.

"I know I told you that hallway is strictly off-limits," Grandma Jo continues as though I haven't said anything. "And yet when I woke up this morning, the study door was open and the light was on. How do you explain that?"

I shrug. "Maybe the cleaning lady left it on?"

"The maid wasn't here yesterday. You are to *stay out of that hallway*. Do you understand?"

"*Yes*, I get it," I say. I grab the crispiest piece of bacon from the doily plate, and Grandma Jo glares at me. For a second I think she's going to smack it out of my hand.

"You will use silverware while you're under my roof,

Annemarie," she says. "I will tame you if it kills me. Four weeks with me and you'll be the very definition of a respectable lady."

To spite her, I impale the whole piece of bacon with my fork at once and take loud, crunchy bites. "Yeah, right. Good luck with that," I say, but she ignores me and turns back to her paper.

After a few minutes, Grandma Jo gets up. "I have things to attend to," she says. "You are not to disturb me. You may go outside and *walk* around when you're finished eating."

I nod, and she heads toward the forbidden hallway.

I don't want to sit here at this massive table by myself, so I grab a muffin and a few slices of cantaloupe and leave the rest of the monstrous breakfast untouched. When I go upstairs to get my shoes, my phone is blinking with a new text from Maddie.

sorry yr gma's so evil. wanna come ovr b4 soccr? pool?

lemme ask, I text back. I'm dying to get out of here, and if Grandma Jo says yes, maybe Stanley will drive me over early.

I call my grandmother's name from the entryway, but there's no answer. She must not be able to hear me from the study, where's she's probably attending to all her mysterious secret "things." I'm not sure how I'm supposed to get her attention when I have to stay away from the forbidden hallway but I'm not allowed to shout, either. I make my way to the very end of the hall and call her name again, but there's still no answer. Then I hear her voice coming from the storage room.

"Come here, my pretty," I hear her crooning. "Oh yes, you're such a good boy, aren't you? Such a beautiful boy."

"Walk the plank, matey!" shouts the bird.

"Such a smart boy," says my grandmother's voice. I've never heard her sound so affectionate with another human being, especially not me.

Anger wells up in my chest again, just like yesterday. Seriously, why should I even bother asking my grandmother for permission to go to Maddie's? It's not like *she* wants to spend time with me, not when there are creeptastic birds to hang around with. She probably won't even notice if I leave a couple hours early.

I go back upstairs and text Maddie: *on the way, be there in half an hour.* I put my bathing suit on under my T-shirt and shorts, stuff a towel and sunblock into my duffel with my soccer stuff, and go out to the garage, where I'm hoping to find the one person in this house who actually seems to like me.

Stanley's out in the driveway with his earbuds in, buffing the silver parts of the town car with a big fluffy rag and doing this goofy dance to the music on his phone. For a second I stand there staring at him—he's *so* cute— but then I realize I'm acting like a weird stalker. I call his name, but he doesn't turn around, so I move into his line of sight and wave my arms. He looks a little surprised to see me, but he doesn't look embarrassed at all that I saw him dancing. I wonder if I'll be that confident when I'm in college?

"Hey, Miss AJ," he says. "What can I do for you?"

I should probably tell Stanley that plain AJ is fine, but hearing him call me "miss" kind of makes me feel important and grown-up, so I don't say anything. "Would you mind driving me to my friend Maddie's house?" I ask. "It's right near the soccer field, so you can drop me off now and pick me up at four like normal."

"Did your grandmother say it was okay?"

"She doesn't care," I say. It's not really a lie.

"Okay, sure," Stanley says. "Let me get the keys."

As we start driving, it occurs to me that Stanley has spent more time at Grandma Jo's house than I have; he might have some information that could help me. "Have you ever been in my grandmother's storage room?" I ask.

"Nope, I usually hang out in the kitchen when she doesn't need me. Why do you ask?"

"She's never asked you to help her carry anything heavy in there? Like, I don't know, a cage or something?"

Stanley looks super confused. "A *cage*? No, definitely not. Why would she have a cage?"

"I mean, I guess she wouldn't," I say. "I don't know, it was the first heavy thing that came to mind. So, um, your grandma and my grandma hang out a lot, right?"

"Pretty much every day, I think," Stanley says. "Grandma told me they've been friends since the seventies."

"Do you know what they do when they're together?"

Stanley shrugs. "Probably drink tea and play cards and stuff. Normal old-lady things."

"Huh," I say. I really like Stanley, but I can see he's not going to be any help. I turn the conversation to soccer instead.

Half an hour later, we pull up outside Maddie's house. She's in the front yard, kicking a ball around with her sister Jordan. When Stanley gets out to open my door, Maddie's face changes a little, but it's only a flicker, and then she gives me a sunny wave. Maybe I imagined the uncomfortable expression I thought I saw.

"Thank you, Stanley!" I call as I grab my bag and jog toward my best friend.

"No problem, Miss AJ," he says. "See you at four." He gets back into the car, and Maddie and I both watch him drive away.

When he's gone, she says, "Hey, sorry I didn't see your texts last night. What happened at your grandma's house? Are you okay?"

For a second I think she already knows about the birds somehow. "What do you mean?"

"You said you hated it there and that she was totally evil. Was the etiquette training really bad?" A horrified look passes over her face. "Wait, you didn't *really* have to fold her underwear, did you?"

I'd almost forgotten about the sewing sampler altogether. "No, but *everything* in that house is so much weirder than I thought," I say. "You're not even going to believe what I found in the storage room last night."

Maddie grabs her swim bag, and as we walk to the public pool, I tell her everything. By the time I get to the part about the birds and the snakes and the baby jaguar, Maddie's so amazed that she forgets to keep walking. She just stands there in the middle of the sidewalk with her bag dangling from one hand, gaping at me.

"You went bursting in there by *yourself*?" she says. "I can't believe you did that. Why didn't you call the police?"

I shrug. "I don't know . . . I guess I should've. But I didn't think they'd take me seriously unless I had proof, and I wanted to help whoever was in there as quickly as possible."

Maddie shakes her head in disbelief. "You are *so* much braver than me."

"I'm really not. I was terrified, especially when I saw all those birds."

"You thought someone in there had a knife, and it was still the *birds* that scared you?"

My face goes hot, and I shove her shoulder. Maddie's the last person I'd expect to tease me about this. "Shut up. I feel stupid enough about my bird thing already."

"I'm not making fun of you! I'm just saying I can't believe all that *other* stuff didn't scare you."

"It did!"

"But you went in there anyway, you know? It's like what Mr. Liu always said about bravery, remember? 'Courage is not the absence of fear . . .'"

"'. . . but the triumph over it,'" I finish, rolling my eyes. Our sixth-grade social studies teacher was always making us memorize quotes from famous people, and that was one of his favorites. He must've written it on the board a thousand times last year.

"Whatever," I say. "The real question is, *what* is my grandmother doing with all those animals? She clearly doesn't want anyone else to know about them. It's incredibly weird, don't you think?"

"It is pretty freaky," Maddie says. "I mean, having one or two birds is normal, but fifteen puts you in Crazy Bird Lady territory. Hey, I bet this is why she made such a fuss about you bringing Snickers over . . . she was afraid he'd smell the birds and go crazy and rat her out."

"Oh wow, you're probably right. Snickers has such a good nose, he would've tracked them down in a second." I picture my dog running in circles outside the storage room door and barking up a storm, and I have a pang of longing for him that's so strong it hurts. Man, I'd sew a million samplers if it meant my parents would come back and take me home right this second.

"Do you think Grandma Jo's training the birds to attack people? Like, to be her own personal army?"

Maddie looks doubtful. "I don't think you can train birds to do that, can you? And wouldn't they have attacked you? Otherwise, it's a pretty terrible army."

"Oh yeah. I guess so."

We're at the pool now, and we both pull out our passes and show them at the entrance. The girl guarding the gate used to lifeguard with my brother, and she smiles and waves at me as we go through. We find two empty chairs, strip off our T-shirts, and start rubbing sunblock onto our shoulders.

"Okay, new idea," I say. "My grandma says she does charity work for this animal rescue league. She gave me this huge lecture last night about how people are always buying exotic pets they don't know how to take care of. What if there *is* no league, and she made it all up as a front so nobody will suspect she has tons of illegal pets?"

Maddie rubs some sunblock onto her nose. "But it's not illegal to have parrots as pets, is it?"

"No, but what about the snakes and the jaguar?"

"I don't know. But we can find out if the league is real, at least." Maddie pulls out her phone, and I scoot over onto her chair so I can see it too. Her screen has a huge crack running down the middle, but I know better than to ask when she's going to get it fixed. Her family can't afford that right now.

Maddie types *Josephine Johansen* and *animal rescue league* into her browser's search window. A bunch of hits come up, and the very first one is about Grandma Jo getting an award from an animal rescue league called Friends of Fur and Feathers. When Maddie clicks on it, a picture pops up of my grandmother standing with some people in fancy gowns, a parrot perched on her shoulder.

"I guess the league is real," Maddie says.

I take the phone and look at the picture more closely. My grandmother is wearing her usual black dress, and the parrot's toes are digging into the ruffles around the collar. The caption says, "Benefit honoree Mrs. J. Johansen with animal rescue league directors Barbara Scranton and Kit Golding. Also pictured is Ms. Golding's blue and yellow macaw, Scrooge." The bird has a yellow front and blue wings with one yellow feather right at the tip.

"Whoa, wait a second," I say.

Maddie leans in closer. "What?"

"I think this might be the same parrot that was yelling at me to walk the plank last night. They look really similar."

"So?"

"So, it says here that it belongs to this other lady, Kit Golding. What's it doing in my grandmother's house?"

"Are you sure it's the same bird? Don't most parrots look pretty much the same?"

"I don't know. Maybe. But the one at Grandma Jo's also has one yellow feather right in that exact spot."

"Huh," Maddie says. "Well, maybe it is the same bird. Maybe Kit Golding's on vacation and your grandma's taking care of him until she gets back. They look like they're friends. Maybe she runs, like, a bird babysitting service for people who are on trips."

That would be logical, but something doesn't seem right. I type *Kit Golding* and *Scrooge* and *missing* into the search box.

Just as I suspected, a short article pops right up, talking about how the Goldings' beloved macaw disappeared from their house a week after the benefit. The reward is listed as $2,000.

"Maddie," I say. "What if my grandmother *stole* him?"

"Why would she do that?"

"Look at how high that reward is. Maybe she's going to pretend she found him and collect the money."

"Your grandma's super rich. She probably doesn't need two thousand dollars, does she?"

"But maybe this is how she *got* so rich." Another idea hits me. "What if this is what the bridge club ladies want to use me for? Maybe they want me to return the stolen bird and collect the money so nobody will connect it to my grandmother! I am *so* not doing that."

Maddie nods slowly, but I can tell she's not totally convinced. "I guess that's possible, but it might not even be the same bird. I definitely don't think you can confront her about it or go to the police until you have more proof."

"How am I going to get that?"

Maddie chews on her lip for a few seconds while she thinks, and then her eyes light up. "Okay, parrots are pretty smart, right? If the bird in your grandmother's storage room really is Scrooge, maybe he'd know his name. Maybe he'd know his owner's name, even. Can you break in there again tonight and talk to him a little—see if you can get him to say something incriminating?"

I don't love the idea of getting close enough to a parrot to have a personal conversation, but catching Grandma Jo in the act could mean getting out of her house and going to live with Ben for the rest of the month. Visions of playing Xbox and eating Cheetos with my brother dance through my head, and I can't help smiling.

"Wow," I say. "You're totally brilliant."

"Film the whole thing with your phone," Maddie says. "That way your grandma won't be able to deny that it happened."

I nod and smile to myself. It's the perfect plan. I can't *wait* to see a bird take down Grandma Jo.

6

When I get home that afternoon, my grandmother is furious. I thought maybe she'd go easy on me for sneaking out because her bridge club friends are there, but no—she takes me into the kitchen and yells at me for a good twenty minutes. All I did was go swimming with my best friend, but from the way she's acting, you'd think I'd stolen all her jewelry and sold it on the black market.

"You *must* act responsible, Annemarie," she snaps at me. "It reflects very badly on me if you get yourself into trouble. I nearly had to call the police when you disappeared, and it would've been an unparalleled disaster if people had seen squad cars in my driveway."

The fact that Grandma Jo cares less about my safety than how she looks to the neighbors makes me insanely angry. "I was *fine*," I say. "You could've asked Stanley where I was. It's not like I can go anywhere without him."

"Since you obviously have too much unoccupied time, you can do some chores for me in the mornings in addition to your afternoon etiquette lessons," Grandma Jo continues, completely ignoring me. "You will go straight to soccer at the proper time, and you will come straight home afterward. You will not spend any more time with this Maddie character. She's clearly a bad influence on you."

I feel the beginnings of tears pricking in my eyes, but I swallow hard and dig my nails into my palms—I refuse to let my grandmother see me cry. "Maddie's not a bad influence! Mom and Dad always let me go over there."

"I'm not your mother, and you didn't have my permission to go," she snaps. "You flagrantly disregarded my instructions, and that is unacceptable. While you're here, you answer to me and me alone, and if you break the rules, you will deal with the consequences."

I think about shouting back that she has no right to talk about breaking rules, seeing as she's stealing people's pets for ransom, but I can't go there until I have the proof I need. "I tried to ask your permission, but I couldn't *find* you!" I say instead.

"Then you shouldn't have left. It is imperative that you

learn patience, self-control, and responsibility." Grandma Jo holds out her hand. "Give me your cell phone, please."

"What? Why? What are you going to do to it?"

"For heaven's sake, Annemarie, I'm not going to do anything to it. I'm going to keep it until you've proven to me that you're responsible enough to have it back."

"That is *so* unfair!" I'm so frustrated now that I'm positive I'm going to burst into tears.

"If you ignore my perception of what's fair, you can't expect me to abide by yours," she says. "The device, please, Annemarie."

I dig my phone out of my soccer bag and slap it into her palm a little harder than necessary, and it disappears into a hidden pocket in Grandma Jo's huge black skirt. Now how am I supposed to record the birds saying incriminating things so I can get myself out of here? I decide I'll break into the storage room again tonight regardless, just to see what I can find out. If the birds don't say anything I can use, maybe I can teach them some things that would make Grandma Jo look really bad. I wonder how fast parrots learn.

As if my grandmother hasn't tortured me enough for one day, she dismisses me to finish my stupid sewing sampler while she hangs out with her bridge club friends. The absolute last thing I want to do right now is nitpicky, delicate work. I'm so angry I'd like to smash the glass door of the china cabinet into a million pieces with this idiotic embroidery book. But I tell myself I only have to keep it together for a few more hours, and then I can put my plan into action and get out of here for good.

My grandmother goes to bed at exactly the same time she did last night. She's such a creature of habit that she probably goes to sleep at the exact same time *every* night and has the exact same dreams, all full of black dresses and old-lady card games and tea. I sit silently for half an hour after her door shuts, waiting to hear her chain-saw snoring start up. It doesn't, but I don't hear anything else, either, so I figure it's probably safe to sneak downstairs. I gather my flashlight and library card and tiptoe down to the storage room.

It takes me much less time than it did yesterday to open the door, and I think of how proud Maddie will be when I tell her how much I've improved. My heart starts racing when I hear the birds rustling around on their perches, but I know I have to keep it together if I want to execute my plan. "Hi, guys," I croon softly to them as I reach for the light switch, careful to keep my back to the wall and one arm up to protect my face from attacks. "It's me. Don't freak out."

The light goes on, and then *I'm* the one who freaks out. Because sitting on a chair in the middle of the room is my grandmother, fully dressed and wide awake.

"Just as I thought," she says.

"I . . . um . . . I was . . . ," I start, but there's absolutely no explanation that makes sense. I mean, she *saw* me break into the storage room. I can't exactly pretend I came downstairs for a glass of water and got lost.

There are several empty chairs arranged in a semicircle, and she pats the one closest to her. "Come here," she says, and bizarrely, she doesn't sound mad. "It's time we had a little chat."

I inch toward the chair, glancing behind me every few seconds to make sure there's no parrot flying silently behind my head, and Grandma Jo raises an eyebrow at me. "Annemarie, why are you walking like that? Are you injured?"

"No, I . . . um. I don't want the birds to, like, fly up and attack me from behind?"

My grandmother sighs heavily. "That's not going to happen. Their wings are clipped."

I'm not sure what that means, but she makes it sound like it's something to prevent attacks. Maybe it's like declawing a cat, though all the parrots' claws look totally intact. I perch on the very edge of the chair, my spine not even touching the back. My heart is pounding even harder than it was last night when I first found the birds.

"Grandma Jo, I'm so, *so* sorry," I say. "I wasn't—"

"Quiet," my grandmother snaps. "We'll wait for the others to arrive. In the meantime, I'll make us some tea." And then she gets up and *clomp-click-rustle*s out of the room with her cane, shutting the door behind her and leaving me alone with the birds. If this is supposed to be my punishment, it's a really, really good one.

I sit rigid in my chair in the bird-filled storage room for what feels like forever, wondering who "the others" are and what will happen to me when they get here. Did Grandma Jo call the police? Is it illegal to break into a room in the house where you're living? I can't go to jail for this, can I? I twist my bracelet around and around on my wrist.

The white bird with the Mohawk-style head feathers is sitting closest to me, and when I look at it, it shrieks, "Let me out, let me out!"

"Trust me," I tell it. "I know exactly how you feel."

But when the doorbell finally rings, it's not the police—it's Cookie and Edna and Betty. None of them have taken the time to get dressed, and they tromp into the storage room in their pajamas like this is some sort of bizarre sleepover party. Cookie's in a red silk kimono with droopy sleeves and a dragon on the back. Edna's wearing a long, shapeless dress that doesn't look much different from what she wore during the day, but her hair is up in some sort of turban. Betty has on a flowered nightgown with ruffles around the neck and wrists, a blue terry cloth robe, and slippers shaped like rabbits, and her hair is in pink plastic curlers. If I'm on trial, this isn't exactly the scariest jury I've ever seen.

"This is so *exciting!*" Cookie gushes as she takes the chair next to mine. She gives my leg such a hard squeeze that I flinch. "I've always wanted to be called out of bed for a secret meeting! Something to check off the ol' bucket list."

"Definitely," I say, though I have no idea what she's talking about. What the heck is a bucket list?

Betty beams in my direction. "I'm so thrilled you're going to join us, dear. I knew Jo would come around about you."

"I don't . . . what?" I ask. "Join you?"

Grandma Jo comes in with a tray of tea things before they can say anything else. Even though it's the middle of the night, she's brought all the proper serving things:

saucers, little silver sugar tongs, a separate plate of lemon slices. "Be quiet," she snaps at Betty. "She doesn't know anything yet." Everyone's silent as she pours tea into five matching china cups, and then she settles down in her chair and looks at me expectantly. "Go on, Annemarie, show them what you did."

I feel like 90 percent of this conversation is happening over my head. "What I did with what?"

She rolls her eyes. "What you did with the *door*."

"You want me to open the lock again?"

"Have you done something else to the door of which I'm not aware?"

"No, I . . . no."

"Out you go, then." She shoos me out of the room, shuts the door between us, and clicks the lock into place. At least I'm separated from the birds now. And the tea.

I can hear Cookie's excited murmurs on the other side as I do my trick with the library card. When the bolt pops open a few seconds later and I step back into the room, she and Betty break into riotous applause. Edna holds her hands above her head and wiggles her fingers, which seems to be her weird way of clapping.

"AJ, darling, that was amazing!" raves Cookie. "Such finesse! Where did you learn to do that?"

"The Internet?" I say.

"Amazing device." Cookie shakes her head. "My granddaughter told me you can learn to build explosives on the Internet! Can you believe it? I must try it some-time."

Grandma Jo is not to be distracted. "I've changed my mind," she says to the other ladies. "I think we should use Annemarie. Let's put it to a vote. All in favor?"

Three gnarled hands shoot into the air. "Aye," all the ladies chorus.

"Then it's decided."

Cookie springs out of her chair and hugs me, her kimono sleeve flying up to hit me in the face. "I'm so glad to have you in our society," she says, planting an enthusiastic kiss on my cheek. "It's going to be wonderful!"

I twist away. "Could someone *please* tell me what's going on here?" I say. "It's the middle of the night, and you guys are making me demonstrate my lock picking and talking about secret societies, and we're in a storage room full of stolen birds, and everyone's acting like this is completely normal, and none of this is even *remotely* normal!"

"Jo, I thought you didn't tell her about the birds," Betty says.

"I didn't." My grandmother turns on me, her eyes full of steel. "Why do you think these birds are stolen?"

"The Internet," I say again.

Cookie shakes her head. "Remarkable."

I wait for someone to tell me there's a perfectly reasonable explanation for all these animals, one that doesn't involve my grandmother's being a criminal, but nobody does. "So these birds *are* stolen," I say, letting that sink in. I can't wait to see the look on Maddie's face when I tell her I was right. Bird babysitting service, my butt.

For the first time I can remember, Grandma Jo actually looks uncomfortable. "It depends on what you mean by 'stolen,'" she says.

"I mean they don't belong to you."

"Wild creatures don't belong to anyone," Grandma Jo says. "They belong to themselves."

"That's your excuse? I can't believe you! You're always talking about being a respectable lady and following the rules and how actions have consequences, and this whole time you've been stealing other people's birds and snakes and jaguars? If you want me to return them for the reward money, I am *not* doing it. That's—"

"It's not a jaguar," Edna says. "It's an ocelot. Jaguars are much larger."

"I don't care what it is! It's not yours!"

"Sit down and listen!" snaps Grandma Jo. "There's no reward money involved. You don't understand anything that's going on here."

"Then explain it to me!"

"Sit down, AJ," Betty says much more gently, patting the empty chair next to her. "We'll tell you everything. We promise."

Betty seems like the most trustworthy person in the room, and she looks like she's totally okay with everything that's going on here. Maybe it's worth hearing out my grandmother and her friends, just for a minute. I sit.

"What your grandmother has here is a sort of safe house for animals," Cookie begins.

"The so-called animal rescue league I work for is useless at rescuing animals," says Grandma Jo. "They're stellar at throwing galas, but when it comes to taking action, they're absolutely abysmal. There's so much red tape that nobody ever manages to *rescue* any animals, and the poor innocent creatures languish in terrible situations while those cowards drink champagne and congratulate themselves on being so noble."

"So your grandmother has taken matters into her own hands," Betty says. "She uses the league to locate animals who live in stifling or unsafe environments, and then we help her liberate them."

I think about the time Maddie stole a pack of Skittles from the cafeteria by stuffing them up her sleeve and assured me that she wasn't stealing, she was *liberating* them. This seems like pretty much the same thing.

"What kinds of bad conditions?" I ask.

"Most of these birds never left their cages before they came here," Grandma Jo says. She gestures to a gray and red parrot on a perch near Cookie. "Lorna here lived in a cage made of two shopping carts welded together. She was kept in a dark corner, and she didn't have any toys or even a water bowl. Birds are very social—they need to play and interact with people, and they need affection. Right, Lorna?" She reaches out to the parrot, who hops onto her hand eagerly and climbs up onto her shoulder. Its needle-sharp beak is inches from my grandmother's face, but Grandma Jo seems completely unconcerned.

"Let me introduce you to my trusty knife," says Lorna.

I scoot my chair backward as far as I can without being rude. "Why does it keep saying that?"

My grandmother strokes the top of Lorna's head with one finger. "Parrots can imitate practically any sound, as long as they hear it repeatedly and find it interesting. Lorna's previous owner must've watched the same movie over and over with her in the room. She can also do a creaking door sound and a very convincing scream. Can't you, my darling?"

"Why don't you love me anymore?" demands Lorna, totally out of nowhere, and against my will, I giggle.

"Okay, so you steal them and then you . . . what, release them into the wild?"

"Of course not," Grandma Jo scoffs. "Don't be ridiculous. These animals were born in captivity. They wouldn't have the slightest idea how to survive in the wild. I find them homes in aviaries and captive breeding programs, where they'll be cared for by professionals."

It's not like I approve of stealing people's pets, but this isn't nearly as bad as I thought. I mean, no matter how I personally feel about Lorna, it does sound pretty awful to live in a shopping cart in the dark. "How long have you been doing this?" I ask.

"Oh, for quite some time," Grandma Jo says.

"See that portrait over there, dear?" Betty asks, pointing to the opposite wall of the storage room. I hadn't noticed it until now, but there's a big painting of a young woman with her arms around a German shepherd. "That dog was your grandmother's first conquest."

"*That's* Grandma Jo?" The girl in the painting does look kind of like my grandmother, but I'm totally thrown off by the fact that she's smiling and wearing a blue shirt and a white skirt instead of a black dress. "How old were you?" I ask.

"Twenty-two," Grandma Jo says. "That's Byron, God rest his soul. Our neighbor used to beat him, so the day we moved out of that neighborhood and into this house, I removed him from harm's way. And then I thought, why stop with one?"

"Wait—I've heard stories about Byron," I say. "Did Dad know he was stolen? Did he know about *all* your animals?"

"Certainly not," Grandma Jo says. "I began renting a storage facility for the other animals as soon as your father was born. I couldn't possibly keep my projects a secret with a child in the house; children are so indiscreet, and they draw so much attention. Byron was the only one we kept as a house pet. He and I were inseparable." She gazes up at his portrait, and I swear there's actual love in her eyes.

All this information is making my head spin. Not only is prim and proper Grandma Jo a huge rule-breaker, she also used to have a dog she adored, just like I do. I've never considered that we might actually have something in common, but if Snickers were being abused, I know I'd do anything to help him, including dognapping him. What she's doing isn't exactly legal, but it still kind of makes me respect her more.

"So, you guys are, like, an animal rights society?" I ask. "That's what you want me to join? 'Cause I'm okay with that."

"That's part of it," Betty says at the same time as Edna says, "Not exactly."

"This is ridiculous," Cookie says. "The girl deserves the truth. We're not an animal rights society, AJ. We're a heist club."

"When my daughter saw my calendar and asked why it said 'HC' every day from three to six, I told her it stood for 'Hobby Club,'" Edna says. "She thinks we knit and play games and bake things." Betty and Cookie start giggling, and Grandma Jo smiles tightly, which is the closest she ever really gets to laughing.

"Baking!" Cookie howls. "I haven't used my oven since 1975, except as a shoe rack."

I'm having a hard time processing all of this. "So, do you steal other stuff, too, or only animals?"

"We all have our causes," Edna says vaguely.

"We rotate being in charge," says Cookie.

"Well, *most* of us rotate." Betty shoots Cookie a slightly unfriendly look.

"Betty, you brought your situation on yourself, and you know it," Cookie says.

"What situation are you—" I start to say, but Grandma Jo cuts me off.

"Enough! Right now, there's a gorgeous green-winged macaw languishing at Fran Tupperman's house, and we need to get him out. She keeps him shut up in the attic, poor darling. She thinks he makes too much noise."

"If she doesn't even like the bird, couldn't you ask her to give it to you?" I ask.

"A bird is not an 'it,' Annemarie," my grandmother says. "Fran keeps Picasso because he can sing snippets of songs. She brings him out to entertain guests at dinner parties."

"Nobody would go otherwise," Cookie adds. "She's an unbelievable bore."

"So, what would you need me to *do*, exactly, if I joined your . . . heist club?" Saying that feels really weird. This kind of thing only ever happens on TV.

Betty reaches out and grasps my hand. Her palm against mine is warm and soft and dry, so fragile I feel like

I could break it if I squeezed too hard. "You'd be such an amazing asset to us, dear," she says. "I used to do all the inside work—I could slip into a house and out again like a shadow, with no one ever the wiser."

"She really was spectacular," says Cookie.

Betty shoots her a grateful smile. "But I had to have this silly hip replaced last month, and let's just say I'm not as sneaky as I used to be." She pats the walker sitting beside her.

"Knock it off, Tommy," one of the birds contributes.

"So, you want me to steal the green-winged whatever? Why can't Cookie or Edna do it?" I don't even suggest Grandma Jo; there's no way she could be stealthy with her foot in that boot.

"We could certainly try," Cookie says. "But there are so many stairs up to the attic. It would take us *ages* to climb them, and Fran would probably find us up there in the morning, still trying to catch our breath. But an athletic girl like you? You wouldn't even be winded."

"It's an easy job," Betty reassures me. "Edna will pick the lock on the front door and disable the alarm system. All you'd need to do is the snatch-and-grab."

Maybe stealing a macaw would be super easy for *her;* she doesn't have a history of birds breaking her fingers. Then again, this bird would be in a cage. If I grabbed it by the top and held it far away from my body, it wouldn't be able to attack me. "What will you guys do?" I ask Cookie and Betty.

"We're the lookouts," Cookie says. "There's not a lot of foot traffic in Fran's neighborhood in the middle of the night, but we'll distract anyone who happens to wander by."

As I'm waffling, my grandmother turns to me. "We could really use you, Annemarie." She swallows hard, and I wonder if that's what people mean when they say someone swallows her pride, because the next thing she says is, "I would be very grateful for your help."

Having power over Grandma Jo is such a weird feeling. I'm pretty sure I'm going to say yes—this really does seem like a good cause—but I can't resist being in control for a minute.

"If I agree to help you, can I have my phone back?" I ask.

Grandma Jo's mouth tightens into a thin line, but she reaches into a hidden pocket in her cavernous black skirt and pulls out my phone. It's disgustingly warm from her body when she hands it back to me, but I'm so happy to see it that I don't even care.

"And am I allowed to go over to Maddie's?"

"Joining us doesn't negate the fact that you betrayed

my trust today, Annemarie," Grandma Jo says. "What I said about leaving the house still stands. However, should you decide to join us, you will not be required to do chores, and you will begin training for the heist after your sporting rehearsals every day instead of receiving etiquette and sewing lessons."

No more sewing? That's the best news I've heard in weeks. And if I do really well with the heist training, maybe my grandmother will actually see that my athleticism is useful, even if it's not as ladylike as sewing your name onto a pillowcase. Maybe she'll stop looking down her nose at me every time I go to soccer or mention my skateboard. Maybe, for once, I'll feel like the two of us are on the same team.

"That seems like a good compromise," I say, trying to make my voice sound as grown-up as I can.

"Needless to say," my grandmother continues, "should you decide to participate, we will require absolute discretion from you. If you speak of this to anyone else, I will know, and I will make you *very sorry* you let our secrets slip. Is that understood?"

Her tone sends a shiver down my back, but I look my grandmother straight in the eye and smile. "Don't worry; I can keep a secret," I say. "Count me in."

7

It's really late by the time Grandma Jo's friends go home, and I should be falling asleep on my feet. But I lie awake most of the night, hugging Hector the armadillo and mulling over everything I've learned tonight.

My grandmother is a crook.

All my grandmother's friends, including sweet blue-haired Betty, are crooks. Classy crooks, but still.

I am about to become a crook.

Worst of all, I have to keep this information to myself. How am I supposed to hide it from Maddie? This is the weirdest, freakiest thing that's ever happened to me, and I can barely keep from telling my best friend what I've gotten her for her birthday every year.

When a sliver of morning light starts to creep through

my curtains, I finally give up on trying to sleep. It's a good thing there's no soccer on Fridays, because there's no way I'd be able to concentrate today. My grandmother is already at the table when I come downstairs, and I kind of expect her to shoot me a conspiratorial smile now that we're planning to do something illegal together. But she doesn't even look up from her paper.

"Good morning, Annemarie. How did you sleep?" she asks, like last night wasn't the weirdest ever.

"Not very well, honestly," I say. "I couldn't stop thinking about—"

"I'll have the cook make you some warm milk before bed tonight," she says, cutting me off. "It'll help you sleep."

Wow, I guess I'm not even allowed to talk about this stuff when nobody else is around. So I shut up and nibble on an English muffin, trying not to think about how gross warm milk sounds.

When Grandma Jo finishes her breakfast, she dabs her mouth with her napkin and pushes her chair back. "I have things to attend to. I trust you can entertain yourself in a ladylike manner until the bridge club arrives?"

I roll my eyes. "Yeah, I think I can handle that."

"Good." She gives me a stern look. "Don't disappoint me, Annemarie."

I end up taking a stack of comic books, a blanket, and a glass of lemonade out into the backyard and sprawling on the grass in the sun all morning. I'm probably not lying in a super ladylike way, but there are tall hedges around the entire yard, so it's not like any nosy neighbors can report me to Grandma Jo. I'm almost starting to feel relaxed when my phone rings and Maddie's picture pops up on the screen. I consider not answering—I don't want to lie to her about what happened last night—but I'm going to have to get it over with sooner or later. It's probably easier to do it on the phone than in person, anyway. I can always tell when Maddie's lying to my face because she scrunches up her chin in a certain way.

"Hey," I say, hoping my voice sounds breezy and casual.

"Hey!" Maddie says. "What's going on over there? Tell me everything!"

"About what?" I say.

"About what?! Seriously? About the *storage room full of exotic birds*, you weirdo! Did you break in again? What did you find? Are the birds really stolen? Did you tell your brother? Is he going to let you move in?"

I want to tell her everything so badly, but my grandmother's face pops into my head: *If you speak of this to anyone else, I will know, and I will make you very sorry.* "Oh, right." I sigh. "You can't laugh at me, okay? 'Cause I feel really stupid about this whole thing."

"Are the birds not stolen after all?"

I swallow hard and pull out the explanation I thought up while I was trying (and failing) to sleep. "Turns out my grandmother's animal rescue league is renovating the building where they usually keep the rescued animals, so she volunteered to keep them in her storage room in the meantime."

"Really? That's so boring!"

"I know," I say, relieved that she's buying it. "You can't tell anyone, though, okay? Grandma Jo's house isn't up to code for this kind of thing, and she could get in really big trouble."

"Okay. I know this is weird, but I'm kind of disappointed. I mean, it's obviously good that your grandmother's not a criminal, but it was sort of exciting that there was something freaky and mysterious going on, you know?"

Of course, my grandmother is a criminal, and there are all kinds of freaky things going on. But I just say, "Yeah, I know. Anyway, thanks for helping me investigate, but I guess it's back to everything being boring."

"Do you want to come over?" Maddie asks. "We could

play *Mega Ninja Explosion*. Jordan said I could borrow it."

"I really want to, but I'm grounded because I snuck out yesterday. I'm not allowed to go anywhere but soccer."

"Seriously? For how long?"

"I don't know, but I'm working on it."

I hear the glass door of the house slide open, and a voice calls, "Yoo-hoo, AJ!" When I look up, Cookie's standing in the doorway. She's wearing a red dress and red tights and motioning for me to come inside.

"I have to go," I tell Maddie. "Grandma Jo's making me do chores."

"Ugh. Good luck. Text me later."

"I will," I say. My stomach twists with guilt as I hang up the phone. Then again, it's hard to feel too bad for Maddie when she gets to play *Mega Ninja Explosion* all day.

"Hello, my darling," Cookie says when I get to the door. "How are you this beautiful morning?"

"Um, pretty good," I say. "A little sleepy. You guys must be tired too."

"Oh, I feel fresh as a daisy," Cookie says. "Follow me!"

I assume we're going to the storage room, but Cookie heads for the stairs instead. "We've made you a surprise!" she says, and even though I have no idea what's about to happen, her excitement is contagious.

I follow her up to the attic, where the rest of the ladies are waiting. They've been busy while I was lounging in the yard; there are a whole bunch of storage boxes and old furniture shoved into various shapes in the center of the floor, sort of like a maze. Some of the boxes are stacked up tall and look like they might topple over any second, and some are pushed together in rows. Clouds of stirred-up dust swirl around in the overhead lights like swarms of tiny bugs, and for a second I worry my grandmother's about to put me to work cleaning. But the ladies are beaming at me, so I'm guessing they have other ideas.

"Do you like it, dear?" Betty asks.

"I . . . umm . . ." I look around, hoping there's a clue I've missed. "Of course I do—this looks like a lot of hard work. But . . . what is it, exactly?"

"It's your training obstacle course," Cookie explains. "During the heist, your job will be to navigate quickly and quietly through unfamiliar territory. So we've made you a place to practice."

"These are for you," Edna says, holding out a pair of black gloves. "We always wear them for heists so we don't leave fingerprints behind. They'll help you get into the right psychic space if you wear them now."

"Thank you," I say. I don't know what a psychic space

is, but when I pull the gloves on, I do feel a little more professional. They're a perfect fit, lightweight and sturdy, and my initials are embroidered along the wrist cuffs in silver thread. "Wait, did you *make* these, Edna?"

She shrugs modestly. "I whipped them up last night."

"But you were here last night. When did you sleep?"

"I don't really sleep," Edna says, like this is totally normal. "I get all the rest I need when I meditate."

"Let's get started," Grandma Jo orders, pulling a stopwatch out of her pocket. "Start here, Annemarie, and let's see if you can make it to the other side in less than two minutes without any of us hearing you."

Cookie switches the lights off, and I start creeping forward through the box maze, arms stretched out in front of me like a zombie. I don't do so well at first—an entire box wall comes tumbling down on me when I turn a corner too quickly—but I soon learn that smooth, controlled movements are the key. I concentrate on shifting my weight carefully from heel to toe as I walk, sweeping my arms in slow, graceful arcs so I can find the walls without knocking anything over. Whenever a floorboard creaks or I brush against a box corner, the ladies hiss, "Freeze!" and I have to freeze in place, barely daring to breathe, for as long as I can. As soon as I get used to one configuration of boxes and furniture, they make me close my eyes while they rearrange everything. Sometimes I have to crawl or limbo through small spaces, and though I doubt I'll actually have to do that in Fran Tupperman's house, the fact that I *can* is pretty cool. Every time I make it through the maze without giving myself away, Betty and Cookie and Edna whoop and cheer and high-five me, and it makes me feel like a celebrity.

"You're a natural," Cookie tells me after a couple of hours, when I'm covered in dust and sore from creeping around. "I'm so impressed, AJ."

"Such a competent aura," Edna muses.

Betty gives me a huge, warm smile. "You're a marvel, dear," she says. "I wish we could keep you forever."

I glance at my grandmother, and she gives me a slow nod. It's not exactly praise; *she* clearly doesn't wish she could keep me forever. But at least she's being respectful, and that's a big step in the right direction.

"Thanks for this, you guys," I say, trying not to sound too cheery and excited. Grandma Jo doesn't approve of fun. "That was really helpful. Are we practicing again tomorrow?"

My grandmother frowns. "Let's not get ahead of ourselves, Annemarie. Hydrate yourself and then come downstairs so we can practice with the birds."

I take the bottle of water she hands me, but there's suddenly a lump in my throat, and I'm not sure I'll be able to swallow any of it. "Wait," I say. "Practice how? All I have to do is grab the cage in that woman's attic and carry it downstairs, right?"

"Annemarie, we're liberating a green-winged macaw."

I don't understand why it matters if the bird has green wings or red wings or hot-pink wings with polka dots. "So?" I say.

"Green-winged macaws are three feet tall from head to tail. The cage Picasso lives in is about as big as you are. Can you carry that down two flights of stairs in the dark?"

My heart is suddenly doing Olympics-level gymnastics. "I have to carry the bird? In my *hands*?"

Grandma Jo sighs and looks at the other ladies like, *I told you she couldn't handle this.* "Is that going to be a problem? If so, I need to know now so we can make alternate arrangements for next Friday."

I know Grandma Jo didn't want to let me be part of this heist in the first place, and if I back down now, she's going to think she was right about me all along. Plus, then I'll have to go back to embroidering things and learning to set a table properly. "I never said I couldn't do it," I say.

"Fine. Then come with me."

The four of us follow Grandma Jo down the stairs and into the storage room, and I quickly count the birds and take stock of where each one is—I don't want any of them hiding and surprising me. But they're all there in plain sight, grooming themselves or eating or shredding their toys. None of them pays us the slightest bit of attention. Grandma Jo fetches a massive red, green, and blue bird from across the room and returns with it perched on her arm. When it reaches up and starts biting the lace around her collar, she doesn't even flinch. It better not try that with me, or I'm definitely going to scream.

"This is Fireball," Grandma Jo tells me. "He's a green-winged macaw like Picasso. When you hold him, you must keep your arm level, like this, and refrain from making any sudden movements. Do you understand?"

"Yes," I say. The bird looks perfectly calm and relaxed, but I can't stop staring at his razor-sharp beak and eye-gouging claws. If I make him remotely angry, I'll be in trouble. I take a small step backward.

"Hold out your left arm, please, Annemarie," Grandma Jo instructs. "You'll want to keep your right hand free for opening doors and such."

Betty gives me an encouraging little nod and reaches out to hold my other hand for moral support. Thank goodness there's *someone* here who cares how I feel. I grip her hand tightly, squinch my eyes shut like I do when I have to get a shot, and offer Grandma Jo my arm. Fireball's weight transfers onto me, but his claws don't hurt like I thought they would, and he's not quite as heavy as I expect, either. For a second I feel a little more confident—something that only weighs a couple of pounds couldn't do that much damage, right? I open my eyes and sneak a peek at him, and he stares right back, tilting his head this way and that.

"I think he likes you," Cookie says.

"Good job, AJ," says Betty in a soothing voice. "You're doing great."

"This isn't as bad as I thought it would be," I admit.

The minute I say it, Fireball leans over and starts pecking at the bracelet Maddie made me. I shout "No!" in the same stern voice I'd use to reprimand Snickers, but the bird doesn't listen, and tiny glass beads fly everywhere as the string snaps. I jerk my arm up involuntarily, and Fireball screams and unfurls his wings, which are—oh no—really, really big. My mind flashes back to those giant white swan wings looming over me when I was a kid. I scream, drop to the floor, and curl up to protect my stomach, and Fireball launches off me like a feathery torpedo.

His nails leave thin scratch marks where they scrape across my forearm. Our shrieks have set off some of the other birds, and I lock my arms over my head as the air fills with grating, high-pitched screams. It's like when all the car alarms on my street go off at the same time after an especially loud clap of thunder.

I hear my grandmother soothing Fireball—of course she'd go to him first, before she makes sure her human granddaughter is okay. But the other ladies are right next to me in a moment, and I feel several gentle hands on my back. "Are you hurt, dear?" asks Betty.

I'm trembling, but technically I'm more humiliated than hurt. *Why* can't I get over this stupid bird phobia? "It's just a couple of scratches," I say. "And he totally wrecked my bracelet."

"It's only jewelry, dear," Cookie says. "We can get you a new bracelet."

"No, my best friend made—" I start to say, but Grandma Jo cuts me off.

"Annemarie, what did I say? *No sudden movements.*"

"I know, okay?" I snap. Tears prick the corners of my eyes as I realize I've probably just undone all the progress I made with Grandma Jo this morning. This was all her stupid bird's fault, not mine.

"Here," my grandmother says, shoving Fireball at me. "Try again."

Betty pushes her walker between my grandmother and me to keep her from coming any closer. "Leave her alone, Jo. You're making everything worse. AJ has plenty of time to practice with the birds before the heist. Let her catch her breath."

"There is not *plenty of time*," Grandma Jo huffs. "The heist is a week from today. She's the weak link in this equation, and I need to be sure she's prepared. We can't use her if the results are going to be unpredictable."

My phone starts ringing in my back pocket, and I fish it out, glad for an excuse to look down so Grandma Jo can't tell how much her comment hurt me. I don't think I've ever been happier to see my brother's name on the screen. "It's Ben," I say. "I have to take this, okay? I'll be right back."

"But we're not done with—" Grandma Jo starts, but I'm out of the room before she can finish.

I pause on the stairs and take a few deep breaths before I answer. When I finally say "Hello?" it comes out sounding pretty calm.

"Hey, kiddo," Ben says, and his voice in my ear is almost as good as a hug. "How's it going at Grandma Jo's? You settling in okay?"

I've made it to my room now, and I close the door and sit down on the floor with my back against it. There's so much to say, and I can't tell my brother any of it, which makes all my limbs feel heavy. "Things are okay, I guess," I say.

"Yeah? Are you and Grandma Jo getting along? I know she's not your favorite person sometimes."

"I'm not really hers, either," I mutter. "But I guess things could be worse."

Ben laughs. "My sister, the eternal optimist."

"Shut up," I say, but I'm smiling a little. Ben's the kind of person who always makes you smile, even when you don't really want to.

"How's soccer? Tell me about your last game."

I try to tell him, but all I can pay attention to is how many birds there are out my bedroom window—a flock of pigeons crowding together on a telephone wire, a sparrow on my windowsill, a couple of crows on a tree branch, staring at the neighbor's house like they're casing the joint for a robbery. Why are they *everywhere*?

"Why is who everywhere?" Ben says.

"Nobody." I didn't realize I'd said it out loud.

"Are you okay? You sound all weird and distracted. Is this a bad time to talk?"

THE CLASSY CROOKS CLUB

"No, it's a fine time. It's nothing."

"Come on, AJ, it's clearly not nothing. If you tell me, I might be able to help."

He sounds so kind and concerned that I almost blurt out everything. If I decided to shut this whole heist thing down, I know he'd help me. But shutting it down isn't even what I want—I want to do the heist, and I want to do it well enough to earn some respect around here. But if I'm going to prove that Grandma Jo shouldn't underestimate me, I need to overcome my fear, and I have no idea how I'm going to manage that.

"Can I ask you something?" I say.

"Of course."

"When you're really afraid of something but you have to do it anyway, how do you deal with it?"

"What kind of thing?"

"Like, what if you were really afraid of spiders, but you had to go camping in a place where there were tons of spiders?"

"Grandma Jo isn't taking you camping, is she?"

I picture Grandma Jo roasting marshmallows over a campfire in her lacy black dress, and I burst out laughing. "Oh my gosh, *no*, that's just an example."

Ben's silent for a minute—I love how he always thinks

hard before he talks. "I guess I would spend some time thinking about why I'm so afraid of spiders and figuring out if the fear is rational," he finally says. "Maybe it would help if I knew there weren't any spiders at the campsite that were actually dangerous."

"What if they might be dangerous, but you weren't sure?" I ask.

"I guess I'd prepare myself to deal with the worst-case scenario," Ben says. "Like, maybe there's some good bug spray I could use. Or maybe there's some special medicine I should have on hand in case one bites me. You're not actually in danger, are you?"

"Probably not," I say, and I hope it's true. "Just trying to deal with some stuff."

"Sometimes it's as simple as mind over matter, telling yourself over and over that you can do it until you believe it. You're incredibly brave, AJ. You always have been. I'm sure that whatever it is, you're going to kick its butt."

"I'm not brave at all." If today has proven anything to me, it's that.

"Are you kidding me? Who tried to do an ollie her very first time on a skateboard?"

I snort, remembering the way I limped home that day, my elbows and knees bleeding and embedded with tiny bits of gravel. Ben had to half carry me. "That wasn't brave," I say. "That was idiotic."

"Who got up in front of the whole school and made a speech for student council last year?"

"That wasn't scary. Who cares about student council?"

"Okay. Who leaped in front of her best friend to keep her from being bitten by a swan? You can't argue with that one; that was *brave*. And you were like five years old."

"What? That swan didn't go for Maddie. It came straight at me, and Maddie ran away."

"That's not what happened, AJ. Is that how you remember it?"

"Well, yeah." I think of the sequence of events that has played out over and over in my head for more than half my life—the pain in my fingers, the giant white wings rearing up, the hissing, the breath-stealing whack in the stomach.

"The swan bit your hand first, and you pulled away and started screaming," Ben says. "And then it went for the bread Maddie was holding out. But you jumped in front of her and started waving your arms and yelling at it to leave her alone, and that's when it got scared and hit you. You had two broken fingers, and all you cared about was protecting your best friend."

"Seriously? I did that?"

"Ask Mom when she gets back, if you don't believe me."

It's an incredibly weird feeling, being told I've been remembering this huge event in my life wrong all this time. It's like the ground has suddenly tipped slightly to the side and I have to adjust to a new way of standing. That swan didn't attack me out of nowhere, like I thought. When it hit me, it was because I screamed and flailed at it first, like I did with Fireball. Maybe birds aren't as unpredictable as I thought. Maybe every bird startles and rears up when it gets scared.

"I never knew that," I say. "Thank you. That helps."

"Knowing what happened with the swan helps . . . with the spiders?"

"Yeah, actually." I stand back up. "Hey, listen, I've gotta go. But I'll call you again soon, okay?"

"Okay," Ben says. "Good luck, I guess?"

"Thanks."

"Love you, AJ."

"Love you too. Bye."

I pull my gloves back on, and with renewed confidence, I go back down to the storage room. "I'm ready to try again," I say to Grandma Jo. "Where's Fireball?"

My grandmother looks impressed, and it's such a rare

occurrence that I almost don't even recognize the expression on her. Maybe I haven't ruined everything between us after all. She fetches Fireball, and when she puts him on my hand and he starts picking at my sleeve, I manage not to flinch. Betty, Cookie, and Edna are quiet and still as I parade him all the way around the room once, careful to keep my gait slow and steady like I did in the dark obstacle course. Maybe he can sense that I'm calmer than before, because this time he just sits there, grooming himself.

When I hand him back to Grandma Jo, she looks at me as though I'm a competent person for maybe the first time ever. This warm, proud feeling spreads through my chest, as if my heart is pumping hot chocolate instead of blood, and when she says, "Very good, Annemarie," I can't help the goofy smile that breaks out on my face. I've clearly passed an important test.

Betty comes up behind me and squeezes my shoulders. "Such a brave girl," she says.

And this time, I actually believe it.

8

I get to soccer a little early on Monday, and the Bananas are the only ones there, stretching and gossiping by the fence. I'm about to sit down by myself and wait for my friends, but Sabrina calls hello and scoots back to make room for me, so I sit down next to her and start putting on my cleats. Ordinarily, Brianna wouldn't bother to acknowledge my existence, but today she smiles and says, "Hi, AJ, how's it going?"

For a second I wonder if she's really talking to me, but it's not like there's another AJ here. "Um, fine, I guess," I say. "How're you?"

She rolls her eyes. "Ricky is servicing our pool, so we haven't been able to use it in two entire days. I'm dying for a swim, but it's not like I'm going to go to the *pub-*

lic pool. I'm sure you know what I mean; your grandmother's house has a pool, right?"

Grandma Jo's house doesn't have a pool, but before
I answer, Maddie arrives and plunks down next to me.
"Hey," she say to me, ignoring Brianna. "I was trying to
call you all weekend. Where have you been?"

I did have a bunch of missed calls from Maddie this
weekend, but I didn't call her back because I had no idea
what to say; my life was suddenly full of birds and obstacle
courses and other things I couldn't tell her about. "Sorry,"
I say instead. "Um, my grandmother's cook accidentally
knocked my phone into the sink, and it stopped working.
But my grandmother says she'll get me a new one, one of
those superfancy ones that came out last week." I've heard
Brianna complaining to the other Bananas that her dad
won't buy her the newest phone, so I figure this is a good
opportunity to slip in a little jab at her. Brianna's mouth
falls open, jealousy stamped all over her face. *Yes.*

"Oh," Maddie says. "That's cool, I guess." She doesn't
seem to realize I'm lying to make Brianna jealous, and
when I remember her cracked screen, I realize I've accidentally made *her* jealous too. I try to send her a telepathic
message that the phone thing is fake, but she's staring
down at her cleats.

"Bring it to practice so we can play with it," Sabrina begs. "I hear there's this game on it where pizzas fall from the sky and you have to slice them up with lasers before they hit the ground."

"Definitely," I say. Hopefully, everyone will forget about this before I actually have to produce a new phone.

Maddie turns so she's facing me, obviously trying to cut the other girls out of the conversation. "So anyway, the reason I was calling is so I could ask if you wanted to sleep over on Friday. Mom says we can make those peanut butter cookies with the Hershey's Kisses on top, and Lindsay's going on this overnight thing for youth group, so you know what *that* means." I do know what that means—Maddie and I have spent hours poring over Lindsay's diaries when she's out with her friends. They're really fascinating and totally bizarre at the same time; I can't imagine I'll ever be that boy crazy, even when I'm sixteen. Once she liked four guys at the same time, and they were all named Mike.

Ordinarily, snooping in Lindsay's room would be an offer I couldn't refuse, but Friday night is heist night. I should tell Maddie I'm still grounded, but Brianna's sitting right there, and that won't go very far toward making her jealous of me. So instead I say, "Oh man, I'd love to, but I can't this week. I have to go to this fancy gala with my grandmother."

It's so unrealistic that Grandma Jo would take me to a gala that I expect Maddie to see through my lie right away, but her face falls. "Oh no. Really?"

"Those things are *sooooo* boring," Brianna says. "My father took me to one last Christmas when his company was getting an award, and I almost fell asleep at the table during the speeches. But at least the food was really good. The cake they served had little flecks of gold leaf on the top."

I want to say, "You can eat *gold*?" but maybe if I'd grown up as rich as Brianna, I'd already know that. So instead I try to look bored and say, "Yeah, they'll probably have stuff like that at this one too. And they're going to have a bunch of ice sculptures." I only remember it's July after that's out of my mouth, and I'm scared Brianna's going to call me out, but instead she nods like what I said was totally normal.

"I hope your grandmother's friends are more interesting than my dad's," she says. "All they talked about the entire night was their yachts. I mean, come on, we all have yachts. It doesn't make you special, you know?"

Maddie gives me a look like, *Is she for real?* I have a hard time biting back a laugh, but I don't let it show. "I know," I say. "My grandmother's friends are always going on about their private jets. But seriously, if you've seen one private jet, you've seen them all, right?"

Brianna nods, but I can tell she's impressed. "Totally," she says.

Sabrina and Elena are staring at us with wide eyes. "You guys have been on private jets?" Elena asks. "You're so lucky!"

I really don't want her to ask me what a private jet looks like on the inside, so I shrug and look down like I'm embarrassed by how good I have it. "It's really not as exciting as it sounds," I say.

"So, what are you wearing to the gala?" Brianna asks. It's the first time she's ever sounded truly interested in something I have to say, and it's pretty unnerving to have her full attention. What is *happening* right now? I'm trying to make her jealous of me, and it seems like I'm just making her like me more. Maybe I need to step up my game.

"Oh, I'm getting something new," I say. "Everyone knows you can't wear the same gown in public twice."

Brianna snorts out a laugh. "Yeah, seriously. You wouldn't want to look like *someone* we know." To my dismay, she looks very pointedly at Maddie, and the other

Bananas snicker. I glance over at my best friend and see that her face is turning bright red.

What am I supposed to do now? I want to stand up for Maddie, but that'll derail this whole gala conversation, which I started completely for Maddie's sake. Since the whole "make Brianna jealous" thing was her idea, I figure I should stick with that, so I don't say anything.

"You should get something that sparkles," Brianna says. "It'll look really elegant in the candlelight. And you should wear your hair up—that way you'll look older. My mom's stylist did mine kind of like this for the last gala. . . ." Brianna twists up her long, thick rope of hair and turns around to show me the result. "There were rhinestone pins here and here and here."

"What color dress do you think you'll get?" asks Sabrina.

My mind races, grasping for something, anything, that'll put snotty Brianna in her place. "Probably blue, since my grandmother says I can wear one of her sapphire necklaces," I say. "She says it'll bring out my eyes."

"Too bad you don't have your ears pierced," says Brianna. "I have some sapphire earrings you could've borrowed."

"Thanks for the offer, but I'm sure I'll have plenty of jewels without them." I toss my hair and try to make a haughty face at her. "I mean, it's not like I care about looking nice for the crusty old people at the benefit, but Stanley's driving me there, soooo . . ."

All three of the Bananas giggle. "He really is cute," Brianna says. "You're so lucky you get to hang out with him all the time."

I did it. Brianna Westlake actually admitted she was jealous of me! I look over at Maddie, sure she's going to be loving this whole exchange, and I'm surprised to find her gone—she's a little ways down the fence, laughing at something with Amy. I didn't even notice her getting up. When I catch her eye, she turns right back to Amy without even the smallest smile.

For a second, I wonder if she's mad about the "not wearing the same dress twice" comment. But she can't think I was actually being serious. She knows I don't care about dresses and that the only jewelry I ever wore was the bracelet she made me, before Fireball destroyed it. I tell myself it was a coincidence that she got up when she did; maybe Amy called her over and I didn't hear. But as Elena taps my shoulder and asks if I'm going to wear heels to my imaginary gala, I can't help feeling like I've done something wrong.

Maddie and I don't get to talk at all during practice. Coach Adrian's drills are tougher than usual today, and he makes us run suicides, back and forth and back and forth across the field until we're too winded to say anything. He finally lets us scrimmage at the end of the day, and he names Amy one of the team captains. I'm relieved when she picks me first and Maddie second, and as soon as my best friend jogs over to our side of the field, I approach her and touch her shoulder. "Hey," I whisper. "You know I wasn't serious about any of that stuff I said earlier, right?"

Maddie glances up at me. "What do you mean?"

"There's no gala or ice sculptures or new phone or anything—I made it all up. I would never wear sapphires or go dress shopping with my grandmother. I mean, can you even imagine? I was just trying to make Brianna jealous, like you told me to."

"*Oh*," Maddie says. She looks as relieved as she did that time she got a B on a geography test she thought she'd failed, and something in my chest releases. "I thought . . . I mean . . . wow. Okay. You were really convincing."

"I think she totally bought it. Did you see her face when I was talking about Stanley? She flat-out said she was jealous of me."

"I didn't hear that part," Maddie says. "So, if there's no gala, does that mean you can sleep over on Friday? We can think up more good lies to tell Brianna."

"No, I really can't," I say. "I'm still grounded from the other day."

"Oh. Maybe I could come over there, then? I could sneak Lindsay's diary out of her room after she leaves for youth group."

"I don't think that's going to work. I'm not even allowed to have friends over when I'm *not* grounded."

Maddie rolls her eyes. "Ugh, your grandma's so annoying. If I invite Amy over on Friday, maybe you could Skype with us?"

"I don't have a computer, remember?"

"Right. Jeez, it's like you're in prison or something."

"It feels like that sometimes," I say, though my grandmother's house is infinitely weirder than any prison.

"Okay. Well, next time, I guess. She can't ground you forever, right?"

I want more than anything to tell Maddie what's really going on, but I remember Grandma Jo saying she'd make me sorry if I let her secrets slip. It seems like it would be safe to talk about it in this open field; how could she possibly find out about it? But for all I know, she's bugged my cleats or something. I have no idea how that kind of thing works. So I just say, "Right. Next time."

Talking to my best friend has always been the easiest

thing in the world. But right now, for the first time, it feels a lot like running around in my grandmother's attic in the pitch dark, never knowing when I'm going to slam into a unsteady pile of boxes and send them crashing to the ground.

9

Now that she sees I can be useful to her, Grandma Jo finally seems to be warming up to me a little. She stops being quite so strict about my bedtime, speaks more gently when she reminds me which one is the salad fork, and even lets me have seconds on dessert sometimes. On Wednesday morning, she actually *does* take me shopping, though it's certainly not for a gala dress. Instead, she buys me a black stocking cap and some skintight black clothing that doesn't make even a whisper of noise when I move around. When the saleslady tells me I look adorable and asks what it's for, Grandma Jo tells her I'm playing a ninja in a community theater production. I'm impressed by the way the lie rolls off her tongue; I could probably learn a thing or two from her for the next time I have to talk to Brianna.

The night of the heist, Betty, Cookie, and Edna arrive early, and we pass the time playing Hearts until a quarter to twelve, when Grandma Jo sends me upstairs to get dressed. I pull on my new black turtleneck, pants, gloves, and soft-soled shoes, then put on my black knit hat. I'm way too hot, but I guess it's more important to be stealthy than comfortable tonight. I clip the utility belt Grandma Jo got me around my waist and make sure all the objects are in place: a flashlight, a tiny can of WD-40 in case the attic door creaks, some peanuts for Picasso, and my library card, in case I have to swipe open any dead bolts. When I look in the mirror and see myself all decked out in serious gear, it makes this heist seem real, and my heart starts hammering.

"Annemarie," Grandma Jo calls up the stairs, "are you ready?"

"Almost," I call back. At the last minute, I grab my broken friendship bracelet from my night table and shove the remains into my utility belt for luck.

When I come downstairs, I see that Edna's dressed in a skintight black bodysuit, to help her blend into the shadows while she picks the lock on the front door. Her tall, willowy frame looks even skinnier when it's not draped in all its usual scarves, and I feel like she might disappear if she turned sideways. Cookie and Betty are wearing regular clothes, since they have to look like normal pedestrians while they act as our lookouts. I was really hoping Grandma Jo would be wearing a ninja suit too, but she's in her usual black dress.

Cookie's holding a large wrapped present with a big red bow on top, and she holds it out to me. "For you," she says. "Your very first heist! We're so proud." She says it in the same teary way most parents talk about their kid's first day of kindergarten.

"Thank you so much, Cookie," I say. I take the present, which is lighter than it looks. "You didn't have to get me anything."

"It's from all of us," she says, and I start feeling a little less excited. If Grandma Jo had anything to do with this present, it'll probably be a dress or a device to monitor my posture or something. I try to keep an enthusiastic smile on my face as I rip open the wrapping paper and lift the lid off the box inside.

There, sitting in a nest of tissue paper, is . . . actually, I have no idea what this is. It's certainly not a dress. I lift out the object, which looks kind of like a camera with a long lens and two big, soft eyepieces. Attached to one side is a plastic ring and a bunch of crisscrossed straps. "Wow," I say. "I . . . um . . . what *is* this?"

"They're night vision goggles, dear," Betty says. "You didn't think we were going to send you into a dark, unfamiliar attic completely blind, did you?"

"*Whoa.*" This is by far the best thing Grandma Jo has ever gotten me. "Thank you so much! I did all those drills in the dark, so I assumed . . ."

"It's always good to be prepared to do the job without equipment, in case something malfunctions," Cookie says. "But if you have tools to help you, it would be stupid not to use them. Go ahead—try them on!"

The goggles look expensive, and I'm suddenly terrified I'm going to drop them. I carefully slip them over my head, and Cookie's bracelets clink and jangle and clatter next to my ears as she helps me tighten the straps. When the goggles fit snugly against my face, Edna kills the lights, and Cookie shows me where the power button is. The room springs back into focus before me, crisp and clear as if it were the middle of the day, except everything is bright green.

"Oh *man*," I whisper. "This is awesome! I can see *everything!*" Then I realize that these goggles will protect my eyes from Picasso's claws and beak, and I love them even more.

A neon green Cookie moves to stand in front of me.

"Aren't they wonderful?" she crows. "I knew you would love them!" She does a ridiculous little dance that only I can see, shimmying her shoulders and hips, and I start giggling.

"What's so funny?" Betty asks.

"Oh, nothing," green Cookie says, turning around and shaking her butt at me.

Edna flips the lights back on, and I push the goggles up onto the top of my head while Grandma Jo distributes little black earpieces to everyone. "I'll be listening from the van the whole time," she says. "Even if you whisper, I'll be able to hear you. If you're in trouble, say 'Mayday,' and I'll find a way to bail you out."

"Your grandmother's an amazing getaway car driver when her foot isn't all Velcroed up in a boot," Cookie says. "You should've seen the way she drove in '79 when we were being chased by—"

"Earpieces in," Grandma Jo orders, and to my extreme disappointment, Cookie takes the hint and stops talking. I watch what the other ladies do with their earpieces, then put mine in the same way.

"This is Agent Condor," my grandmother says when it's all secure, and it's so weird to hear her voice directly in my ear that I jump. "Agents, do you copy?"

"Agent Cardinal copies," says Cookie.

"Agent Sparrow copies," says Betty.

"Agent Heron copies," says Edna.

Grandma Jo looks at me. "What would you like your code name to be, Annemarie?"

I wish I'd known before now that we got to choose code names so I could've thought up something really cool. But everyone else has a bird name, so I guess I should stick to the theme. I try to think of a bird that's calm and graceful and bold and fierce all at once, all the qualities I'll need while I'm doing this heist.

And then it comes to me, and I smile to myself.

"Agent Swan copies," I say.

Fran Tupperman's house is twenty minutes from my grandmother's, and Cookie drives us over in Grandma Jo's black van with tinted windows—of course, *this* is what it's for. There's a giant dog carrier fitted with a bunch of perches strapped into the trunk so that Picasso will be comfortable on the ride home. Sitting in the backseat in my ninja clothes, I feel like a legitimate spy, and I'm starting to understand why the grannies like doing this so much. I love the feeling of being part of a team, and even though the heist hasn't even started yet, I can already feel the adrenaline rushing all the way to the tips of my fingers.

We park across the street and a couple houses down, close enough that Grandma Jo will have a good visual on us. Fran's house is almost as big as my grandmother's, and I realize for the first time how long those hallways I have to sneak down are going to be. But when I pull my night vision goggles back down over my eyes and turn them on, I feel a little calmer. *You can do this,* I tell myself. *You're way braver than you think, remember?*

"It's showtime," Grandma Jo says. "Everyone ready?" She sticks her hand out between the seats, and it's such an uncharacteristic move that it takes me a minute to realize she's doing a "Go team!" thing like Coach Adrian always has us do before our games.

"Ready," says Cookie. She puts her hand on top of Grandma Jo's.

"Ready," says Betty, adding her hand to the pile.

"Ready," says Edna dreamily. Her hand drifts down onto the pile like a floating leaf.

All of a sudden I really have to pee, which always happens when I'm nervous. I try to concentrate on willing the feeling away.

"Agent Swan?" Cookie says. "Everything okay?"

I swallow hard, then rest my hand on top of theirs, praying I can get through tonight without letting anyone down. I want so badly to see that impressed expression on my grandmother's face again.

"Ready," I say.

"'Heist' on three," Grandma Jo says. "One . . . two . . . three. . . ."

"Heist!" I shout, and as everyone's hands spring to their earpieces, I realize I should have whispered. "Oh God, sorry, sorry."

Grandma Jo sighs. "Well, now that Annemarie's woken the entire neighborhood, I suppose it's time to begin," she says. "Operation Freebird, commence. The faster we get this over with, the better."

Everyone but Grandma Jo gets out of the van, and the doors automatically slide closed behind us. Betty and Cookie blow me kisses as they head for opposite ends of the sidewalk, and I blow some back. It reminds me of how my parents always blow me kisses from the sidelines at my soccer games. I'm so glad they have no idea what I'm up to right now.

Fran's porch light is off, and Edna and I slip up the front steps in the darkness, quiet as shadows. Edna gently caresses the lock on the front door with one finger, then bends down and whispers into it, almost like she's asking it to open for her. Then she pulls out her lock picks and gets to work.

It doesn't seem like it would be exciting to watch someone pick a lock, but watching Edna is weirdly fascinating. She sticks a bent piece of metal into the bottom of the keyhole, then uses a sharp tool that looks like it belongs in a dentist's office to fiddle around in the top part. In my night vision goggles, her green, willowy form sways back and forth, like she's dancing with the lock, and she hums a soft, tuneless song that sends shivers up my spine. I've never seen Edna focus so intently on anything before. I've barely even seen her make eye contact.

"Stop humming, Heron," says my grandmother's voice, and the song comes to an abrupt halt.

I've heard that lock picking is really difficult, but it takes Edna less than a minute to open the door. When the lock turns, I feel a spark of *wanting* ignite deep inside me, like the first time I saw professional soccer players on TV when I was a little kid. Suddenly, more than anything, I want to learn how to do that.

"First barrier has been breached," Edna whispers. "Heron going in."

"Roger that," says my grandmother. I really hope I'll

get to say that later. It sounds so cool and professional.

Edna swings the front door open, and a faint beep-ing sound starts up inside the house—the security system. "Wait for my signal, Swan," Edna whispers, and then she pulls a pair of small wire cutters out of her utility belt and disappears inside.

Cookie did some recon work at Fran's last dinner party and determined that the alarm would beep for forty-five seconds before notifying the security company of a break-in. My grandmother counts down the seconds over the earpiece so Edna knows how long she has left, and everything feels like it's moving too quickly and too slowly all at once. If I were Edna, there's no way my fin-gers would work under this kind of pressure.

"Fourteen . . . thirteen . . . twelve . . . ," counts Grandma Jo, and I wonder if Edna's heart is beating as quickly as mine. Maybe all her meditating makes her immune to nerves.

"Eleven . . . ten . . . nine . . ."

I lower myself into a sprinter's crouch, ready to bolt back toward the van if the alarm goes off.

And then the beeping stops.

Everything is silent, but I barely have time for a sigh of relief before I hear Edna click her tongue twice, then three times, then twice more. That's my signal to come inside.

I try to move toward the door, but I suddenly start thinking about how breaking and entering is a crime. I haven't even started seventh grade yet, and in a second I'm going to be a legitimate *criminal*. I take a deep breath and think about what Ben said about mind over matter, but my muscles refuse to move. What if can't do this after all and I end up frozen on the doorstep all night? Will my grandmother kick me out of the house? Will Edna be able to climb all those stairs to get Picasso? What if she hurts herself and it's all my fault?

"You are a hollow reed, Swan," I hear Edna's voice whisper, as if she knows my body has turned into one giant knot of anxiety. "You are pliable and strong, swaying whichever way the wind shifts, always bending, never breaking."

I have absolutely no idea what she's talking about, but her tone is soothing, and weirdly enough, it calms me down. Before I know it, I'm moving over the threshold.

Edna points me toward the staircase, and I start to climb, testing each step to see if it creaks before I put my full weight on it. Cookie determined from her snooping that Fran's bedroom is the first one on the right, and I'm horrified to see that the door is halfway open—what if the beeping of the alarm has already awakened her? But as I creep closer, I'm comforted by the noise of soft, heavy breathing tinged with the slightest hint of a snore.

I cross my fingers, hold my breath, and tiptoe past the room. A floorboard creaks under my feet, and I freeze, but the rhythm of Fran's breathing doesn't change. The attic door is directly in front of me at the end of the hall, and I make my way toward it, step by stealthy step, wishing Fran had rugs on her ancient hardwood floors. The attic door is closed, and for a second I panic that it might be locked. But the knob turns smoothly, and I slip through and close it just enough that it'll open with a gentle push when I come back down.

The attic stairs are a lot creakier than the ones in the main house, but I do the best I can with them, creeping up on all fours to distribute my weight. Finally, after what feels like years, I reach the top. And directly across from me, in a cage not much bigger than the dog carrier in the back of the van, is the bird.

"Swan, what's your 20?" says Grandma Jo's voice in my ear.

I have no idea what that's supposed to mean. "What?" I whisper.

"She wants to know where you are," explains Cookie.

"Do you have eyes on the target?" Grandma Jo asks.

"Yup," I say. "He's right here."

Picasso rustles a little as I approach; he's probably not used to company at this time of night. I can see him clearly with my goggles on, but he probably can't see me at all, so I turn on my flashlight and set it on the floor next to his cage, pointed up at the ceiling. I push up my goggles up onto the top of my head so I won't look like an alien, and whisper, "Hi, Picasso."

"Hello," he replies, louder than I would've liked. His voice is higher than Fireball's, and I wonder if he's imitating Fran.

"My name is AJ," I say, even though I know he can't understand me.

"Hello, hello," Picasso says again, very loudly.

"Shhh, we have to be very quiet, okay? I'm going to get you out of here."

I approach the cage, careful not to make any sudden movements, but Picasso doesn't seem the least bit agitated. When I grab a peanut from my utility belt and hold it out to him, he goes right for it, and I snatch my fingers back as he chomps down on it.

"Good boy," I say, fiddling with the latch on his cage. "You're a very good bird."

"Stupid bird," he replies.

I stop. "What did you say?"

Picasso ducks his head under his wing, ruffles up some feathers, and smoothes them back down into place. When he's done, he squawks, "Stupid bird! Shut up, stupid bird!"

Grandma Jo makes a *tsk* sound over my earpiece, and I remember how she told me that birds repeat sounds they've heard over and over. I suddenly feel incredibly bad for Picasso, and I'm more convinced than ever that liberating him is the right thing to do.

"You're a *nice* bird," I tell him as I swing the cage door open. "You're a *very* sweet bird. And once we're out of here, nobody's ever going to call you stupid again." My heart is pounding, but I grit my teeth and reach my hand into his cage.

"Stupid bird," Picasso says. He hops onto my wrist with no hesitation at all.

I pull him out slowly, and he immediately starts picking at my glove, the edge of my sleeve, the seam down the center of my shirt. I know he's not trying to hurt me, but I still don't like his beak so close to me, so I hold him as far away from my body as I can. "Hang on a couple more minutes, buddy, and you'll have plenty of stuff to play with," I say.

"Have you acquired the target, Swan?" asks Grandma Jo's voice.

"Yes," I whisper back. "Everything's going fine." Carefully, I gather up my flashlight, push my goggles back into place, and head for the door.

And that's when Picasso bursts into song.

"*I'm dreaming of a whiiiiiiiite Christmaaaaaaas . . . ,*" he belts at the top of his lungs. "*Just like the ones I used to knoowwwww. . . .*"

"Shhhh!" I hiss at him, but it doesn't make any difference. Picasso is in full-on performance mode now, and he continues to sing about sleigh bells in the snow.

"Mayday!" I hiss into my earpiece. "How do I get him to shut up?"

"That idiotic woman," grumbles my grandmother. "She only takes him out when she wants him to perform. He associates being out of his cage with singing."

"*Whiiiiiiite Christmaaaaas . . . ,*" Picasso warbles.

"But what do I *do*?" I'm frantic now—what if Fran Tupperman comes upstairs to see what the racket is and finds me here? What if this stupid Christmas song sends me to jail?

"Keep him busy with something else!" Grandma Jo says.

I pull another peanut out of my pouch and hold it near

Picasso's beak. To my great relief, he pauses for a second and gulps it down. Then he leans over and starts biting at the Velcro on my glove, which I don't exactly appreciate, but at least he's being quiet.

I start creeping down the stairs as quietly as I can, but even with the night vision goggles, it's really hard to see with a three-foot bird on my arm. I try to hold him down lower so he's not directly in my line of vision, but he doesn't seem to like that, and he starts climbing my arm. "Picasso, down!" I hiss as he inches up my forearm and into the crook of my elbow. Before I know it, he's halfway up my biceps. I shake my arm a little, but that only makes him grip me more tightly, and I can feel his claws biting into the fabric of my skintight shirt.

"Step up," he insists. "Stupid bird."

I try to grab his feet with my other hand so I can make him switch arms, but he doesn't like that either, and he pecks at my hand. I yank it away, barely managing not to cry out, and Picasso seizes the opportunity. In two more quick hops, he's up on my shoulder, very, *very* close to my face, and he starts biting at the straps on my goggles. When I crane my neck and twist my face away from him, I lose my footing, crash down a couple of steps, and land on my butt. My whole body is sweating inside my suit.

"Everything okay in there, Swan?" says Grandma Jo's voice in my ear.

"Roger," I whisper, wishing I could've said it under better circumstances.

I stay as still as I can for a minute and listen, trying to determine whether my clumsiness has woken Fran, but I can't hear anything over the pounding of my heart and the rustling of Picasso's feathers. I take my earpiece out for a second so I can hear better, but even that doesn't help, since Picasso chooses that moment to belt, "*May alllll youuuur Chriiiiiistmasses be whiiiiite. . . .*"

"Oh my God, shut *up*," I whisper frantically, and Picasso agrees, "Shut up, shut up!" He's inching around to the back of my neck now, and his long tail feathers brush my spine, like I'm wearing a bird backpack. I'm completely freaking out now that I can't see him—he could do *anything* back there—but I can't seem to get him to move no matter how I contort. It looks like I'm going to have to run all the way out to the car like this.

I start creeping toward the bottom of the attic stairs again, and Picasso stays quiet for a minute, occupied with picking at the back of my goggles. But when we reach the bottom and I pause to open the door, he starts up again. "*I'm dreeeeeaming of a whiiiite Christmaaaas. . . .*"

I hear the unmistakable sound of rustling from the bedroom. "Shut *up*, stupid bird," a voice says sleepily.

I freeze in my tracks, not sure which direction to flee. Should I bolt for the front door? Or would it be better to go back up to the attic and wait for Fran to go back to sleep? How will I know when it's safe to come down? How long is it going to take for Picasso to get bored of my back and climb up onto my head? The need to get him off me is visceral, like the need to smash a mosquito when you notice it sucking your blood. It probably won't be long before I panic, and then I'll be completely useless.

Forward it is.

Somewhere in the back of my mind, I remember how much Grandma Jo's birds seem to enjoy ripping stuff up. In a last desperate attempt to keep Picasso occupied and quiet, I pull off one of my gloves and dangle it behind my head, approximately where I think his beak might be. "Here you go, boy," I whisper. "Go ahead and destroy it." I feel terrible offering Edna's hard work to a bird, but I don't really have another choice. To my relief, he takes it, and I bolt through the attic door and down the hallway while he's busy figuring out what to do with it. The hallway floor squeaks under my feet a lot more than it did on my way in, but speed is more important than stealth right now. Picasso absolutely *cannot* launch into another musical number outside Fran's bedroom door.

The only sound I hear as we dash down the stairs is the quiet ripping noise of my glove coming apart at the seams. I try not to think about how quickly Picasso is shredding it and what that implies about the things he could do to the back of my head.

Edna is waiting for me at the bottom of the stairs, and she whispers, "Swan incoming," into her earpiece.

"Copy that," says my grandmother's voice, followed by a quiet, "Thank the Lord."

Out onto the front steps I go, and Edna slips out behind me and closes the door. I sprint across the street, adrenaline pumping through my blood, praying Picasso doesn't decide to make a break for it—I can only imagine how my grandmother would react if I managed to get him out of the house only to accidentally release him into the wild. But he doesn't let go of me as I make my mad dash; maybe riding on my shoulders is fun for him. I used to love it when my dad ran around with me on his shoulders. Soon I'm at the van, and my grandmother whispers, "Swan is in the nest." She opens the van's back doors, and then I feel the sweet sensation of Picasso being lifted off my neck. My hand flies back to feel for broken skin and brush all the bird molecules off me.

"Hello, beautiful boy," my grandmother croons to Picasso as she snaps open the latches on the dog carrier. "You're safe now. You're going to be so happy here with me."

I did it. I actually *did it*. Grandma Jo didn't believe I could handle this heist, but I managed it, even though there were problems I never could've foreseen. We couldn't have liberated Picasso if it weren't for me, and now he's safe, headed for a life of treats and cuddles and never being forced to sing on command. I watch as he drops the shredded remains of my glove and hops up onto his new perch to investigate.

"Say thank you to Annemarie for rescuing you," Grandma Jo says to Picasso, and when she glances at me out of the corner of her eye, I realize that's *her* way of thanking me for participating in the heist.

"You're very welcome, Picasso," I say. "It was my pleasure."

"Shut up, stupid," Picasso says.

It's so quick and quiet that it's possible I'm imagining things, but before she turns away, I swear I catch my grandmother laughing.

10

My heist adrenaline keeps me up most of the night, and by the time I leave for soccer the next morning, I'm completely exhausted. We're playing the Falcons—seriously, why is my entire life filled with birds?—and it would be hard to beat them even under normal circumstances. But today I have more to worry about than sloppy playing. As far as the rest of my team knows, I spent last night at a gala in sapphires and heels, and I know they're going to pepper me with questions the second I arrive. This whole "make Brianna jealous" thing was fun when it just involved gushing about Stanley, but I feel like I've taken it too far now, and I'm not sure I can keep lying convincingly.

To make matters worse, I know absolutely nothing about galas. It would be one thing if I were trying to trick a bunch of other clueless people, but Brianna has probably been to a million *real* galas, and I'm sure she's going to see right through me. My brother always warned me that lies feed on themselves and get more complicated with time. Why didn't I remember that before I got myself into this mess?

Stanley has been talking for the last five minutes, telling me a story about the time he and his roommate got locked out of their dorm and had to break in by climbing up the fire escape. It's a good story, and ordinarily I'd be laughing my head off, but I'm having a lot of trouble paying attention today. Finally, he reaches over and raps the top of my head with his knuckles.

"Knock knock," he says. "Anybody home in there?"

"Sorry, I'm so sorry," I babble. "I'm totally listening."

Stanley laughs. "I don't care if you listen to my dumb story. Are you okay? You look worried."

It's kind of cool that he's tuned into my moods enough to notice when I'm distracted; according to Maddie's sister's diary, guys usually don't pick up on stuff like that. I'm about to tell him everything is fine, but then I realize he might actually be able to help me. "Have you ever been to a formal event?" I ask.

"Um, I went to prom," he says. "And I went to a superfancy

Christmas party at my dad's boss's house once. Does that count?"

"I don't know. I guess," I say. It's certainly way better than any experiences I have to work with. "Can you, like, describe them to me? With a lot of details?"

He gives me a weird look. "Is your grandmother taking you to an event? You don't have to be nervous—I'm sure she'll tell you what to expect."

"No, it's not that." I take a deep breath. "Here's the thing. I might've tried to make someone jealous by telling her I was going to a gala with my grandmother on Friday but I didn't really think it through and now she's going to ask me all these questions about it and I don't know anything about galas." It all comes out in one rushed run-on sentence.

I brace myself for Stanley's laugh, but instead he nods, like he knows exactly how I feel. "I did the same thing once," he says. "In fifth grade, there was this guy at school who always made fun of me, so I told him my dad got us tickets to the World Cup in Germany. I mean, I watched it on TV and everything, but I had no idea what it was like to actually *be* there."

The most surprising thing about this isn't that Stanley lied about going to the World Cup—it's that someone used to make fun of him at school. Did he use to be dorky? I want to ask him about it, but I figure that's probably private. "What did you do?" I ask.

"When he asked me about it, I barely talked about the games at all. I made up all these other stories that he couldn't possibly check, about the people sitting near us and the amazing food I ate and how my dad let me watch movies in the hotel room all night. I told him I got lost on the street and one of the players gave me directions."

"You think Brianna—um, I mean, this person—would believe stuff like that?"

"Definitely. Try to look confident and she'll swallow it right down."

I nod, already starting to formulate stories. "Thanks," I say. "That's a really good idea."

We pull up in front of the field, and Stanley puts the car in park and gets out to open my door as usual. But when I stand up, before I even know what's happening, he reaches out and pulls me into a one-armed hug. He's so much taller than I am that my face is right by his armpit, and I can smell his boy deodorant, which is super embarrassing for some reason. I wish I'd had more time to prepare for being this close to him so I could actually enjoy it.

"It's going to be fine, kiddo," he says. "Try not to worry. Okay?"

I open my mouth to answer, but there are absolutely zero words left in my brain. Before I manage to form a sentence, he's gone.

I'm still standing there, frozen like a statue, when Brianna rushes over to my side and links her arm with mine. "Oh. Em. *Gee*," she squeals. "Is there something going *on* between you and the cute chauffeur?"

"I . . . um . . . ," I stammer as the car pulls away. I put my hand to my cheek, which is *burning* hot. There's definitely nothing going on between us, but the way Brianna has misinterpreted things is kind of perfect, so I force a secretive smile onto my face. "Maybe."

"Have you kissed him yet? Isn't kissing the *best*? This one time, I was at a swimming party with these supercute boys, and . . ."

Brianna launches into this whole kissing story, but I'm not even listening, because I've just noticed Maddie across the parking lot. She's staring at our linked arms with this hurt, surprised look on her face. I try to pull away, but Brianna has a good, strong hold on me and is steering me toward the field. Oh no, she's acting like we're actual *friends*. This whole plan has totally backfired.

"AJ!" Brianna snaps, and I realize she's waiting for me to respond to whatever she's been talking about. We're on the field now, and Sabrina, Elena, and three other girls have crowded around us, closing me in. I can't even see Maddie anymore.

"What?" I ask. I finally manage to extract myself from her grip.

"I *said*, how was the gala last night? Were you bored out of your mind? Did your grandmother make you stay the whole time? My parents never leave those things until the very end. I always tell them it's more fashionable to leave early, because it makes you look like you have some- where even cooler to go, but they never listen."

"What did you wear?" Sabrina asks. "Did your grand- mother really let you have her sapphires?"

It's the weirdest feeling ever, looking into their eager eyes. Not one of these girls has ever been remotely inter- ested in what I had to say before, but now that Brianna has made it clear that I'm someone worth knowing, they look ready to hang on to my every word. I know this isn't real friendship, but at the same time, it's interesting to see what popularity would be like. I hate myself for even thinking that, but it's hard not to appreciate the attention.

"I ended up getting a green dress, so the sapphires didn't

really match," I tell Sabrina. "I wore one of my grandmother's diamond pendants instead."

"How many carats?" asks Brianna.

"Were there really ice sculptures?" Elena asks at the same time.

I have no idea what Brianna's question even means, so I pretend I didn't hear her. "There were ice sculptures for a while," I say. "But it was kind of warm in the room, so they started melting right away, and one of them, this big swan, started dripping all over the floor. One of the waiters walked by with a huge tray of shrimp, and he slipped in the puddle and fell right into the dessert table, which had all these little mini tart things and chocolate-covered strawberries and stuff. The table collapsed under him, and the swan smashed into a million pieces, and the guy was, like, *covered* with custard and fruit." Stanley's right—the girls seem totally rapt. I could tell them anything right now and they'd believe it.

"Man, what a waste of dessert," says Sabrina. She seems genuinely sad about it, like I told her someone died.

"Do you have pictures?" Elena asks. "Are they on your new phone? Can I see it?"

I shake my head. "I don't have any pictures—I'm sorry."

"Aw, not even of your dress?"

"Nope. I tried to teach my grandmother how to work the camera, but . . ." I make a face like, *You know how old people are.*

"You could've asked Stanley," Brianna says, wiggling her eyebrows at me. "You guys should've seen them hugging in the parking lot when he dropped AJ off! It was sooooo cute!"

Everyone squeals and jumps up and down, and Sabrina throws her arms around me like it's something she does all the time. I'm so surprised that it doesn't even occur to me to hug her back. "Oh my God, you are *so lucky!*" she shrieks.

"It's really no big deal," I say, but I know I'm turning red again, which must make it look like there's more going on than I'm willing to spill. "He did like my dress last night, though. He told me I looked stunning. And he gave me a flower." It occurs to me that when Stanley told me to make up detailed stories, he probably didn't mean stories about us being all lovey-dovey with each other. In my head, I silently apologize to him.

"What kind of flower?" Sabrina asks.

"A pink rose."

She sighs. "That's *soooo* romantic." I can't believe how well I'm pulling this off, and a rush of pride surges through me. But then Sabrina bends over to fix her shoe, and I catch a glimpse of Maddie standing across the lawn with Amy, laughing at some joke I'll never hear. Suddenly, everything I'm doing over here starts to feel really, really wrong.

"Hey, I've gotta to talk to Maddie for a second before the game starts, okay?" I say.

"Whatever." Brianna turns to Elena. "Ugh, look at Becky's *hair*."

Elena scrunches up her nose like she smells rotten eggs. "Hasn't she ever heard of conditioner?"

"She clearly needs us to educate her," Brianna says. Elena giggles and takes her arm, and they set off across the grass toward our poor, unsuspecting teammate. Sabrina trails along behind them, but she doesn't look happy about it.

I jog over to Maddie and Amy. Maddie's saying something about cookie dough, and Amy's laughing and shoving her, but they both go quiet as soon as I arrive. "Hey," I say.

"Hey," Amy answers, and Maddie echoes her, but then she suddenly pretends to be very busy redoing her ponytail. Amy's face looks friendly, but instead of launching into some crazy story like usual, she just stands there and waits for me to say something.

"What're you guys talking about?" I ask. I know it sounds kind of desperate, but I feel desperate.

"Nothing," Maddie says at the same time Amy says, "I may have eaten a little too much cookie dough last night. But it was totally worth it."

"We only had enough left to bake, like, ten cookies," Maddie says.

"Yeah, and who ate *all* of those?"

"Jordan had at least three," Maddie says, and I realize she really did invite Amy to sleep over when I said no. I'm not sure they've ever had a sleepover without me before, and even though I was the one who turned them down, it makes my stomach squirm like I've swallowed a live goldfish.

"I'm really sorry I couldn't come," I say. "Trust me, I would way rather have been with you than with my grandmother. Do you guys want to have another sleepover this week? Maybe Thursday, since we don't have soccer on Friday?"

Maddie looks skeptical. "You're not grounded anymore?"

It's not like I've asked my grandmother, but I did such a good job with the Picasso heist that I feel like I can use it as leverage. "No, I'm totally free," I say. "Grandma Jo will freak out if I bring anyone into her house, though. Do you think we could do it at one of yours?"

Maddie and Amy look at each other, and for a second, I think neither of them is going to volunteer. But then Maddie says, "I guess we can go to mine. I'll ask my mom."

"Great," I say. I'm trying to sound perky, but I kind of come off sounding like a cartoon character, and Maddie gives me this look like, *Why are you acting so weird?* "Right after soccer on Thursday, then?"

"Sure," Maddie says.

Amy nods. "Sounds good." Fortunately, Coach Adrian blows his whistle, and I breathe a sigh of relief as I jog into a huddle with the rest of the team before things have a chance to get too awkward.

I try to leave my baggage at the door, like Coach Adrian always says, and I have a better game than I expected— one goal, two assists. We end up beating the Falcons three to two. But even though my body's moving freely, doing everything I tell it to do, I feel like my brain is all tied up in knots, tripping over its own feet at every turn.

11

Since the heist is over, I expect to find the grannies in the parlor when I get home, relaxing and playing cards like on the first day I met them. But the parlor is empty, and I hear voices coming from the storage room. As I'm heading upstairs to change out of my uniform, the door opens and Cookie's voice calls, "Is that you, AJ?"

"Yup. Hi, Cookie!"

"Come join us when you're ready. I brought pie to celebrate."

"Don't worry—she didn't bake it herself," calls Betty's voice.

I smile to myself and tell them I'll be right down. The grannies and I have never really gotten to hang out and have fun together before, and I'm excited to see what they're like when they're not busy planning something important. Now that we have the heist out of the way, maybe we can just chat and get to know each other. After all the awkwardness today at soccer, I'm pretty sure spending time with them will be way less weird than talking to my own friends.

But when I get down to the storage room, they're not relaxing—they're huddled around the table in the center of the room, examining some blueprints. When Cookie spots me at the door, she drops the pen she's holding, picks up a pie plate, and starts dancing it toward me. It says GO AJ! across it in big, sloppy whipped cream letters, which reminds me of something my parents would do, and it makes me miss them all over again. Once, when I won an essay contest at school, I woke up the next morning to find a snowman in the front yard holding a flag that said AJ = #1!

"For she's a jolly good fellow, for she's a jolly good fellow . . . ," Cookie sings.

Edna starts doing strange interpretive dance moves, dipping her head and fluttering her hands in the air as Betty joins in on the song. When they get to the last line, all three of them stop and look at Picasso, who's sitting on Grandma Jo's shoulder.

"*Which nobody can deny*," he squawks, and everyone bursts into laughter and applause. Even Grandma Jo claps, though I suspect she's clapping more for the macaw than for me.

"My dear, you were absolutely brilliant last night," Cookie says, handing me the pie.

"We couldn't have asked for a better accomplice," Edna says.

Betty puts her arm around me. "This girl is no accomplice. She's the main event. Wasn't she wonderful, Jo?"

Grandma Jo sighs; I can tell she thinks they're making way too much of a fuss over me. To her, accomplishment is its own reward. But she says, "You did very well, Annemarie," and then she gestures to the tea tray. "Here, have a drink."

There are four cups of disgusting tea on the tray, but in the fifth spot is a tall glass of Coke with ice and a lemon slice perched on the rim. I'm so surprised that I just blink at it for a second; Grandma Jo has never taken my likes and dislikes into account before.

"Well?" she says. "Do you want it or not?"

"Yes. Thank you," I say. I pick up the Coke, take a long sip, and smile at her. Then I turn to Cookie. "You guys are so nice. I was happy to help with the heist; you really didn't have to get me a pie."

"Well, it's not *all* for you." She snatches the pie away and starts cutting it.

I peek at the blueprints on the table. "What're these for?" I ask.

"They're for our next project, of course!" Betty says. "Take a look."

"Already?" I ask. "Don't you think you guys deserve a day off?"

Cookie looks at me like I'm crazy. "Why would we want that? This is such *fun*. Didn't you have a good time last night?"

I think back over the evening—my nervousness when I thought Edna wouldn't be able to disarm the security system, my terror that Picasso's singing would wake Fran, my revulsion at the feeling of bird claws on the back of my neck. But the adrenaline and the pride and the feeling of success outshine all those other things, and I realize I *did* have a good time. "Yeah," I say. "It was actually really fun."

"Excellent." Cookie beams, then taps the blueprint in front of her. "Now, our next project requires very specific timing. We have to do it in the next eight days if we're going to do it at all. This house belongs to—"

Grandma Jo cuts her off. "I don't know if—"

"Jo, it's not fair to expect her to help us if she's not part of the process right from the get-go." Cookie turns to me. "You want to help us plan, don't you, AJ?"

I concentrate on serving myself a piece of the pie so I have a second to think. I kind of expected I'd be gone already by the time they did their next heist, but if there's time for me to be involved again, I guess I *do* want to. I definitely don't want to be exiled back to the dining room with the sewing book.

"Sure," I say. "I'm happy to help, if it's for a good cause. Are we stealing another bird?"

"Bird, bird, stupid bird," Picasso chimes in.

"Oh no, dear," Cookie says. "We only steal birds when it's Jo's turn. This time it's *my* turn." She rubs her hands together, thrilled as a kid who's winning at Candy Land.

"What did you pick to, um, liberate?" I ask.

"We're going to pay a little visit to my ex-husband. He got *quite* a few things in our divorce settlement that are rightfully mine."

"It's ex-husband number three this time," Betty clarifies.

My mouth drops open. "You have *three* ex-husbands?"

"Four, actually. Five divorces altogether—I married one of the suckers twice. I was young and stupid." Cookie shrugs like it's a mistake anyone could make. "Wait for the right boy, AJ. Don't marry the first Romeo who names his boat after you and sails you around the Caribbean."

I can't imagine anyone ever doing that for me, but I nod anyway. My brain unhelpfully provides an image of Stanley in a sleek white sailboat called *The Annemarie*, and I push it away.

"So, what are we taking from ex-husband number three?" I ask.

"A stuffed bear," Cookie says, in that same "This is totally normal" voice.

"Really? You want to steal a stuffed animal?"

Cookie, Betty, and Edna burst into laughter. "Not a plush toy, dear," Cookie explains. "A *taxidermy* bear."

"*Oh.*" That's a completely different story. "How big is it?"

"About six feet? It's not a prizewinning specimen or anything. It's very old, though—my father shot it back in the twenties. It was in his hunting lodge all through my childhood, and I moved it into our parlor when my father died. But when Bill and I split up, he convinced the judge he'd shot it himself. What a dunderhead—any idiot who looked closely should've been able to tell it hadn't been stuffed using modern taxidermy techniques." Cookie shakes her head. "In any case, it's time for good ol' Teddy Roosevelt to come home to Mama."

"So, what do you say, darling?" Betty asks. "Will you help?"

It's definitely strange, but it doesn't seem morally *wrong* to steal something that technically already belongs to you. "All right, I'm in," I say. "But I'd kind of like to learn how to do more stuff this time, if that's okay. Maybe you could teach me how to pick locks, Edna?"

Edna beams mistily at me. "Of course," she says. "I've been hoping you'd ask. I could tell right away from your aura that you'll be good at this. So few people understand the grand art of lock picking, and I need to pass down my knowledge before I lose my dexterity. You'll be the perfect protégé."

I think of how the lock sprang open under Edna's fingers as if by magic last night; she doesn't seem remotely close to losing her dexterity. But I like hearing myself and the word "protégé" in the same sentence, so I don't protest. I wonder if my grandmother will argue that I'm not ready, but instead she gives a small nod.

"Awesome," I say. "When can we start?"

"No time like the present." Edna springs up from the table, and her four green scarves billow out like tentacles. "Jo, where have you put my locks?"

"They're in the Sunkist box near the ocelot," Grandma Jo says.

"This project will be an excellent opportunity for you to learn, since we won't be in any hurry," Cookie says as Edna retrieves her equipment. "Bill's on his yearly fishing trip, so it's the perfect time for a break-in."

I know I shouldn't feel excited about the prospect of breaking into someone's house, but I can't help it—I do. And I like the way Cookie calls what we're doing a "project." It makes me feel like I'm learning a skill for school, totally normal and aboveboard.

I hope my parents and Ben never find out what a delinquent I've become.

Edna rummages around in the box for a minute, then brings a ring of keys and a bunch of locks back to the table and drops them on top of the blueprints with a clatter-crash. I was expecting the kind of padlocks you use on a gym locker, but these are much bigger, and I realize they're the kind that get embedded in doors. Then she takes a smooth, worn leather case out of her purse and snaps it open, revealing a set of silver lock picks. I extract one that has a funny squiggly end and turn it over in my hands. Just holding it makes me feel weirdly powerful.

"This is really cool," I say. "So, how do I start?"

Edna explains how a lock works, which is something I've never really thought about before. There are a bunch of little pins inside it that are all different lengths, and they stop the plug inside the lock from turning because they don't line up. But the jagged teeth on a key push them up so all the tops are in the same place, and then the plug can turn. Edna shows me how to insert a tiny wrench into the bottom of the keyhole and turn it slightly for tension. Then she inserts one of the picks and explains how you have to feel around until you've pushed each of the pins up, one by one. Sometimes you can bounce more than one of them into place at the same time by "raking" the lock, which means doing this sort of scooping motion with the pick. I recognize it from what she was doing at Fran Tupperman's house.

It's finicky, intricate work, and even though she has tons of practice, it still takes Edna a couple minutes to get this lock open. While she works, she stares into the middle distance, like she's watching a movie being projected on the air, and hums that same eerie little song from last night. Finally, the lock turns, and we all applaud.

"Watching you do that never gets old," Cookie says.

Edna rewards her with a misty smile. "I'd imagine not," she says.

She finds the right key and turns it in the lock, and

the bolt pops back out. "Go ahead and try, AJ," she says, sliding the lock and the picks over to me.

I shove the wrench in like she showed me, ready to blow everyone away by how great I am at this, and the lock promptly slips out of my hands, slides across the table, and crashes to the floor. Grandma Jo winces at the sound, and one of the parrots screeches, "*Walk the plank, matey!*"

"Thanks," I grumble at him. "I really appreciate your encouragement."

"Stupid bird," Picasso agrees as Cookie hands the lock back to me.

"You can do it, dear," Betty says. "Edna probably didn't get it on her first try, either."

"I did, actually." Edna doesn't sound like she's bragging, just stating a fact.

I try again, and this time the wrench holds, so I stick the pick in above it. "Use your third eye to see inside," Edna suggests. "Sometimes it helps if you politely ask the lock to open for you."

I'm pretty sure I'd feel stupid talking to a lock, so I stay quiet and jiggle the pick around, but I'm not even really sure what I'm feeling for. A couple times, it catches on something that might be a pin, but I can't figure out how to push it up. All four of the grannies are looking at me expectantly, like maybe I'll be some sort of superstar at this, and I hate that I'm going to disappoint them. The pick and the wrench grow slick as my hands start to sweat.

"I, um, I think my third eye might need glasses," I say, and Cookie lets out a guffaw. I even catch the corner of Grandma Jo's mouth twitching a little, the ghost of a smile.

Edna comes around behind me and puts her hands over mine on the pick and the wrench. She smells like my mom's spice drawer. "Relax," she says to me, and I loosen my grip. Edna starts moving the pick in tiny, prob-ing motions. "Listen to what the lock is telling you. Oh, there's a pin—we've got it . . . feel for the little click it makes when it slips into place." She makes the smallest motion, and she's right, there is a tiny click. It's barely enough to feel, but a thrill runs through me.

"I felt it!" I tell her, and she nods against my hair.

"Four more to go," she says.

Edna stays behind me, and together we manipulate three more of the pins into place. "The last one's yours," she says, and before I can get nervous again, she says, "Take your time. We have nowhere else to be. Keep breathing. You're a hollow reed. You can do it."

And as it turns out, I *can*. It takes me half an hour to get the last pin, but I try to stay calm and quiet and breathe through my impatience, and finally, *finally*, I feel that telltale little click. "I did it!" I say quietly, hardly daring to move. "Edna! I got it!"

"Very good, dear," she says mildly, and I wonder what it would take to get her really excited. "Now turn the wrench in the same direction you'd turn a key . . . slowwwwly, now. . . ."

I do, and I let out a cheer as the bolt retracts. "Yeah!" I scream, pumping my fist. "I did it! Did you guys see that?" Grandma Jo puts her hand to her heart at the sudden noise, but Cookie throws her arms around me and we hug-jump around in a circle. Betty whoops and does a little happy dance, pushing her walker from side to side, and I laugh and hug her, too. She reaches up to pat my cheek, her eyes shining with pride.

"Knock it off, Tommy," says one of the birds.

"Well done," Edna says. "If you do this again and again, it'll eventually become second nature. I'll bring you some picks to practice with tomorrow."

"Thanks," I say. "I'd love that." When I glance over at Grandma Jo, she gives me one of those slow nods that mean *I respect what you've done*, and I smile. I'm pretty sure I've impressed her.

The grannies go back to their planning, and I spend the rest of the day at the table with my plate of forgotten pie, poking and prodding at the insides of the locks. It's funny—lock picking involves the same kinds of repetitive, small, precise motions as sewing, but this doesn't bore me at all. It's like a puzzle, and every time I make one of the tiny pins click into place, I feel a rush of joy. This is going to take a lot of practice, but I know I'll put in the work. What's the use of being a thief unless I'm the best thief I can be?

After all, a lady strives for perfection.

12

Grandma Jo agrees to let me sleep over at Maddie's house on Thursday night as long as I spend all my afternoons practicing my lock picking in preparation for Friday's bear heist. On Thursday morning, she sits me down and gives me a talk about how I am not to mention the heists to my friends *under any circumstances*, no matter how tired I get, but she's not nearly as snippy about it as usual. I can't believe I've actually started to prove to Grandma Jo that I'm a responsible person, but shockingly enough, it seems like I'm on the right track.

Before I go, I cut three big pieces of the leftover chocolate cake in the kitchen, wrap them in aluminum foil, and sneak them into my bag as a peace offering for Maddie. It's only fair that my friends should get to taste

Debbie's baking even though they're not allowed in my grandmother's house.

I avoid Brianna all through soccer practice, and I'm pretty sure Maddie notices, because things between us don't feel awkward at all. I wonder if maybe I imagined the weirdness between us the other day. As we run our laps, she and Amy and I talk about nothing—whether Skittles or M&M'S are better, how Maddie's sister wants to audition for a reality show, whether or not my parents have killed any anacondas in the Amazon. When Amy wants to know how to kill an anaconda, Maddie and I tag-team, explaining what my dad taught us, talking over each other and making wild hand gestures like we always used to do. Is it possible things have gone back to normal without me even having to try?

I'm changing out of my cleats at the end of practice, feeling pretty relaxed about the evening ahead, when Brianna jogs over. She doesn't say hi to Amy or Maddie; it's like she doesn't even see them. "Here," she says as she holds out a thick silver envelope to me.

On the front, my name is written in calligraphy—not *AJ*, but full-blown *Annemarie*. The paper is thick and expensive, and I feel bad for touching it with my sweaty hand. "What is this?" I ask.

"It's for my birthday party next week," Brianna says. I can feel Maddie and Amy exchanging a look behind my back, but I say, "Okay, cool," because what else am I supposed to do? It's not like I can refuse to take the invitation.

"Let me know if you can come as soon as possible, okay? We need to know how many cosmetologists to hire and how many lobsters to order." Brianna spins around and stalks off, and Maddie shoots her a look of such pure hatred that I'm surprised Brianna's head doesn't explode, showering brains and diamond earrings and clumps of perfect hair everywhere.

"That was really rude of her," I say; maybe the damage won't be so bad if I get that out in the open right away. "I'm sorry she did that in front of you guys."

Maddie snorts. "As if I'd actually *want* to go to her party. Lobsters are disgusting; they're like giant underwater bugs. And what the heck is a cosmetologist? Is that like a Russian astronaut?"

"I think that's a cosmonaut," Amy says. I try to stuff the silver envelope into my bag, where we can all forget about it, but she snatches it right out of my hand. "Let me see that."

I want to tell her to give it back, but that'll make it sound like I actually want it, so I sit quietly while she rips it open. "Oh my *God*," she says, holding it out so Maddie can see it too. "Can you even *believe* this? 'Please join Brianna Westlake for a celebratory makeover and lobster boil on the occasion of her thirteenth birthday.'" She reads it in a snooty British accent that doesn't sound anything like Brianna, but it makes Maddie laugh.

"I mean, I'm not going to go," I say. I take the envelope back and stuff it out of sight.

Maddie shrugs. "You should go if you want to." It almost sounds like a dare.

"I *don't* want to. Why would I want to?" I throw my cleats on top of the envelope to show her how much I don't care about it, and they make a dent in one of the pieces of cake. I'll be sure to take that one for myself.

"Okaaay," Maddie says. "All I'm saying is that if you—"

"Let's just go home, okay?" It comes out a little sharper than I intended, and Maddie gives me a look like, *What is your problem*? Why am I screwing everything up?

"Fine," she says. "Let's go."

We head toward Maddie's house, and I start chattering on about nothing again on the way, trying to get them back into a silly, lighthearted mood, but it doesn't seem to be working. Even when I tell them about Edna's weird clothes and her crazy comments about auras, only Amy giggles, and Maddie barely cracks a smile. This sleepover was such a bad idea. How am I going to make it through an entire evening of this?

Mrs. Kolhein meets us at the door, and she, for one, looks genuinely happy to see me. She pulls me in for a hug even though I'm all sweaty from practice. "AJ! We've missed you! Are your parents back?"

"No, not for another couple weeks," I say.

"Everything going okay over at your grandma's?"

I shrug. "I guess. She's really strict. She doesn't let me go anywhere except for soccer. That's why I haven't been over."

"Well, it's good to have you here now," Maddie's mom says. "Hi, Amy. You left your hoodie over here on Tuesday—I put it in Maddie's room for you."

"Thanks, Mrs. K," Amy says. I didn't even know she was over here on Tuesday. It kind of seems like she's over here all the time now.

Amy suggests we play *Mega Ninja Explosion*, and I breathe a sigh of relief—blowing up bad guys will probably cheer Maddie up, and maybe she'll forget about Brianna's party. We lug our stuff up to her room, and Amy pulls a package of Oreos out of her bag. "Look what I brought," she says, dangling them in front of Maddie's face.

"Ooh, Double Stuf." Maddie grabs them and rips them open.

"Oh, hey, I just remembered," I say. "I brought this superfancy chocolate cake my grandmother's cook made the other night. Do you guys want some? I could run downstairs and grab forks. It's seriously so, so good." I dig around in my bag until I find one of the pieces of cake and hold the aluminum foil package under Maddie's nose. "Here, smell."

She sniffs. "Mm," she says, but she doesn't sound very enthusiastic. "Maybe later. I think we're good with the Oreos for now." When Amy offers me the package of cookies, I take one, but it doesn't really taste like anything.

We spend the rest of the afternoon staring at our little ninja avatars on the screen, blowing up walls and bad guys and collecting lucky swords and jewels. When Maddie's dad gets home, he tells us he's ordering pizza from Zappetto's, and I perk up a little—the food at Grandma Jo's has been amazing, but there's something about a super cheesy slice with extra pepperoni that no fancy rich-people food can ever touch. There must not be an expensive way to make grease. Mr. Kolhein delivers the pizza to us upstairs when it arrives. Usually, Maddie and I are thrilled when her parents don't make us eat with the rest of the family, since we always have an endless list of things to discuss privately. But tonight it seems like everything we have to say to each other has been tied up in a big, tangled, confusing knot. I'm afraid to pull on any individual thread, because I can't tell what it's attached to or what it might unravel, so I mostly stay quiet.

When we finish dinner, nobody mentions the cake, so I don't bring it up again. Amy digs through her backpack, pulls out a bunch of DVDs—*The Wild Winds of Love, The Rose's Kiss,* and *Sweetness and Sorrow*—and holds them up with a hopeful smile. The covers are overwhelmingly pink, and all feature swooning ladies and brooding men.

I make some exaggerated gagging sounds. "No *way.* Let's borrow one of Jordan's alien movies. I really want to see *Tentacle.*"

Amy scrunches up her nose. "Too much screaming, not enough kissing." She turns to Maddie. "What do you think?"

I expect Maddie to agree with me, but instead she says, "We can watch one of yours, if you want."

What is up with her tonight? "But you hate these," I say. "We both do."

"They're not that bad," Maddie says. "Maybe you're not the only one who wants to try new things." She glances over at my bag, where the top of the stupid silver envelope is poking out.

I take a deep breath. "Hey, if this is about—"

"It's not about anything—we're just picking a movie." Maddie randomly grabs a DVD out of Amy's hand. "Come on, let's go downstairs."

I tell myself she probably doesn't want to talk about our private stuff in front of other people. Maybe later, after Amy falls asleep, we can have a real conversation, and I can reassure her that I don't even like Brianna and that she'll always be my best friend, no matter what.

But right now, as I look at her clutching that stupid *Sweetness and Sorrow* DVD box, I'm afraid the feeling isn't mutual.

The movie is exactly as horrible as I think it's going to be. It's about a woman who's in love with the ghost of this guy from the Renaissance, and the only place they can be together is this enchanted gondola, but then the gondola sinks, and they're separated forever. Ordinarily, Maddie and I would laugh our heads off and talk over the movie with our own silly dialogue, and I can see her rolling her eyes on the other side of the couch. But when I make a snarky comment out loud, Amy shushes me, and Maddie doesn't take my side, so I shut up.

When the movie ends, Amy is all teary, which is totally ridiculous. I mean, the word "sorrow" is *in the title*; she can't have expected it to end well. "So romantic," she says, wiping her eyes.

"I guess, if you like wispy dudes in boats," I say, and the corner of Maddie's mouth twitches up a little. She pulls it back down before Amy can see, but it still feels like a reward.

"Want to watch another one?" Amy asks.

"I think I might go to bed," I say, even though it's only eleven. "I'm really tired." I look at Maddie, sending her a telepathic message that she should leave Amy down here to swoon over *The Wild Winds of Love* and come upstairs with me so we can have a real talk.

But she either doesn't get the message or chooses to ignore it. "I'm up for another one," she says. "Should I get more popcorn?"

"Sure," Amy says. "See you up there later, AJ."

"Okay. Good night," I say. I hope they don't notice how strained my voice sounds.

"'Night," Maddie calls as she heads into the kitchen.

I change into my pajamas and get into the second twin bed in Maddie's room, the one I've slept in so many times

I think of it as mine. The sounds of the Kolheins' house wrap around me when I close my eyes—Jordan and Lindsay playing competing music in their rooms, Maddie's parents watching some late-night talk show down the hall, the whir of the air conditioner as it flips on and off. This house has always felt like a second home to me, but tonight all the familiar sounds make me feel homesick. If Maddie were up here too, breathing quietly in the other bed, I'm sure I'd be able to fall asleep, but knowing she's downstairs with Amy keeps me wide awake. I find myself straining for the sounds of their voices and laughter, and a couple times I hear it, but I can't tell if they're talking about important stuff or just messing around.

Finally, a little after midnight, I can't stand it any longer. I've gotten really good at sneaking around now, and I tiptoe down the hall and onto the first landing without making a sound. I crouch there out of sight, my arms tight around my knees. At first I hear only the TV—they really are watching another one of Amy's stupid romances—but then Maddie says, "She was never like this before, you know?"

My heart starts galloping in my chest. I try to tell myself they're talking about something in the movie, but I know it's not true. They're talking about me.

"What do you mean?" Amy says.

"Like, she never cared about having fancy stuff or talking to the popular girls. Brianna's always so mean to everyone, and after she did that thing with the dresses, I thought it would be funny if AJ bragged about all the nice stuff her grandmother had and rubbed it in her face. But now it kind of seems like AJ's taking it seriously, you know? It's like she's turning into one of them or something."

"She still seems like herself to me," Amy says, and I want to hug her.

"But did you see the way she and the Bananas were acting at soccer the other day? All that giggling and whispering about gowns and ice sculptures and stuff? Even that thing with the cake earlier tonight, when AJ was all like, 'Look how much better *my* dessert is than *your* low-class dessert.' Sometimes I can't even tell whether she wants to be friends with me anymore."

"I wonder where that cake went," Amy says. "I kind of want it now."

"Amy, that is *so* not the point!"

"I know. Jeez. It didn't seem that way to me, though. I think she was actually just trying to give us cake."

I hear Maddie sigh. "Do you think she'll go to Brianna's party?"

"She didn't seem like she wanted to," Amy says. "She

probably didn't know how to react when Brianna gave her the invitation. I really don't think it's a big deal."

"Maybe you're right."

"The whole situation was super awkward, but I bet everything will go back to normal when her parents come back and she goes home. It's only a few more weeks, right?"

"I guess," Maddie says. "Maybe I'm being paranoid. Can I have the popcorn?"

Part of me wants to run down the stairs, throw my arms around my best friend, and tell her I don't care about expensive stuff at all and I still think the Bananas are idiots and of *course* I want to be friends with her. But I know she'd be super embarrassed and angry that I've been eavesdropping, and if this is really what she thinks of me now, she wouldn't want me to comfort her anyway. She'd probably rather talk to Amy.

So instead I creep back upstairs and curl up in a tight ball in the guest bed, cursing that stupid silver invitation in my bag. There's no *way* I'm going to that party.

I'm going to make everything right again if it kills me.

13

I spend most of Friday shut up in my room, practicing my lock picking and stewing over the Maddie situation. Every half hour or so, I pull up her name in my phone and consider pressing the talk button, but I have no idea what I'd say to her. I wasn't supposed to have overheard her conversation with Amy, so it's not like I can tell her the stuff she said is wrong. Maybe I could get back on her good side if I convinced Grandma Jo to send us somewhere really cool with Stanley—Six Flags or a water park or a show or something. But that might make me seem even *more* like Brianna, flashing all my cool stuff around to make people like me. I guess I'll have to hope that staying far away from the idiotic lobster boil will be enough to show my best friend I haven't changed.

Cookie, Edna, and Betty show up late in the evening

for our bear heist, and hearing their excited voices downstairs perks me up and reminds me I have a job to do. I immediately start to feel better when I put on my ninja clothes. These heists are so wonderfully clear-cut, with no gray areas or confusing feelings to deal with. You go in, you liberate your target, and if you get out without being caught, you win. It's a lot like soccer that way; either you score a goal or you don't, and either way, you know exactly where you stand.

I come down the stairs and join the grannies in the front hallway. Edna's wearing her skintight black suit from last time, and tonight, Cookie and Betty are dressed in black too—the bear is so large that this heist will require all of us. Betty has even wrapped her walker in strips of black fabric so it'll be invisible in the dark, though the tennis balls still glow bright green on the bottom. Grandma Jo will stay in the van because of her foot, but she's wearing black anyway because she's Grandma Jo.

"There's our star," Betty says, and she reaches out to hug me. "How are you feeling, dear?"

"I'm a little nervous," I admit.

Betty pats my hand. "You're going to show that lock who's boss."

"Darn tootin'," Cookie says, and Edna raises both

hands and does her wiggly fingered applause thing at me. Just having them all around me, knowing how much they believe in me, calms me down a lot. I squeeze Betty's hand and smile. When Grandma Jo asks if I'm ready to go, I say yes, and I mean it.

When we pull up in front of Bill's place in Grandma Jo's black van, that delicious nervous-excited feeling starts bubbling up in my center and fizzing outward into my arms and legs. I'm surprised by how tiny the house is; it's low and squat and made of dark brick, and Bill hasn't made much of an effort to make it look like a home. One of the porch lights is burned out, and the other illuminates a bunch of dead potted plants, a broken vacuum cleaner, and a sagging wicker chair with one arm. Cookie takes it all in with a snort. "I bought those drapes in 1990," she scoffs. "I can't *believe* he hasn't replaced them. He probably hasn't even *cleaned* them."

"Nineteen ninety," Betty muses. "Is that when we lifted the Fabergé egg, or was that the year with the lion cub?"

"I'm not surprised you don't remember," Cookie snorts. "You had *other things* going on in 1990, didn't you, Betty?"

"Wasn't that 1991?" Edna says. "I remember the trial wasn't front-page news because the USSR dissolved."

"What trial?" I ask.

"Oh, just a trial we were all following closely," she says.

"Betty was following closest of all," Cookie says.

"Cookie, *don't*." Even in the dark, I can tell Betty looks a little scared. I don't know why it's such a big deal that she was interested in a trial, though.

"My mom really likes true crime stuff, too," I say to make her feel better. "There was this one time—"

"*Focus*," Grandma Jo snaps. "Is everyone ready?"

"Ready," the ladies say, stacking their hands up in the middle of the van, and I add my hand to the pile. She's right, I really do need to focus. This time, I remember to whisper *"Heist!"* instead of shouting.

"Operation Teddybear, commence!" Grandma Jo announces.

The four of us slip out of the van, and Edna and I make our way around to the back of the house while Betty and Cookie guard the front. We cross a small yard that's more dirt than grass, pass a ramshackle toolshed, and tiptoe up to the back door. There's one of those motion-sensor floodlights over the patio to our left, and we're careful to stay out of range.

"Swan attempting to breach first barrier," I whisper into my earpiece. "Do you copy?"

"Copy that," says Edna. "Go ahead, Swan."

"Go, Swan, go! Do your thing!" Cookie whisper-cheers, and Betty's sweet voice says, "I know you can do it, dear."

Grandma Jo doesn't say anything, and my temper flares. She's the only one here who's actually related to me, and she still can't bring herself to support me, even when I'm being a huge help to her. "Agent Condor, do you copy?" I whisper.

"Condor copies," Grandma Jo says. "Good luck, Swan."

It's not exactly warm and fuzzy, but it's better than nothing.

I pull the screen door open and inspect the lock in the dim light from the neighbor's house. It looks exactly like the ones I've been practicing with, and I breathe a sigh of relief. I wonder if I should stroke the lock and whisper to it, like Edna did during the Picasso heist, but that would probably look stupid and fake, so I go straight for my tools. I pull out the medium-size tension wrench, but my hands are trembling, and I gasp as it clatters to the porch.

"Steady, Swan," whispers Edna gently. "Keep breathing. You're a hollow reed, remember?"

"Right. A hollow reed." I retrieve the wrench, take a couple of deep, centering breaths, and try again to insert it into the lock. This time it holds, and I pull out my first pick, the one with the squiggly end. I tell myself this is no different from what I've been doing all week in Grandma Jo's spare bedroom.

"Good," Edna whispers. "Now rake the pins very gently."

I do, thinking how cool it would be if I could make all the pins pop up on the first try. But only a couple of them bounce into place, so I reach for a different pick to do the rest of them individually. The neighborhood is dead quiet, and the only sounds I hear as I poke around inside the lock are cicadas whirring away in the trees and the shushing sound of four old ladies breathing in my ear.

It feels like it takes an eternity to open the lock, and for a few minutes I'm afraid it isn't going to work at all. But I finally feel the last pin click into place, and when I slowly, carefully turn the wrench in the keyhole, the cylinder rotates. I'm so excited it's like there are fireworks going off in my brain, and I do a quiet little happy dance on the porch, shaking my butt and doing a hula motion with my arms.

"First barrier has been breached," I whisper, like Edna did during our last heist, and it makes me feel super professional. "Heron and Swan going in. Do you copy?"

"Roger," Grandma Jo says. "Cardinal and Sparrow, you may proceed."

"Copy that," says Cookie.

Edna and I slip into Bill's small mudroom and pull tiny flashlights out of our utility belts. There are dirty boots scattered all over the floor, and I think of how disgusted Grandma Jo would be by this mess. It's a good thing she's staying in the van. I kick the shoes to the side to make room for Betty's walker.

"Eight minutes, Swan," Edna says, now that we're inside and free to talk. Even though I can't see her face in the dark, I can hear that she's smiling. "That's a record for you. Very well done."

Eight minutes! That's way faster than I've ever picked a lock before. "That's awesome!" I say. "I guess I work better under pressure?"

"Focus," says Grandma Jo's voice, and for a second, I'm furious—can't she let me celebrate for one second? But then her voice comes through the earpiece again. "Well done, Swan."

"Thanks, Condor," I whisper back, and I get that rare warm feeling in my chest that happens when I've made her proud.

The mudroom opens onto a wood-paneled den with a huge flat-screen TV and a pool table. There are hunting and fishing magazines, empty beer bottles, and old pizza boxes scattered everywhere. What a slob—this guy is way worse than my brother. I was hoping the stuffed bear would be in this room so we wouldn't have to squeeze it through any doorways, but I don't see it anywhere. Edna points toward the hallway. "You go right, I'll go left," she says.

"Copy that," I reply.

All I find on my end of the hallway is a filthy bathroom with no toilet paper, a linen closet, and a guest bedroom with a ruffled pink bedspread. I wonder if Cookie bought that in 1990 too. Then Edna says, "I have eyes on the target. I repeat: I have eyes on the target."

"What's your 20, Heron?" I say.

"The target is in the study."

"Copy that," I say. "Swan incoming."

I make my way down the hall in the other direction, and the first thing I see when I enter the study is the bear's face, lit from below by Edna's flashlight. Its mouth is wide open to show off a set of enormous teeth, and its glass eyes reflect the light, making it look disturbingly alive. I sweep the beam of my flashlight over its body and find that it's standing on its hind legs, front paws outstretched like it's going to grab Edna and devour her like a snack cracker. I'm pretty sure it's bigger than Cookie told us, and the rock it's standing on makes it seem even taller.

There's a creaking sound from a few rooms away, and for a second I freak out that Bill might be home after all, but then Cookie whispers, "Cardinal and Sparrow incoming."

"Copy," I say. "Turn left down the hall."

Cookie and Betty appear soon after—Betty shuffles along with her walker, and Cookie is lugging a hand truck like the ones the FedEx guys use to move heavy boxes. Both of them swoop in and hug me, squashing me between them as though I'm the meat in an old-lady sandwich. "Such impressive dexterity," Cookie whispers. "I knew the first day I met you that you'd be a great asset to us."

"I'm so proud of you, dear," whispers Betty. "My talented girl." I love how she talks about me as if I belong to her, like I'm her real granddaughter.

Cookie shines her flashlight across the room and puts her hand to her heart when the beam lands on the bear. "Teddy Roosevelt!" she says, her voice a little teary. "I'm so happy to see you!" She hurries over and hugs the bear around its furry middle, then gazes up into its toothy face. Her eyes are level with its lower jaw. "He's a bit bigger than I remembered," she muses. "Maybe I've shrunk."

Edna is behind the bear now, inspecting its feet with

her flashlight. "This base isn't attached to the floor," she says. "We should be able to scooch him right onto the dolly." She pushes gently on the bear's back, then a little harder, but it doesn't budge. "It's heavy," she says.

"You three get behind him and tip him back toward you, and I'll shove the dolly under the base from the front," Cookie says. "Don't pull on his fur—I don't want any bald spots. Ready?"

We arrange ourselves around the bear, Edna in the middle, me on the right, and Betty and her walker on the left. Cookie counts to three, and I brace both hands against the bear's furry shoulder and pull. He tips back toward us for a second, but none of us are expecting how bottom-heavy the base makes him, and he slips out of our grip. The bear rocks back toward Cookie before righting itself with a solid *thwack*.

"No harm done," she reassures us. "Pull a little harder this time, okay? Ready? One, two, three!"

We rock the bear back toward us again, and this time Cookie jams the dolly under the base. "Perfect!" she crows, and Grandma Jo hisses, "Keep your voice down, Cardinal."

"It's fine, Condor," Cookie reassures her. "There's nobody here but us. Target acquired—we're headed for the back door. Help me turn this thing around, Heron."

Together, Cookie and Edna tip the dolly toward them and the bear leans forward, its head looming sinisterly over them. They back up three steps and rotate the dolly ninety degrees so the bear's butt is pointed toward the study door. The whole operation is surprisingly smooth, as if they move huge, heavy things together all the time, and it makes me wonder what else they've stolen.

Betty watches them wistfully. "I miss my young, strong back," she whispers to me. "I used to be able to do that, and now I'm completely useless."

I pat her shoulder. "You're not useless at *all*. And you can borrow my back anytime."

"Thank you, dear."

"And forward!" Cookie says. "Hang on, the wheel's caught on the rug. Let me just—" She reaches out a black-sneakered foot and gives the wheel an enthusiastic kick.

A little *too* enthusiastic.

The rug springs free, the dolly's wheels shoot forward, and suddenly everything seems to be happening in slow motion. Edna and Cookie pull back on the dolly's handles to stop it from falling, but that makes everything worse, and the bear topples toward them face first. For a second I'm afraid it's going to flatten them both, and I lunge toward them, but there's nothing I can do. Cookie and Edna leap to the sides, and the bear's entire upper body crashes through the plate glass window that overlooks the patio. I fling my arms up to protect my eyes as the dolly smacks the hardwood floor with a sharp metallic clang.

Then everything is silent except for the neighbor's dog, who starts barking like crazy.

"What is going *on* in there?" hisses Grandma Jo. "What's your 20?"

Cookie ignores her. "Is everyone all right?" she whispers.

I'm almost afraid to open my eyes, terrified I'm going to see one of the ladies sliced up and gushing blood all over the floor. But one by one, everyone confirms she's fine, and when I stand up and search my arms and legs for cuts, I find that I'm unharmed too. There's not even any glass on the floor—it all seems to have exploded outward into the yard. The window ledge has caught the bear across the chest, and it's leaning out over the patio, the curtains hanging on either side of it like it's part of some sort of deranged puppet show. The security light over the patio clicks on and bathes the bear's furry head in a yellow spotlight.

We all gaze at it for a good ten seconds, and then Cookie whispers, "Well, this isn't ideal."

"Report your status, Cardinal!" says Grandma Jo's

voice. She sounds like she's hovering halfway between panic and fury.

"We, um." Cookie looks around, as if she might find a magical solution lying on the ground somewhere. "We . . . sort of broke a window?"

"*Sort of?* What do you mean, *sort of?*"

"We definitely broke a window. But I'm sure it'll be fi—"

Cookie breaks off when an awful, high-pitched shriek echoes through the sleeping neighborhood—it sounds as though someone's being murdered next door. "Marlene? Are you okay? What happened?" a man's voice calls.

"A bear! There's a *bear* in Bill's house!"

Cookie springs into action, righting the dolly and grabbing the bear's left side with both hands. "Help me tip it back!" she whisper-screams. "Swan, brace the dolly! Everyone be careful of the edges of the window!"

"A bear?" we hear the man next door say. "Are you sure? I don't think we have bears here, hon. Maybe it was a raccoon or something."

"A *raccoon?* You don't think I can tell the difference between a bear and a raccoon?"

"Marlene, calm down!"

"Don't tell me to calm down! Its head and paws are sticking right out the window! Look for yourself!"

"One, two, three, tip!" whispers Cookie, and we all pull on the bear as hard as we can. Thankfully, it rights itself, and the base thumps back down on the dolly with a crash. Tiny shards of glass rain down around us, and I squeeze my eyes shut. When I shake my head, a few pieces fall out of my hair.

"Listen!" says the woman next door. "Did you hear that? Do you see it?"

All of us freeze in place and hold our breath. Then the man's voice says, "Hon, I'm looking, and there's nothing out there. I don't know what you saw, but it's gone now. How would a bear get inside the house, anyway?"

"I don't know, I'm just telling you what I saw! Look, the window's broken! Don't you see the glass all over the patio?"

"It was probably some kids throwing rocks or something."

I know I shouldn't do anything without explicit instructions from Cookie or my grandmother, but when he says that, I have an idea I can't resist. I sneak up close to the window, let out a loud giggle, and then hiss, "Shhh! Go! Go! That way!"

"Annemarie, what are you doing?!" bellows my grandmother over the earpiece, not even bothering with my code name.

But the misdirection works exactly as I'd hoped. "There

is someone out there," the man says. "I'll bet you anything it's that little punk Zach Wheeler."

"Nicely done, Swan," Edna whispers.

"Such a smart girl," whispers Betty.

"I could swear I saw something sticking out the window," says the woman's voice. "Will you go over and check, Hank? Just to make sure? What if Bill comes back from fishing and some animal is nesting in the middle of his living room?"

There's a pause, and then the man says, "Fine. Let me put on some pants."

"Take the shotgun," the woman says, and all of us startle.

"Don't be ridiculous. I'll be fine with the baseball bat."

"Report your status!" Grandma Jo demands.

"The neighbor's heading over with a baseball bat to check out the broken window," Cookie reports.

"Lord have mercy," Grandma Jo mutters. "Abort Operation Teddybear. Abort mission! Do you copy?"

"I'm not leaving without Teddy Roosevelt!"

"Cardinal, I said, *Abort mission!* I'm in charge here, not you! Do you copy or not?"

Cookie gets a defiant look on her face. Then she reaches up and switches off her earpiece, and a little thrill goes through me—I've never seen anyone disobey my grandmother outright. "She always thinks she's in charge," Cookie grumbles. "It's my turn to be Mission Control for once. Betty, grab that afghan from the back of the couch and help me get it over the bear. Edna and AJ, look in the mudroom and see if you can find some bungee cords."

"Exit through the front door this instant," Grandma Jo orders. "I want you clear of the house before that idiot starts poking around."

"Roger that, Condor," Edna says, but she's heading off to the mudroom and gesturing for me to do the same.

We rummage through the overstuffed shelves, which are packed to bursting with gear for pretty much every outdoor activity—fishing, snowshoeing, hunting, skiing. After a minute Edna says, "Aha!" and holds up a handful of brightly colored bungee cords.

"Nice!" I say. We dash back to Cookie and Betty, who have mummified the bear in crocheted blankets, and start strapping the flowered, puffy bundle to the dolly.

"*What is your 20?*" Grandma Jo roars through the earpiece.

We hear the neighbor's back door open. "You know where the spare key is?" calls the woman next door.

"Yes, Marlene. It's been in the same place for the last eight years."

There was a spare key? I suddenly don't feel so special for having picked the lock.

"Forward!" Cookie whispers. "Quick quick quick! Edna, help me push! AJ, clear a path, open the front door, and get ready to brace the bear so we can get it down the steps! Betty, get yourself out of here as fast as you can!"

I race ahead, unlock the front door, and help Betty outside. "Cardinal, Heron, Sparrow, and Swan incoming," Edna reports.

"Copy that," mutters Grandma Jo. But then she sees what's coming out of the house behind us, and she gasps.

"How *dare* you defy me," she snaps into our earpieces, her voice low and threatening. "I specifically instructed you to abort this mission! How do you expect me to run a professional operation when you so flagrantly disrespect my authority? How do you think—"

"Oh, come off it, Condor," whispers Cookie, who has turned her earpiece back on. "We're hardly a professional operation. This was my mission, not yours, and I got it done. Brace the back now, Swan. Ready? First step."

The dolly and the quilt-wrapped lump of bear bump down the first step. For a second, the bear tips precariously in my direction, and I'm afraid it's going to fall, but the bungee cords hold fast. We take the second step the same way, then the third, while Grandma Jo continues to rage and sputter.

" . . . there are rules for this sort of thing, and it's imperative that you follow them! I can't believe you—"

"That's enough, Jo!" Cookie snaps. "Sometimes life requires a little flexibility. Stop being so sanctimonious, open the back of the van, and help us get the target in. Or do you want us to get caught so you can teach us a lesson about obedience?"

I expect Grandma Jo to argue—I don't know what "sanctimonious" means, but from the way Cookie said it, it's obviously not a compliment. But I guess my grandmother wants this to be a successful heist as much as we do, because she climbs out of the front seat and *clomp-click-rustle*s toward the back of the van. I can just about see the steam coming out of her ears.

The bear bumps down the last step, and I run back up to the front door. As I shut it quietly behind us, I hear the sound of Bill's neighbor calling, "Hello? Anyone in here?" I flee down the steps and toward the van.

Cookie and Edna wheel the bear into position and turn it so it'll go into the trunk faceup. "Condor, you help me lift from this side, and Swan and Heron will get that side," Cookie instructs. "Lift from between its legs and under its arms. Ready? One . . . two . . ."

I take a deep breath and grip a fistful of fur, and on three, we heave the bear into the van. The last row of seats has been removed, but the feet still stick out the back in a ridiculous way. Cookie climbs in and secures a couple of the bungee cords under the bear's arms and around the seats. Its paws stick straight up in the air, tenting the blanket and making it look like we're carting around some sort of petrified zombie. "Well, it's not perfect . . . ," she says when she's finished.

"It'll have to be good enough," Grandma Jo snaps. She secures the back doors as best she can with another bungee cord. "We need to get out of here. Everyone in."

Cookie hops into the driver's seat, and I help boost Betty into the back and fold up her walker. When she's settled between Edna and me, she takes my hand and squeezes. "Thank you, dear," she whispers. "Mission accomplished. You were absolutely wonderful."

I squeeze back, not too hard so I won't hurt her fragile fingers. As we zip away from the crime scene, we both turn and watch out the rear window as the corners of a flowery blanket flap in the breeze around two stuffed, furry, very liberated bear feet.

14

The grannies don't come over all weekend. I wonder if Grandma Jo told them to stay away for a while—she's still incredibly grouchy about the end of the bear heist, and she spends dinner every night telling me stories about armies that got flattened because they didn't obey their generals. It seems unfair that I have to deal with her bad mood all alone—it was Cookie's idea to defy her, not mine. I miss the ladies for other reasons too; our last two heists have been so exciting that I was hoping to fit in one more before I go back home to my safe, normal life. But if we don't start planning right away, there won't be time, and my career as an ethical thief will be over just as I was getting really good at it.

Soccer used to be my escape when things weren't

going well at my grandmother's house, but practice on Monday doesn't feel like a relief at all. It's impossible to enjoy playing—or even concentrate on it—when I'm constantly thinking about whether every word I say is going to make someone mad. Instead of focusing on my technique, I spend the entire practice watching for signs that Maddie hates me and avoiding Brianna so I won't have to tell her I'm not going to her party. Rejecting the invitation is definitely the right thing to do, but who knows how she might punish me once she decides I'm not cool after all?

I relax for the first time when I get home from soccer on Monday and hear Cookie's raucous laughter coming from the storage room. I change into jeans and a clean T-shirt and dash in to see everyone, even though I know I'm not supposed to run in the house. Cookie beams when she spots me and beckons me over. "Look!" she says, holding out her phone. "Stanley showed me how to use the camera! Doesn't Teddy Roosevelt look wonderful in the master bedroom?"

I had assumed Cookie would keep the bear in her parlor or her study, like Bill did, but there he is on the phone's tiny screen, looming over the bed like he's contemplating chowing down on the fluffy pillows. Cookie's wallpaper, carpeting, and enormous canopy bed are all a startling shade of red; it looks kind of like a meat locker in there. I scroll to the next picture, and my heart does this stupid fluttering thing when I see Stanley posing next to the bear, in shorts and sandals, making a goofy face like he's scared he might get eaten. I consider texting it to myself, but Cookie would probably notice if I started typing away on her phone.

"He looks great," I say, then turn off the phone really fast before anyone notices I'm not actually talking about the bear. "You did a good job taking the picture, Cookie."

"I wish I had a grandchild to teach me how to use all this newfangled technology," Betty says quietly. "I can barely make my phone dial someone properly."

"I'll help you with your phone anytime," I say. "You can pretend I'm your grandchild. I'm sure Grandma Jo won't mind sharing."

"What's that?" asks Grandma Jo, who's feeding Picasso small pieces of mango.

"Nothing, Jo," Betty says. She winks at me like it's our secret, and a little bubble of happiness expands in my chest.

I peer down at the new blueprints on the table. "So,

what are we working on this time? Whose turn is it to pick the target?"

"It's my turn," Edna says. She has so many scarves on today that I can't even tell if she's wearing a shirt underneath.

"What are we stealing?"

"Liberating," Betty and Cookie correct me in unison.

"A painting," Edna says.

I suddenly feel uncomfortably hot. Stealing Picasso isn't even remotely the same as stealing *a* Picasso. "Like, from a *museum*?" I ask, and my voice comes out high and squeaky.

"No, no," Edna says. "From a house."

"Might as well be a museum, though," says Cookie. "Look at this place!"

I take a look at the drawings. I don't know how to read blueprints, but it looks like there are at least forty rooms, and the swimming pool and four-car garage are labeled, so they're easy to spot. When I lean in close, I see the words *Entertainment Area* penciled onto a room on the basement level. It looks big enough to be a private movie theater.

"This is amazing," I say. "So, what's so special about the painting?"

"I made it," Edna says, totally matter-of-factly.

"Really?" I say. "You paint?" What I really mean is, *You paint well enough that other people hang your work in their houses?*

"She's quite well known in the art world, actually," Betty says.

"Wait, was painting, like, your job?" Up until this moment I've never considered that the grannies might've had actual jobs. In my mind, they've always been retired, planning heists and playing cards. But of course they must've done other things before I met them.

Edna nods. "It still is my job. I paint every morning from five to noon."

"Wow." I turn to Cookie. "What's your job?"

"I used to sell real estate for a living. But that wasn't my *real* job." Her eyes get misty behind her giant bug glasses. "I was a muse."

I wait for her to say more, but she seems to think this is self-explanatory. Finally I say, "Um, what does that mean?"

"I inspired people to make great art, darling," she says. "Sculptures, music, dance pieces." She lifts her arms in a slow ballet move, then lets them drift back down, and her bracelets clink back into place. "Most art made by men is inspired by beautiful women, you know—men rarely think about anything else. And I was very beautiful when I was young."

"You're still beautiful," I say, and Cookie pats my cheek.

"Flatterer," she says, but I can tell she likes it.

"Betty, what was your job?" I ask.

"I was a teacher, dear. Second grade. Oh, I loved those children with all my heart. I never had any of my own, you know."

That makes total sense—Betty actually looks kind of like what my second-grade teacher, Ms. Colbert, might look like when she gets old. They have basically the same haircut. "When did you retire?" I ask.

"Oh, I can't remember exactly."

"It must've been around 1991. Right, Betty?" Cookie asks.

Betty shoots her a sharp look. "Yes," she says. "That sounds about right."

I'm pretty sure 1991 is the year they were talking about the other night, when Betty was super interested in someone's trial. There has to be a connection; maybe she got so wrapped up in her true crime stuff that she stopped doing her job properly. "Why did you—" I start to say, but Betty cuts me off.

"It was time," she says. "It was just . . . time."

I want to ask more about it, but her voice sounds final; this subject seems to be off-limits. She's probably embarrassed about whatever happened; maybe she got fired or something. I don't want to make her uncomfortable, so instead I ask, "What are you going to liberate when it's your turn?"

Betty shakes her head, and for a second she looks a little sad. "I'm just in this for the thrills, dear."

"Really?" I say. "You're going to skip your turn?"

"I already have almost everything I need."

"There must be something you *want*, though, or a cause you believe in." It doesn't seem fair that Betty should put herself at risk for her friends over and over without ever getting any payback.

"I don't need to liberate anything to be happy, darling AJ," she says. "All I want is to be here with you."

"Well, okay." If Betty doesn't *want* to take her turn, I certainly can't force her. I turn back to Edna. "So, why are we stealing—um, liberating—your painting? Did someone take it from you, and we're getting it back, like with the bear?"

"No, no, nothing like that," Edna says. "They bought it at auction, but I miss it so. My paintings are parts of me, and I need them near me to give me strength as I head into the third act of my life."

Okay, this isn't quite as bad as stealing from a museum, but it still doesn't sound as ethical as the other two heists. "So, you've stolen other paintings, then?" I ask.

Grandma Jo puts Picasso down on a perch and joins us at the table. "Goodness, Annemarie, there's no need for you to ask so many questions. We're wasting time."

"Jo, she's one of us," Cookie says. "There's no reason to keep information from her."

"She's one of us right *now*, but she won't be in a week," Grandma Jo says. "It's far too risky to tell her everything and then send her back to her family. Information should be distributed on a need-to-know basis."

Of course, there are lots of reasons I'm excited to go back home next week—I get to see my parents and Snickers, and I'll finally be able to walk to soccer and skate around the neighborhood and watch TV again. But the way Grandma Jo's talking, it sounds like she expects our entire relationship to be over after I leave. It's not like we've become friends or anything, but it *did* seem like she was finally starting to trust me and respect me a little. I don't want things to go back to how they've always been between us, where I see her on holidays three times a year and she sighs at my unladylike interests. We actually have things in common now, and it hurts that she still doesn't want me to be part of her life. I've been trying pretty hard to get into her good graces, but now it seems like I haven't made any progress at all.

"Do you want me to leave you alone?" I ask, and my voice sounds shakier than I meant it to. "I promise I'm not going to spill any of your secrets, but I guess I don't have to help this time, if you guys don't want me to."

I expect Betty or Cookie to jump in and stand up for me, but it's Grandma Jo who says, "Don't be ridiculous. You're here for eight more days, and you can be very useful to us in that time. There's no reason for us to be inefficient with our resources. Now, come here and help us figure out how to get this painting out of Westlake Manor."

At least my grandmother's giving me a little credit for being smart and useful; that's way better than the first week I was here, when she called me an irresponsible savage. But I don't want to be a resource. I want her to see me as a person, as part of the team.

I go over to the table and look at the blueprints anyway. Maybe I can pull off something really spectacular during this heist and Grandma Jo will never look down on me again.

"The first step is *finding* the painting inside the manor," Cookie says. "There are forty-three rooms, and it could be anywhere. I'm sure the security system is no match for our Edna, but we're going to want to be in and out. This is a heist, not a scavenger hunt."

"I'm terrible at scavenger hunts," Edna says faintly.

"Stupid, stupid," Picasso agrees.

Grandma Jo ignores them both. "We'll need some inside recon."

"I could try my trick where I play the helpless, dotty old lady desperate for a bathroom," Betty says. "If they let me in, maybe I could give them the slip and take a look around?"

Grandma Jo looks pointedly at Betty's walker. "You're not exactly the master of stealth you once were, Betty. The Westlakes will never fall for that."

Betty heaves a sad sigh. "I guess you're right."

Something suddenly clicks inside my head. "Wait a minute. Did you say the *Westlakes*?"

"They own Westlake Systems," Edna explains. "It's a software company."

"Do they have a daughter named Brianna?"

"I think that *is* their daughter's name," Grandma Jo says. She looks at me sharply, like I've been eavesdropping on conversations I wasn't supposed to hear. "How did you know that, Annemarie?"

"I know her," I say. "She goes to school with me, and she's on my soccer team."

"AJ, that's *wonderful* news!" Cookie crows. "Are you two friends?"

"Do you think you could finagle an invitation to go inside the house?" asks Betty. "Oh, that would be *marvelous*."

Up until this moment, I had no intention of going to Brianna's party. If Maddie found out I was even considering it, I know our friendship would be in serious trouble. But how can I pass up this opportunity to prove to Grandma Jo once and for all that I'm worthy of her respect? This is my last shot to make her see me as something more than a silly, useless, wild kid.

Maybe Maddie would never have to know. If I can keep secrets about breaking into someone's house and stealing a taxidermied bear, surely I'm sneaky enough to keep a secret about a stupid lobster boil at Westlake Manor.

"Here's the thing," I say to the four ladies assembled in front of me. I pause dramatically, drawing out the moment before my big reveal, and then I drop the bomb. "I *already* have a way in."

"What do you mean?" asks Cookie.

"Brianna's turning thirteen on Saturday, and I'm invited to her birthday party," I say. "If you need an inside woman for this job, I'm your girl."

The delighted look that blooms across Grandma Jo's face is worth braving a hundred parties with the Bananas.

15

The last two heists have required learning new skills: navigating in the dark, getting used to birds, picking locks. But this project requires a whole different kind of training. By Saturday, I have to learn to blend in with Brianna's friends so I can carry out my mission without attracting unwanted attention. If anyone finds me skulking around remote parts of the house, I'll need to seem like I'm the kind of girl who belongs there, like I'm over at Westlake Manor all the time and know exactly what I'm doing.

And that means I'll have to go undercover as a girly girl.

I consider asking Amy what I should wear to the party, since her super fashionable stepsister takes her shopping sometimes. But I can't risk the conversation getting back to Maddie, and the two of them seem to share everything these days. So instead I start spending my evenings investigating the pictures on the Bananas' Instagram feeds. I've never really paid that much attention to what I wear as long as it fits, but I quickly discover that nothing I own is remotely appropriate for Brianna's party. The Bananas seem to wear cute little dresses to one another's celebrations, and the only dress I have is this horrible flowery thing my mom made me wear to Ben's high school graduation.

The next morning, while Grandma Jo's reading the *Wall Street Journal* and taking tiny sips of tea with her pinkie extended, I swallow my pride and ask her to buy me a dress. She usually answers my questions without even looking up, but this time she actually lays her paper down on the table, as though my request deserves her undivided attention. Behind her half-glasses, her eyes are wide with surprise. "I'm afraid I must have misheard you," she says. "I could have sworn you just asked for some proper clothing."

I concentrate on serving myself some more bacon so I don't have to look her in the eye. "Um, yeah," I say. "Is that okay?"

Grandma Jo blinks, and for once she actually seems at a loss for words. Finally, she says, "I'd be delighted to buy you a dress, Annemarie. It will be nice to see you looking feminine for a change."

"It's mostly for camouflage," I say so she won't get her hopes up too much. "I need to look like I belong in Brianna's house, you know? But, um, I guess it couldn't hurt to look nice, too."

"It certainly couldn't," Grandma Jo says. "I don't have time to take you myself—the Brookfield Zoo is coming to collect the ocelot and three of the birds this week, and I have a lot of things to attend to. But I won't be needing Stanley on Friday, so I'll have him drive you to the mall then."

My stomach does an uncomfortable little somersault. I can't quite decide if the thought of parading around in dresses for Stanley is thrilling or too mortifying for words; it kind of feels like both at once. But I can't back out without explaining why to my grandmother, so I agree. Maybe he'll help me find the right stores and then wander off on his own to shop for ties or shaving cream or whatever else guys buy.

"I trust you'll pick out something classy," Grandma Jo continues. "The skirt should be no shorter than your knees, and the top should be decently cut. There is no need to show your bosom to the world."

I turn bright red, but I just nod. It's not like I have any "bosom" to show the world, even if I wanted to. My chest is about as flat as this dining room table.

By Friday morning, I'm so nervous I can barely manage three bites of breakfast. Under normal circumstances, I'd call Maddie and tell her how terrified and excited I am, but then she'd ask why I was going to the mall in the first place, and I don't want to lie to her any more than I have to. I try to spend the morning practicing lock picking in my room, but I can't concentrate at all, and I end up playing *Zombie Squirrels* on my phone instead. When it's finally time to go, I brush my hair and put on a little lip gloss Amy gave me, then head down to the garage. Of course, then I chicken out at the last second and wipe the lip gloss off with the back of my hand. I don't want to be too obvious.

Stanley's leaning on the hood of the town car and reading a magazine, and he smiles when I come out. "Hey, Miss AJ," he says. I love how he still calls me that. "You ready to go?"

"Yup," I say. "Thanks so much for taking me."

"It's my pleasure," he says, and I wonder if he really means it. Is it possible he might actually *like* spending this extra time with me? I start wishing I'd kept the lip gloss on.

I act like a complete idiot at the beginning of the drive, fidgeting and laughing too loudly at Stanley's jokes and repeating myself. But he doesn't seem to notice, and about halfway through the drive I finally manage to calm down. It's starting to feel like a normal trip to soccer when Stanley turns onto a side street and pulls up in front of a green house with a wraparound porch. "This isn't the mall," I say.

Stanley laughs. "Well spotted," he says. "We have to pick someone up first." He taps lightly on the horn to signal that we're here.

Relief and disappointment hit me at the same time as I realize I'm not going to be shopping alone with Stanley after all. "Who's coming with us?" I ask. It's probably Cookie; when she heard her grandson was taking me to the mall, she probably decided to tag along. She's pretty fashionable for an old lady, so maybe it'll be good to have her around. I watch the front door for a flash of red.

But when the door opens, there's no sign of Cookie. Instead, a tall girl about Stanley's age with a dark ponytail comes out and locks the door behind her. She's wearing jeans, a striped tank top, and flip-flops, but she makes them look elegant somehow. Looking at her makes me feel more like a kid than I ever have in my whole life.

"That's my girlfriend, Talia," says Stanley, making everything five hundred thousand times worse. "Your grandma told me you need to buy a dress, and I don't know anything about that kind of stuff, so I asked her to come along and help. I think you're really going to like her."

I open my mouth, but no sound comes out, and before I manage to say anything, the girl slides into the backseat. "Hey, you," Stanley says, and he smiles at her the same way the girl smiled at the ghost boy in *Sweetness and Sorrow*. It makes me feel sick.

"Hey, babe." The girl leans forward and kisses Stanley on the cheek like it's no big deal. Before I've had time to recover, she turns to me. "Hey, you must be AJ. I'm Talia. It's really nice to meet you. Stanley's told me all about you."

Talia has a dimple in her chin and a smattering of freckles across her nose, and she's so pretty I want to puke. "Hi," I say. I have to force it out, like there's a hard candy stuck in my throat.

"Thanks so much for helping us," Stanley says.

"No problem," Talia says, and then she turns to me and lowers her voice like we have a secret together. "Stanley's hopeless with fashion stuff. His idea of dressing up is wearing Converse instead of flip-flops. You're *much* better off with me."

It seems like the part of my brain that makes words has totally shut off. "Cool," I finally manage. I almost suggest we switch spots—she obviously belongs up front with Stanley. But Talia scoots back and buckles her seat belt like she's totally content where she is, and Stanley pulls away from the curb.

Fortunately, Talia launches into a long story about her friend's birthday party, so I don't have to talk. As she and Stanley laugh together about people I've never heard of, I turn my face to the window so neither of them will see how my cheeks are flushing with anger and embarrassment. How could Stanley never have mentioned he has a *girlfriend*? Has he been hiding it from me on purpose? It doesn't seem fair that she already knows about me but I know nothing about her. What kind of stuff has he been telling her, anyway? When he goes home from Grandma Jo's, do the two of them snuggle up together and laugh about all the stupid things I've said?

I'm so lost in thought that I don't even notice we've arrived at the mall until Talia reaches forward and squeezes my shoulder. "Ready to shop till we drop?"

"Um, I guess," I say.

"Come on," she says. "We're going to get you something beautiful." She hops out of the car and goes around to Stanley's side, where she gives him a big hug and another kiss, this one right on the mouth. "You don't have to come with us if you don't want to, babe. We can meet you back here when we're done if you have other stuff you want to get."

Before I can decide which is worse, spending time with the two of them together or shopping alone with Talia, Stanley says, "Nah, I don't really need anything. I'll hang out with you guys." Talia looks relieved, and I realize she probably doesn't want to be alone with a totally uncool twelve-year-old any more than I want to be alone with her.

"So, what kind of thing are we looking for?" she asks me as we start walking toward the mall. She and Stanley are holding hands now, and her nails are perfect, painted the same light pink as the inside of a seashell.

My only plan had been to wander around until I saw something the Bananas might wear. "Um, just, like, a summer dress, I guess? Not super fancy. It's for this girl's birthday party . . . it's not a dance or anything." I kind of want to say, *I want something like what you would wear,* but I don't want to sound like a total dork.

"Sure," Talia says. "Let's start at Nordstrom. They've got a great juniors' department." I'm pretty sure she's not *try-*

ing to remind me how much younger I am than her, but that's kind of how it feels.

She leads Stanley and me into the massive, air-conditioned department store, and I'm suddenly glad I'm not here by myself; I wouldn't have the slightest idea where to start. We make our way through a maze of makeup counters, and one of those perfume ladies sneak-attacks Stanley with her spritzer so he ends up smelling like the potpourri in my grandmother's bathroom. Talia leads us up the escalator and through a bunch of suits and work-out gear, and finally I start to see some clothes that look like the stuff in the Bananas' pictures. There's a wall of TVs in the juniors' department, and it's playing a music video with lots of shirtless guys and girls in bikinis prancing around. It's super embarrassing to watch with Stanley standing next to me.

"*Ooh, ooh, baby, I'll always be true! When will you see that I'm the one for you?*" croons the singer, and I want to die right there on the spot.

Stanley seems bewildered by the whole situation, but Talia's right at home. "Any favorite colors?" she asks, raising her voice over the music.

"Blue, I guess," I say. "Green, too. Anything is fine, really, if you think it would look good."

"Blue would be perfect with your eyes," she says, and I wish Stanley had been the one to say it. "What size are you?"

That feels like something I should know, but I have no idea; my mom buys most of my clothes. "I'm not totally sure," I say. "I've grown a lot since the last time I needed a dress."

I wait for Talia to make fun of me, but instead she smiles. "That's okay, we'll figure it out." I almost wish she'd laugh at me or make a snarky comment. I want to hate her so badly, but it's hard to hate a really nice person just because she's super pretty and gets to date the guy I'm crushing on.

Talia takes the lead as we wind through the racks, pulling off dress after dress and heaping them into my arms. She always asks me if I like them first, and even though most of them aren't things I would've picked out myself, I always say yes. When I've got so many options I can barely see over the pile of filmy fabric, Talia steers me toward the fitting room. "Do you want me to come in with you?" she asks.

I think about the Wonder Woman underwear I put on this morning and shake my head. "I'll be fine," I say.

"Cool. Shout if you need a different size or something. I'll be right outside."

"Okay," I say, and I shut myself into one of the little

white rooms. I can hear the rise and fall of Talia's and Stanley's voices, but I can't hear what they're saying over the music, which has changed to some guy singing about how his girlfriend's eyes are shy goldfish in a pond. (What does that even *mean*?) I suddenly get paranoid that they're laughing about me now that they're alone, so I open the door as quietly as I can and listen hard. But all Talia's saying is, ". . . got so sick the last time we went to that Chinese place, remember? How about burritos?" I close the door again and start changing into the first dress.

None of the first six looks that great on me, and I remember why I don't like wearing dresses; I always look so gawky and uncomfortable in them. I really like the bright blue color of the seventh one, but it zips up the back, and I can't reach the zipper no matter how I stretch. Why would you even make clothing that's this hard to put on? As I'm bending and reaching and hopping around, I hear Talia's voice right outside my door. "How're you doing in there, AJ?"

I stop hopping, my cheeks hot with embarrassment. "All right," I say.

"Need any help?"

I don't really want to ask her for anything, but none of the remaining dresses are as pretty as this one, so I say,

"Um, yeah. I can't get this zipper." I open the door a tiny bit, then hug the dress close to my body and scoot into the far corner of the fitting room. I don't want Stanley to catch a glimpse of me.

Talia slips inside and shuts the door behind her. "Oh, that color is so nice on you," she says. "Here, turn around." I do, and she brushes my hair out of the way and zips up the dress in one quick, efficient swoop. She smells like pineapple and coconut.

"What do you think?" I say. Locking eyes with her in the mirror is a little easier than looking straight at her.

"It's beautiful. Have you done the spin test?"

I seriously know nothing about shopping. "What's that?"

"Spin around and see if the skirt flares out. It's a very important thing to know about a dress. Go ahead, try."

It sounds so much like something Maddie or Amy would say that I find myself smiling. I spin a few times, and the skirt bells out around me in a really satisfying way.

"Ooh, it definitely passes," Talia says. "Do you like it?"

"Yeah, I think so."

"You want to show Stanley?"

I wonder if it's obvious to Talia how I feel about her boyfriend. "It's okay. I think I'm going to get it."

"No, no, we should get his opinion first. He won't mind." She opens the door. "Babe, come here and tell us what you think."

I hear Stanley's footsteps coming toward the fitting room, and when he sees me, he smiles widely. "Looks great," he says. "I think this is the one."

"Thanks," I say. And when I really inspect myself in the mirror, I realize it *does* look kind of great. It's certainly not the kind of thing I'd want to wear every day, but I do look feminine, and surprisingly enough, I don't hate it.

If Grandma Jo buys me a dress for Christmas this year, I might actually try it on for once.

16

I'd always thought "My mouth dropped open in shock" was a figure of speech, but when Stanley and I pull into the driveway of Westlake Manor that Saturday, my mouth literally drops open. The house is huge and white, and the front is covered with ornate pillars, like what might happen if a wedding cake and a Greek temple had a baby together. It looks like it could eat Grandma Jo's house for a snack. The security system on this place must be insane, and I wonder how Edna is ever going to get past it.

"You okay there, Miss AJ?" Stanley asks when I don't make any move to unbuckle my seat belt.

"Yeah," I say, but I don't sound very sure, even to myself. I clear my throat and try again. "Sure, yeah, of course."

"Well, you look very nice," he says, and my stomach

does a backflip and sticks the landing. Now that I've met Talia, I know I need to get over Stanley, but it's not hurting anyone if I like him a little longer.

"Thanks," I say.

"Have a great time, and I'll be back to get you at eight, okay?"

Stanley starts to get out to open the door for me, but another guy gets there first. He's wearing a uniform with brass buttons up the front, and he reminds me of the frog butler in this book I had when I was a kid. I wonder if his only job is to open people's car doors—judging by the size of this house, the Westlakes are probably rich enough to have a separate staff member just for that.

"Hello, young miss," he says to me, like we're in the eighteenth century or something, and I think about how hard Maddie's going to laugh when I tell her about this. Then my heart twists as I realize I can't *ever* tell her; if she finds out I went to this party, she'll hate me forever. But I can't think about that now, because I have a job to do. I concentrate on getting out of the car without flashing my underwear at the frog butler.

"Please proceed through the foyer and turn right. You'll find the other young ladies in the solarium at the end of the hall."

"Okay," I say, even though I have no idea what a solarium is. "Thanks for the ride, Stanley."

"No problem," he says, and he winks at me like he finds the butler guy as ridiculous as I do. I have to bite my lip so I won't giggle.

I climb the steps, and by the time I get to the top, I'm so nervous I have to pause on the threshold and take a couple long, slow breaths. I've never been on a spy mission before, unless you count reading Maddie's sister's diary. I tell myself this is much less scary than breaking into someone's house; I even have an invitation that proves I'm supposed to be here. But I can hear Brianna's practiced laugh echoing from somewhere inside the house—she always lets out exactly the same number of "hahs"—and this suddenly feels much more daunting. No matter what my invitation says and how good my girly-girl costume is, I know I don't belong here.

"Down the hall to the right, miss," the butler guy reminds me. I nod and hurry inside.

The entryway has white marble floors so shiny I can see my reflection, spindly tables supporting enormous flower arrangements, and a domed ceiling with a chandelier that looks like it belongs in *The Phantom of the Opera*. I look around for Edna's painting, which is abstract with lots of streaks of blue and green, but I don't see it anywhere. I do see a small white box that looks like part of a security system, though, so I flip open the cover and take a picture of it with my phone. I hear a dog barking somewhere in the house, and I make a mental note to tell the grannies about that later. I wonder how they handle houses with dogs? Maybe Edna will bring a steak full of sleeping pills with her when she comes in to disable the security system.

I'm trying to decide whether to snoop around now or wait until later when a voice behind me says, "Are you here for the party, miss?" I jump about fifteen feet in the air. There's a sleek-looking woman standing there, dressed in a black shirt and black pants that are so perfectly creased, it looks like she ironed them when they were already on her body. For a second I think this might be Brianna's mom, but then I notice she's wearing a small apron, like the people who served the appetizers at my great aunt's eightieth birthday party a few years ago. She's probably a caterer.

"Um, yeah?" I say. "I was, um, taking a picture of the flower arrangement because it's so pretty? I wanted to show it to my mom, because she, like, *loves* flower arranging?" I don't know why everything I say suddenly sounds like a question.

"The solarium is straight down the hall," she says. Since it's the third time the staff has told me that, I figure I better actually go before someone drags me there by force.

The solarium turns out to be a large octagonal room with giant screens in every wall, like a really classy gazebo attached to the house. Tall potted ferns stand in each corner, and there are baskets of exotic-looking flowers hanging everywhere, making it smell fresh and green. In the center of the room is a small fountain shaped like a mermaid, circled by about twelve matching wicker loungers with flowered cushions. I know most of the girls here from school, and some of them look a little confused when they see me. But then they smile politely, like they're willing to accept that I have a right to be here as long as Brianna has given her stamp of approval. I hover in the doorway, biting my lip, and I reach out to twist Maddie's bracelet around my wrist before I realize it's not there anymore.

Finally Sabrina spots me, and when she smiles, it looks totally genuine. "Hi, AJ," she calls. "I like your dress."

Her compliment gives me the courage to step into the room. "Thanks," I say. "I like yours, too." I really do—it's patterned in cream and tan and brown and has gold threads all woven through it, and it looks great against her dark skin. Several of the other girls are also wearing summer dresses, and mine blends in perfectly. I grudgingly feel grateful for Talia's help.

Brianna turns at the sound of my voice, but she doesn't get up to greet me or anything. "You can put your present over there," she says, gesturing toward a corner.

I move toward a table piled high with brightly wrapped packages and curly ribbons. Now that all the other girls are watching me, I'm suddenly super conscious of how I walk. Are the steps I'm taking smaller than usual? What do I normally do with my arms? Do I always *have* this many arms?

Calm down, I tell myself. *You don't have to impress anyone. You just have to fit in long enough to find Edna's painting. You're here on a supersecret spy mission, and it makes no difference what these girls think of you.* I desperately want to believe that little voice, but it's really, really hard not to care what they think.

"Grab a chair," Brianna says to me. "Victoria will bring you some punch." She doesn't say "please" or address anyone directly, but another lady in an apron springs into action and pours me a glass of fizzy pink stuff. There's another uniformed woman in here as well, standing next to the door and waiting for instructions, and it seems incredibly weird that there are this many staff people working at a party for kids. Is this what rich-people parties are always like? And where are Brianna's parents?

I want to sit by Sabrina, but the chairs on either side of her are taken, so I sit next to a redhead named Olivia who's a grade ahead of me at school. She shoots me a quick smile, but then she turns right back around and keeps talking to Jasmine Sato about a bonfire they went to on the Fourth of July. I sip my drink and try to keep a smile on my face, pretending I'm enjoying myself and not feeling unbelievably awkward.

After about five minutes a third woman in a uniform shows up at the solarium door. "Excuse me, Miss Brianna," she says, as if she's a little afraid of interrupting. "The cosmetologists have arrived."

I'm still not sure what a cosmetologist is, but the rest of the girls squeal, so I guess it's something good. "Thanks, Emily," Brianna says. "You can show them in." It seems out of character that Brianna would bother to learn the staff people's names, but then it occurs to me that these people must work here *all the time*, not just for the party. I can't even imagine what that would be like.

Emily backs out of the room and calls for the cosmetologists to follow her, and three women carrying big plastic kits come striding into the room. They're all dressed in black shirts and skirts, white lab coats, and high heels, though the heels are different colors—one has pink, one has red, and one has turquoise. It's a little spooky how they all walk in unison, and I wonder for a second if they might be robots. I almost lean over and whisper that to Olivia, but I'm pretty sure she would think it was more weird than funny, and the last thing I want to do is draw attention to myself. All of a sudden I miss Maddie like crazy.

"Which of you is the birthday girl?" asks Turquoise Lady in a clipped accent that sounds kind of like the Russian detective on this crime show my mom watches. Brianna raises her hand and smiles in that closed-mouth way she always does with adults. She must think it makes her look sophisticated, but actually it makes her look constipated.

"Happy birthday, darling," says Turquoise Lady. The word comes out like *dar-link*. "We will do your makeover and manicure first, of course." *Oh*—cosmetologists are makeup people. This party is getting less fun by the second. Except on Halloween, I've never had the slightest desire to wear anything but a tiny bit of lip gloss.

"Would you like to choose two of your friends to join you?" asks Pink Lady.

Almost all the girls' hands shoot up. I expect Brianna to pick Sabrina and Elena, since they're her best friends, but instead she chooses Jasmine and this girl named Kelsey. "They need it the most," Brianna tells the makeup ladies in a low voice, but it's plenty loud enough for the rest of us to hear. Everyone else giggles a little, but it's the half-nervous, half-relieved kind of laughter that happens when you think someone's about to make fun of you and then they don't at the last second. Nobody's really ever safe around Brianna, not even her close friends.

Kelsey's and Jasmine's faces go red, but they don't argue, and they take their places next to Brianna. The cosmetologists set up small folding tables next to the girls' loungers and unpack a bunch of hair products and makeup and nail polish. They talk as they start to paint and primp the girls, giving tips about boring things like how to blend eye shadow. Everyone else huddles around and gapes like they're watching a cat do backflips or something. As Pink Lady uses some sort of scary-looking clamp on Jasmine's eyelashes, I glance down at my dirty, ragged nails, then tuck my hands under my thighs so nobody else can see them. I can pretend to be a proper lady all I want, but my messy, imperfect real self is still right there under the surface.

I wait until the robot ladies are almost done with the

first group of girls, and then I get up and ask the woman who poured me punch where the bathroom is. Everyone's so fixated on the makeup demonstration that I'm able to slip away unnoticed. Perfect. After I wash my hands, I'll investigate more of the house.

I peek into every room I pass—a study, a guest bedroom, and a room full of exercise equipment—but there are no abstract paintings in any of them. When I find the bathroom, I'm surprised to see that the ceiling and all four of the walls are made of mirrors. I stand in the middle of the room and spin slowly; it's kind of fascinating to see myself from so many angles at once. I don't know how anyone manages to pee or take a shower in here. I would be way too distracted.

As I watch the millions of AJs scrub their nails with the tiny shell-shaped soaps, I hear voices outside in the hall. One of them is Brianna's, and when I hear how upset she sounds, I roll my eyes at the AJs in the mirror. What can she *possibly* have to complain about, today of all days? Did her nail polish chip? Did her perfect hair not curl perfectly enough? I leave the water running, tiptoe to the door, and press my ear against its cold mirrored surface.

"Do you really have to go right *now*?" I hear Brianna saying.

"Darling, you know I always meet with my personal trainer on Saturdays," says a voice I don't recognize.

"But couldn't you cancel this week? Or at least reschedule?"

"Callista's in very high demand, and her schedule is completely full. I reserved this spot months in advance."

I hear Brianna sigh. "Daddy's not here either, so I thought maybe you'd—"

"Your father's on an important business trip, Brianna."

"I *know* it's important, but neither of you were here last year either, *or* the year before, and I hoped that—"

"Victoria has everything under control, doesn't she?" says the other voice. "Is there a problem? I can speak to her before I go. Didn't she hire enough cosmetologists? Let me check—"

"Victoria's not the problem!" Brianna shouts. "*You're* the problem! You're supposed to be my *mom*, and you don't even care about—"

"Don't you raise your voice at me," snaps Mrs. Westlake in such a scary tone that I take a quick step back from the door. "You have a very privileged life and a house full of beautiful things, and you're getting heaps of presents today. Don't act like a spoiled brat."

"I'm *not*. I just wanted you to—"

"We can't have everything we want all the time, Brianna. You're old enough to know that."

It's silent for a second, and then Brianna's mom's voice changes back to perky and peppy, like someone flipped a switch inside her head. "I'll be back in time for cake. All right, darling? Victoria got you the five-layer lemon one you wanted from Schusterman's, with the gold leaf and sugared violets on top."

Brianna grumbles something, but I can't hear what it is.

"Have a lovely party, all right? The girl did a wonderful job with your makeup. You look so grown-up."

"Thanks," says Brianna, and from her flat tone, I can tell she'd gladly go right back to being a little kid if it meant her mom would come to her party. Mrs. Westlake's footsteps start moving away, and after a minute, I hear Brianna leave too.

As I stand in the Westlakes' crazy bathroom, I'm struck by a feeling so weird it takes me a minute to recognize it: I actually feel *sorry* for Brianna. I don't have any servants at home to pour me fizzy drinks or do my nails, and I don't have a solarium or diamond earrings or a cake that sounds like it belongs in a bank vault. But both my parents have been at every single one of my birthdays, beaming at me and snapping pictures while I scarfed down Zappetto's pizza, blew out my candles, and opened my presents. I've really missed them the last few weeks, and it occurs to me that Brianna must feel that way *all the time*, even when her parents are right there.

I try to push the thought away. I have a job to do, and feeling bad for Brianna will only complicate things.

It's been long enough now that I'm pretty sure I won't be spotted leaving the bathroom, so I turn off the water and slip into the hall. But instead of heading back to the solarium, I cross the foyer and hurry up one of the curved double staircases that lead to the second floor, my feet totally silent on the plush white carpeting. It feels like I'm walking on a sponge cake. I creep down the halls and glance quickly into each room—a master bedroom wallpapered in gold, four guest bedrooms, a room full of expensive-looking leather books, another bathroom, a room with a pool table and a bunch of squishy couches— but I don't see Edna's painting anywhere.

The only room left on this side of the house has a silver nameplate on the door that says BRIANNA in fancy script, and I approach it nervously. The door is shut, and I know I could get in serious trouble if Brianna caught me poking around in her bedroom. But the grannies would want me to be thorough, right? Plus, I can't pretend I'm not a little curious. How many ball gowns and shoes and pairs of diamond earrings does she actually have? Are there love letters from eighth-grade boys sitting on her night table? Are there Barbies in her closet that she secretly plays with when nobody else is around?

I put my hand on the knob, but as I'm about to turn it, I hear a soft sob, and I jump back. Oh no, Brianna's *in* there! If I catch her crying, she'll probably tell everyone I have a horrible contagious rash or something. Just thinking about what she could do to me makes me want to turn around and run back downstairs. But at the same time I still feel kind of bad for her about the stuff her mom said. Maybe I should get Sabrina or Elena and ask them to come up and comfort her? Then again, if Brianna wanted to talk to them, wouldn't she have called them up here herself?

It occurs to me for the first time that even though Brianna has a lot of followers, she might not have any actual *friends*. Maybe everyone's just afraid of her. Maybe she needs someone to talk to.

Before I can think too hard about it, I tap quietly on the door. "Brianna, it's AJ," I call. "Are you okay?"

I hear a loud sniffle, and then Brianna says, "Yeah, why wouldn't I be?" She's clearly trying to make her voice sound normal, but it comes out wet and choked.

"I was in the bathroom, and I overheard you talking to your mom. I can't believe she's skipping your party."

It's quiet for a second, and I wonder if Brianna's getting ready to yell at me for butting into her personal business. Maybe she'll throw me out of her house altogether— the grannies will be furious if I have to leave before I've found their painting. I'm trying to think up excuses when Brianna says the absolute last thing I ever expected to hear.

"You can come in if you want."

I open the door slowly, like there might be a wild animal waiting to attack me on the other side. But it's just a normal bedroom with big windows and pink curtains and Brianna's jeans and shirts and books strewn all over the white carpet. Hanging over the bed is a huge photo collage of the Bananas; it's a lot like my corkboard at home, only it's more professionally done, and the frame says WORLD'S COOLEST DIVAS across the top in pink rhinestones. Brianna's curled up in the middle of her flowered bedspread, her curled hair falling over her face and a ratty stuffed panda hugged tightly to her chest. As I step into the room, she shoves the panda behind her. The thought of Brianna being embarrassed in front of me is so ridiculous I almost laugh, but I manage to swallow it down.

"What's your panda's name?" I ask instead, to show her it's okay. "I have this falling-apart old armadillo named Hector at home."

She makes a noise that's sort of a half sniffle, half laugh. "That's a dumb name."

"I know, right? I got him when I was a baby."

She pulls the panda back out and sits it in front of her stomach. "This is Coco," she says. "That's kind of stupid too, but whatever." She dabs at her eyes carefully with her fingers. "Is my makeup all smeared?"

I walk over and take a closer look. Her eyes are a little red, but her mascara and sparkly gold eye shadow still look almost perfect. "It's actually fine," I say.

"Thank God. Olga must've used the waterproof stuff. My mom would kill me if I wrecked it."

She grabs a tissue from her nightstand and blows her nose, and when I turn around to give her privacy, that's when I see the enormous painting hanging across from the bed. It's blue and green and silver and purple, all swoops and swirls and splashes that look completely random but totally planned at the same time. The paint is so thick in some places that it actually sticks off the canvas in peaks, like frosting on a cake. It's bigger than my arm span in both directions, and the lower right corner is signed with a silver *E.S.*

Edna Shapiro.

"Whoa," I breathe. Even though Edna showed me a picture of the painting, the real thing is so much more beautiful. I kind of see why she wants it back.

Brianna sits up and scoots closer to the edge of the bed. "I know," she says. "Isn't it awesome?"

"Who made it?" I ask, even though it's obvious.

"I don't know. It's been here since I was a baby. The signature says *E.S.*, but I don't know what that stands for. My dad says I used to lie there and stare at it for hours when I was little. I still do that sometimes, actually. It kind of looks like different stuff on different days, depending on what mood you're in." She glances at me sideways. "That sounds kind of crazy, right?"

What's crazy is that Brianna seems like she wants my *approval.* "I don't think it's weird," I say. "What does it look like to you right now?"

She squints and tips her head to the side. "It looks like a woman holding a kid," she says. "See that curvy silver part at the top? That's her head. And that blue part is her arm, and there's her back, and that green part is the kid's face. Do you see it?"

I do see it. "Totally. That's cool. That part on the right kind of looks like a whale to me."

"Oh yeah, it does." Brianna pulls her knees up to her chest and wraps her arms around them. "Looking at it calms me down for some reason. It's nice to know it's always up here waiting for me, you know?" She laughs a little. "It's kind of lame to care about a painting this much, right? You must think I'm such a freak."

Actually, I like Brianna better right now than I ever have before. For once she's not acting snotty or insulting someone or trying to show off. She always talks about stuff she wants because it's expensive and flashy and impressive, but she never seems to have actual *feelings* about any of it.

"Is it worth a lot?" I ask to test my theory. "Is E. S., like, a famous artist or something?"

Brianna shrugs. "No idea. Honestly, even if it was worth a ton, I'd never sell it. What else could I buy that's this cool?"

"I don't know, new diamond earrings or something?"

She waves her hand like she's trying to swat away a mosquito. "Eh, whatever. Diamonds aren't nearly as interesting."

This is so weird. All Brianna has ever seemed to care about are jewelry and dresses and boats and jets. It suddenly occurs to me that maybe she talks about those things to cover up the fact that all she really *has* is stuff. I've definitely been jealous of her before, but now that I know what her family's really like, I wouldn't want to trade places with her for a second. I have people at home who actually care about me.

And Edna has people who care about her, too. She has her kids and grandkids and my grandmother and Cookie and Betty and me, and probably lots of other people I don't even know about. She doesn't need this painting. She can always make another one. But Brianna's life seems kind of empty, and I don't want any part in taking away the one thing I'm sure she loves.

"I wish I could tell the artist how much I like it," Brianna says. "It's weird that I look at her painting every single day and she has no idea who I even am."

"I'm sure she'd be really happy to know it has such a good home," I say.

And I hope that's true, because if I have anything to do with it, this painting is staying right here.

Sorry, Edna, I think to myself. *I'm out.*

17

When Stanley brings me home from the party, sparkly-eyed and shiny-nailed and curly-haired and looking totally unlike myself, the grannies are waiting for me. It's way past six, when they usually leave, so I thought I'd have until tomorrow to work out how to tell them I'm not on board with this heist anymore. But when I open the door, Cookie's right there in the entryway, dressed in bright red shoes and a red beret covered in sequins. Before I have time to object, she grabs my elbow and steers me toward the storage room.

"Did you find it?" she whispers. "Come in here and tell us everything." Then she notices my makeup and stops dead in the middle of the hallway, and her eyes widen behind her glasses until they practically take up her entire face. "Oh, *AJ*," she breathes. "*Look* at you! You're absolutely *divine!*"

I'm pretty sure I actually look ridiculous—Stanley didn't comment on my makeup at all—but I say, "Thanks, Cookie."

She drags me through the storage room door. "Girls, *look* at our AJ! She could be a little muse-in-training, don't you think?"

Edna looks slightly to my left and makes a sort of *hmm* noise, but Betty beams at me, and her eyes crinkle up until they're almost lost in their nest of wrinkles. "So beautiful," she says, and suddenly I do feel prettier. I smile back at her with my weirdly pink lips.

My grandmother comes over to see what all the fuss is about, a parrot on each shoulder, and she frowns at me. "Good heavens, Annemarie. You looked so lovely when you left. *What* is all that ridiculous goop on your face?"

Did Grandma Jo just give me a backhanded *compliment*? "It was—" I start to say, but Cookie cuts me off.

"Don't get your knickers in a twist, Jo. Young girls are supposed to experiment with these things. It's perfectly harmless."

Grandma Jo makes a harrumphing noise. "It's an enormous waste of time, if you ask me. Did you manage to find the painting, or were you too busy gadding about?"

"I found it," I say.

Cookie and Betty let out happy shouts and pull me into one of their double hugs, and Edna raises her hands above her head and does her finger-wiggling silent applause thing. "Well *done*, my darling," Cookie crows.

Betty beams at me. "I *knew* you'd come through for us."

"Walk the plank!" Scrooge chimes in.

Everyone looks so pleased with me, even my grandmother, that I almost can't bring myself to say the rest of the words that are crouched in the back of my throat. I feel as nervous as I did the first time Grandma Jo made me carry a bird around. I remind myself that Ben and Maddie both said I was brave, but it turns out that the kind of bravery that involves standing up for what you believe in is harder than the kind that involves psyching yourself up to be a daredevil. I'd much rather fall off my skateboard than say no to people who are counting on me.

"Your painting is really beautiful, Edna," I say, stalling. "I love the way the paint, like, sticks up off the canvas. How did you get it to do that?"

Edna gives me a big smile. "Thank you, dear. I used a palette knife to apply the paint. That painting is one of my very favorites; I can't *wait* to see it again."

"Um, yeah. About that." I take a deep breath. "Here's the thing. I, um . . . I don't think we should steal it."

"Liberate," Cookie and Betty correct me.

Grandma Jo's eyebrows pull down into a stern V shape. "What? Why not? Is it alarmed? Is it behind glass? It doesn't matter—Edna can get around it."

Edna nods. "I'm a master."

"It's not that," I say. "It's not protected or anything. It's just . . . I think it's *wrong*."

Nobody speaks for a minute, and the grannies exchange confused looks. Finally Cookie says, "What do you mean, dear?"

"I mean, it isn't right to take something that doesn't belong to you."

"It *does* belong to me," Edna says. "I made it."

"But the Westlakes bought it. Look, I got this dress at Nordstrom. Are you saying it still belongs to Nordstrom, even though I paid for it?"

Edna blows out a puff of air and makes a vague, dismissive gesture with her hand. "Money doesn't *mean* anything. It's the spiritual connection that matters."

"It's not really about the money, though," I say, a little more confident now. "The girl who has your painting now? She *loves* it. It's been hanging in her room since she was a baby, and it's, like, her favorite thing in the whole world. I've never seen her care about anything the way she cares about it, including the *actual pony* she got for her birthday when we were ten. Don't you want someone who cares about your work to have it? If you took it away from her, she'd be so upset, and she has enough stuff to be upset about already."

For a second I think I've gotten through to her. But then Edna says, "It's very nice to know she appreciates it. But I'd still rather have it back."

"Her parents can buy her another painting, dear," says Cookie. "I read in a magazine that her father is one of the richest men in America."

"I know they can *afford* another painting. That's not the point. It's wrong to take someone else's stuff, even if you think you deserve it more! You can't really know what other people's lives are like or what things mean to them."

All four of the ladies look at me like they've never even seen me before. Then my grandmother says, "I told you we shouldn't have trusted her with this."

I hate how she's talking about me as if I'm not even here. She suddenly sounds so cold, and her tone makes me feel like I've been kicked in the soft place below my ribs. "How can you say that?" I snap. "I've been incredibly trustworthy! I've done *everything* you've asked me to do, and I've kept all of it a secret. It's not like I'm going to tell anyone about the other stuff you've stolen. But I think you should call this heist off. Can't you steal another abused animal instead? I'm sure there are plenty of birds that need your help."

"We'll liberate another animal when it's Jo's turn," Cookie says. "It wouldn't be fair to skip Edna."

"But stealing Brianna's painting isn't fair, either!"

"We're going forward with the project," Grandma Jo says. "Loyalty is what matters most, and Edna's a loyal friend who always works hard to help us get what we want. If this is what *she* wants, we owe it to her to help her get it. Good people try to make their friends happy, Annemarie. Since when do you care about this Westlake girl? After all I've done for you, I'd have thought you'd be on my side, not hers."

I haven't felt this red-hot anger bubbling up inside me for weeks, not since Grandma Jo took my phone away and told me Maddie was a bad influence. But now the anger-lava is back, churning in my stomach. After all she's *done* for me? What on earth has she done for me but take me in reluctantly, rope me into an illegal organization, and try to keep me away from my favorite people?

I'm about to shout all of that at her, but that'll prove to Grandma Jo that I really am an impulsive, immature child who can't control myself. So I stand up very straight and take a couple of deep breaths, trying to be a hollow reed like Edna taught me. Then, as calmly as I can, I say, "I know I can't stop you from stealing the painting. But you'll have to do it without me."

I glance over at the other ladies, then wish I hadn't. They've always stood up for me, and now they're looking at me like maybe they've been wrong about me all along. Even though I'm positive I'm doing the right thing, I feel like I'm betraying them. Especially Betty.

My grandmother moves toward me, and even though she's leaning on her cane, it seems like she gets taller and more imposing with each step. She looks furious, and I'm suddenly a little afraid of her. "Tell us where the painting is, Annemarie," she orders, her voice cold and cutting. "You owe us that, at least."

I'm about to snap back that I won't, that I don't owe them anything, but then I get a better idea. Grandma Jo is always talking about how there are consequences for breaking the rules, but she and her friends break the rules all the time, and *they* certainly never seem to pay for it. If I don't tell the grannies about Brianna's dog, there's no way they'll get past the entryway before they'll have to hightail it out of there. Even if the Westlakes manage to catch them and call the cops, I'm sure the punishment for breaking into a house is much less harsh than the one for stealing an expensive painting. They've been lucky so far, but maybe this will make them think twice about what they're doing. I don't want them to go to jail or anything, but I *do* want them to see that this isn't a game.

"Fine," I say. "The painting's in Brianna's room. You go up the curved staircase in the entryway, turn left, and it's the first room on your right." That's actually where the master bedroom is, but in case the dog doesn't bark up a storm, this will ensure that they walk right into a trap.

"And the alarm system?" my grandmother says.

I pull up the picture of the alarm box on my phone, then show it to Edna, who nods like she's recognizing an old friend. She jots down some numbers on the edge of the blueprints and hands my phone back to me. She seems distant, and I wonder if she's furious with me too, but it's hard to tell. Edna always seems distant.

"That's all we need from you, Annemarie," says my grandmother. "Go to your room and wait there until dinner. This hallway is off-limits to you from now on. If I catch you here, you will no longer be allowed out of the house."

There's not a trace of warmth or respect in her voice; I may as well be a total stranger. It stings more than I expect, knowing things might be like this between us from now on. It's not like we've ever been close or anything, but we were finally making progress. The version of Grandma Jo who brought me Coke instead of tea and thought I was smart enough to help plan a heist was way better than the version who sent me an etiquette book for my birthday.

I guess never having something at all hurts less than getting what you want and then losing it again.

"What are you waiting for?" Grandma Jo says. "We have things to attend to."

As I turn and leave the room, I hear Betty say, "Don't you think that was a bit harsh, Jo?"

"Don't question my behavior," my grandmother snaps. "*You* don't exactly have a flawless moral compass." There she goes again, implying that the only person who stands up for me around here is somehow defective. I guess now I'll never find out what Betty did that's supposedly so terrible. Who knows if I'll ever be allowed to speak to her again?

I stomp up the stairs and try to slam the door, but it's too heavy and only makes an unsatisfying, muffled thump. The second I throw myself down on my bed, my phone starts ringing on my night table, and I lunge for it. Maddie's picture is on the screen, and for a second, all I feel is relief. If she's reaching out to me, maybe that means she's over all the stuff she said to Amy at our sleepover about our friendship falling apart. Right now I could really use a friend who loves me no matter what.

"Hey," I say. "You wouldn't *believe* how annoying my grandmother is being. She's such a—"

"I like your new dress," Maddie says, cutting me off. "Did *Brianna* help you pick it out?" Her voice sounds poisonous. I've never heard her use that tone before, not even when Brianna tried to give her the used gowns at soccer.

"My . . . what?" I hold the phone away from my ear and check to see if I pressed the video chat button by mistake, but it's a normal call. She can't possibly see me.

"I saw the pictures, AJ," Maddie spits. "Did you seriously think I wouldn't?"

"What pictures? What are you talking about?"

"The ones on Instagram? Of Brianna's party? For someone who made such a big fuss about not wanting to go, you look like you had a pretty great time."

Oh *no*. I am *so stupid*. Of course all the girls posted pictures of the party the second we left—how did I not think of that before now? Why did I idiotically assume I could keep this from Maddie? "It's not what it looks like at all," I say.

"Oh, it's not? Because what it looks like is that you lied to me and went to that party behind my back, even though Brianna's a raging jerk who makes fun of your best friends right in front of you. I thought you were on *my* side, so I'm not sure exactly what I'm supposed to think when I see you getting makeovers and eating cake with them."

"Maddie, I *am* on your side. I really didn't want to go. It was—"

"If you didn't want to go, you shouldn't have gone! Can't you see what a monster she is, AJ? Or did she brainwash you with all her sparkly, expensive *stuff*?"

"I don't care about her stuff! Listen to me, okay? It wasn't—"

"You don't get to tell me what to do!" Maddie yells. "If you want to eat lobster rolls and get your nails done with the freaking Bananas, fine, I can't stop you. But if you choose them, don't even bother pretending we're friends anymore. Go call your new BFF Brianna if you want someone to listen to you. I am *so* done with this."

"No, Maddie, wait—" I start, but I hear a click, and she's gone.

I call her back right away, but the phone just rings and rings until it goes to voice mail. I leave a long message, and then I send her a bunch of texts, apologizing like crazy for going behind her back and assuring her that I didn't really have fun at the party. But she doesn't answer. Tears prick at the corners of my eyes, and part of me wants to hurl the phone across the room and watch it smash into pieces against my grandmother's stupid mission chifforobe. But instead I pull up Instagram and scroll through Brianna's photos.

There I am, front and center, standing with some of the other girls by a pot of boiling lobsters, my arm linked with Sabrina's. My fake-curly hair is blowing in the breeze, and I'm smiling broadly with my glossy pink mouth. I look exactly like the Bananas, like I belong there with the rich, popular girls. I look like I'm having a great time. But I know how I was feeling as Victoria snapped that picture: awkward, gawky, totally out of my depth. Three seconds after that photo was taken, I'd sneakily checked my phone so I'd know how many more minutes of the party I'd have to endure.

And now, because of this stupid, lying photo, I've lost my best friend.

I wipe my eyes, expecting my hands to come away

black with melted mascara. But I guess they used the waterproof stuff on me, too, because even as my tears drip all over the bedspread, my painted-on face stays right in place, sparkly and perfect and totally fake.

18

The next few days at my grandmother's house are absolutely miserable. As if to punish me for standing up for my beliefs, Grandma Jo takes my phone away again and puts me to work learning how to set a proper table. (She actually makes me measure the distance between the forks with a *ruler*.) To make matters worse, Coach Adrian has some sort of family emergency and has to go out of town, so we don't have soccer for an entire week. I could call Maddie from the wall phone in the kitchen—I know her number by heart—but I'm positive she doesn't want to talk to me, so I don't even try.

As if losing my best friend isn't bad enough, Grandma Jo keeps me completely isolated from Cookie, Edna, and Betty. I've gotten used to seeing them every day, and I miss Cookie's jokes, Edna's weird, nonsensical advice, and Betty's warm unconditional love. I'm pretty sure they've forgiven me for backing out of the art heist—when we pass each other in the halls, they always smile and ask me how I'm doing in lowered voices. But they never linger or try to make conversation, and I have a feeling Grandma Jo has forbidden them to communicate with me.

Even though we eat dinner across from each other every night, my grandmother doesn't talk to me either, unless you count her repeated warnings that if I do anything to alert the Westlakes to the heist, I'll be very, very sorry. She doesn't even bother to correct me when I use the wrong fork anymore, which shows how much she's given up on me. I know it's a waste to gulp down Debbie's delicious food without even tasting it, but I always eat as fast as I can and head straight up to my room to get away from Grandma Jo. I spend the hours before bed rereading all Ben's old comic books for the millionth time. I'd kind of like something new to read, but I won't stoop to asking Grandma Jo to lend me something from her library.

I can't wait to go back to my normal life and forget this stupid month ever happened.

Grandma Jo plans the heist for two days before my parents come back from Brazil, and though I'm totally against what they're doing, I can't help feeling left out as the grannies assemble in the entryway in their black clothes. I sit quietly on the step in the dark, listening to them test their earpiece "Agent Cardinal, do you copy? Agent Heron, do you copy?" and a pang of jealousy shoots through me. After days stuck in this house with nobody to talk to, I'm desperate for an adventure. I miss the feeling of my lock-pick pouch strapped snugly around my waist, and even though I know it's stupid, I tiptoe up to my room and clip it on under my shirt. Maybe I'll pick every lock in this house as soon as they're gone, just to prove that I can.

The moment I think that, Grandma Jo appears at the bottom of the staircase. Sometimes I think she can read my mind. "Let's go, Annemarie," she says.

"What?" I say. "I told you I wasn't helping you this time."

"Of course you're not *helping*," she says. "But you don't really think we're going to leave you here alone to sabotage us, do you? You'll stay within our sight until the target is secured."

"What makes you think I won't call the police after you have the painting?"

Grandma Jo rolls her eyes. "Don't be ridiculous, Annemarie. You'll have absolutely no proof. We're obviously not going to leave the painting out where anyone could find it. It'll be your word against ours, and no police officer is going to believe a twelve-year-old over a group of dignified, respectable ladies."

She's probably right, and it makes me furious. I dig my fingers into the banister and try to keep my anger in check. "Fine," I say. "But I'm not getting in that van with you. You can't make me."

"You're coming with me, dear," says Betty, her voice soft and sweet, the exact opposite of Grandma Jo's. "You know I can't do anything more than be the lookout with these creaky old hips. I'll be sitting in the car at the end of the Westlakes' driveway, and I was so hoping you'd keep me company. I need some quality time with my girl before you go."

She smiles up at me, and she looks so hopeful that some of my anger melts away. Betty seems to respect my decision not to be part of this heist; she just wants to hang out with me because she genuinely likes me. It *would* be nice to have some alone time with her before I go back home, and I'd finally get to leave the house for a little while. I've set the grannies up to walk into a trap, but if Betty and I aren't anywhere near the house, we won't get in trouble when the cops come.

"Let me get my shoes," I say.

Edna smiles at me when I come downstairs, and Cookie reaches out to pat my shoulder, but when Grandma Jo glares at her, she removes her hand. "Take route B to the house, Sparrow," she directs Betty, already in Mission Control mode. "The trip should take approximately twenty-three minutes. If we arrive first, we'll wait until you're in place to enter the driveway."

"Copy that," says Betty. "Come on, Agent Swan." It feels like a little act of defiance that she's using my code name, and I smile.

I follow Betty to her car, which is parked in front of Grandma Jo's house. For some reason I had pictured her driving a boxy sky-blue car the color of the flowered dresses she likes to wear, and I'm disappointed to see that it's a boring black one. There aren't even any bumper stickers or fun little toys dangling from the rearview mirror. "Help me get my walker into the backseat, dear," she says.

"Should we put it in the trunk?" I ask. "There's probably more room."

"No, no. The trunk is a little crowded at the moment. It'll be fine back there." So I fold up the walker for her, stash it behind the driver's seat, and give her a hand as she slides behind the wheel. When I close her door for her, I feel like Stanley.

I walk around to the passenger's seat, but Betty stops me when I open the door. "Why don't you sit in back?" she says. "The statistics say it's twice as safe, and I couldn't live with myself if anything happened to you."

This seems a little overprotective—Stanley and my parents always let me ride in the front. But it's not worth it to argue over one ride, and it's kind of sweet that Betty's so concerned about my safety. I slide into the back, and the walker's tennis ball feet rest against my left leg.

"Perfect," Betty says. "Exactly where I want you."

Before she starts the car, she reaches into her cavernous purse, pulls out a pair of white cotton gloves, and puts them on. "What are those for?" I ask. "We're not going inside this time. You don't have to worry about leaving fingerprints."

"This is an *occasion*, dear," Betty says. "It seems right to get a little dressed up, don't you think?"

I look down at my outfit: a shirt with two *T. rex*es trying to high-five each other and fraying jeans that haven't been washed in weeks. "Sorry, I didn't know I was supposed to dress up," I say.

"No, no. You're perfect the way you are." Betty laughs,

and it sounds a little high and strained, like she's nervous. She seemed totally calm during the last two heists, and I wonder why she's more worried about this one. Maybe she's intimidated by the Westlakes.

"Is everything okay?" I ask.

"What? Yes, of course. Oh! I almost forgot. I got you something on the way here." Betty takes a plastic 7-Eleven cup out of the cup holder and passes it back to me, along with a red straw. "I thought maybe you'd like a Coke Slurpee as a little treat."

I *do* love Coke Slurpees, and I haven't had one since my parents left; there's no 7-Eleven near Grandma Jo's house, and even if there was, she'd never let me go on my own. "Wow, thank you so much," I say. "I love these."

"You're very welcome," Betty says. "It's my pleasure."

I take a long sip of the Slurpee. It's kind of melted from sitting in the car, but it's mostly fine once I stir it around. I hold the cup out to her. "Do you want some?"

"Oh, no thank you, dear. I can't have that much sugar anymore; it upsets my tummy."

"Okay. Sorry." I take another sip and let the fizzy, sweet slush melt on my tongue. It really is delicious.

Betty starts the car and pulls away from the curb, and the radio comes on automatically, playing soft classical piano music. It sounds like something Grandma Jo might put on during a dinner party, but I find it kind of soothing. "I'm so glad I finally get some time alone with my favorite girl," Betty says. "It's been cruel of your grandmother to keep us apart this week. She knows I love you like you're my own granddaughter."

It's kind of surprising that Betty feels so strongly about me—she's known me only a few weeks—but I like it anyway. Grandma Jo has definitely never said she loves me. I don't even think she's said it to Ben.

"I've really missed hanging out with you guys," I say.

"Do you love me too, AJ? Do you love me like a grandmother?"

I wouldn't exactly say I *love* Betty, but I certainly like her a lot more than I like my actual grandmother. I don't want to hurt her feelings when she's being so nice to me, so I say, "Sure. I love you like a grandmother."

Betty sighs happily. "I would've been a perfect grandmother for you, don't you think, AJ?" Her voice quavers a little, and I don't know why she's getting so emotional or why she's using my name so much.

"Definitely," I say. "You would've done a great job. Way better than Grandma Jo."

For a second I think she's going to tell me it's rude to

insult my grandmother, that she's doing the best she can. But instead Betty says, "Thank you, dear. It's so nice of you to say that." Then she giggles, a weirdly high-pitched, hysterical sound I've never heard her make before. It sets me on edge, and my heart starts beating a little faster, though I'm not exactly sure why.

"No problem," I say.

"I always wanted children of my own, you know," Betty says. "It's the great disappointment of my life that I never got to have them."

"Yeah, I know. You told me. I'm sorry."

"I thought teaching other people's children would be enough," she continues like she hasn't even heard me. "But it never was, because those children didn't *belong* to me. At the end of the day, they went home to other women, who got to hug them and kiss them and feed them chicken noodle soup and put them to bed. I was allowed to love them only during school hours, and love can't be limited to school hours, AJ. *Love can't be limited at all.*"

I don't know why she's getting so worked up, but it's really starting to creep me out. "I'm sorry," I tell her again, since I have no idea what else to say.

Betty stops at a light and turns around partway. Her eyes look weirdly bright and glassy, like Maddie's did the time she came down with the flu in science class. "Are you drinking your Slurpee back there?" she asks.

"Yes." I suck on the straw loudly to prove it.

"Finish the whole thing. It's important to stay hydrated."

"I will. Don't worry. It's really good."

This seems to make her happy, and she turns back around and hits the accelerator. "If you belonged to me, I would get you Slurpees every day. I would buy you the most beautiful dresses and made you cakes and take you on trips to see the world. I would take you camping in the woods. Do you like the woods, AJ?"

"Sure, the woods are nice," I say.

"They *are* nice, aren't they? No other people for miles and miles around. Nobody to spy on you or gossip about you or tell you that what you're doing isn't allowed. That'll be wonderful. Just wonderful. . . ." She sounds dreamy, sort of like Edna sounds most of the time, but it's much freakier on her. This ride is getting weirder by the second. I'm starting to wonder if Betty should be driving a car while she's like this; maybe I should ask her to pull over until she calms down.

"Are you sure you're okay?" I ask. "You're acting a little strange."

"Oh yes, dear. I've never been better." Betty fiddles

absently with her earpiece, and I notice that the little blue light isn't on. If the other ladies have been giving her instructions, she hasn't been listening. Then she takes it out altogether, rolls down the window, and tosses it out.

I sit up straighter and stare at her. "What are you doing? Don't you need that?"

Betty smiles at me in the rearview mirror. "No, I don't think I'll be needing it anymore."

"But what if my grandmother—" I start, but then the strangest wave of dizziness sweeps over me, and I stop talking and put a hand to my forehead. The road is perfectly smooth, but it feels like the car is rocking back and forth like a boat, and even though I was wide awake a minute ago, I'm suddenly completely exhausted. I take another big gulp of my Slurpee, hoping the cold will snap me out of it, but it doesn't make me feel any better.

"Whoa," I say. "I feel really weird."

"What's the matter, dear?" Betty asks.

"I don't know. I'm just . . . really tired all of a sudden."

"That's okay," Betty says, and her voice sounds strange, like it's echoing around in my head. "Lie down on the seat and take a little rest. You've had a long, stressful week. I'll wake you when we get there."

"I don't know what's wrong with me," I try to say, but

my tongue has suddenly grown ten sizes and feels much too heavy for me to lift. I slump down sideways and press my cheek to the scratchy upholstery of Betty's backseat, and it's a huge relief to be horizontal. Slowly, the earth starts to rotate off its axis, and when I feel myself floating away and getting lost in the stars, I don't have the energy to fight it.

"Good girl," says a faraway voice. "That's right. You just rest now. Everything's going to be okay."

And then someone flips off a light switch behind my eyes, and everything goes dark and quiet and still.

19

When I become aware of the world again, I have absolutely no idea where I am.

I'm lying down, and I can feel a blanket covering me, so at first I think I'm in my bed at Grandma Jo's house. Opening my eyes feels like way too much effort; all I want to do is let myself drift back into unconsciousness. I feel like I could easily sleep for eight more hours right now, lulled by the soft classical music playing somewhere nearby and the way the whole world seems to be vibrating beneath me. But I'm lying on my arm, which is half-asleep and tingling with pins and needles, so I roll over to get more comfortable and my cheek lands in a freezing-cold, sweet-smelling puddle. *Eww.* How did *that* get in my bed? Grandma Jo won't even let me bring a granola bar up here; she's going to be so mad.

I try to reach up and wipe my face . . . and that's when I realize my wrists are tied behind my back.

My heart, which felt like a sluggish sea creature tread-ing water in my chest a second ago, kicks back into gear and starts thrashing. I force my eyes open, and everything comes back to me in bits and pieces. I'm in Betty's car. We were headed to Brianna's house, and Betty started act-ing all weird and creepy and talking about how great the woods are. Then I got dizzy and tired, so I lay down for a minute. And while I was out, someone tied my hands.

Since there's only one other person here, I'm pretty sure who did it.

I try to struggle into a sitting position, but my feet are stuck together too, so I kick them like a mermaid tail until the blanket falls free. There are fat strips of silver duct tape wound around and around my ankles.

Betty hears me moving around and glances at me over her shoulder. "Goodness, are you awake already, dear?" she says. "They told me it would last much longer."

"Betty, what did you *do*? Why am I tied up? Did you *drug* me? Did you put something in my Slurpee?"

"I'm sorry, darling, but it was the only way," she says. "Just lie back and relax now. We're going to be driving for quite some time."

"The only way to *what?*" I squirm around and try to loosen the tape on my wrists, but it holds fast.

"Please be still, AJ," Betty says. "I promise I'll untie you when we get there. But until then, you're safer this way. I can't have you trying to escape and getting injured."

Now my heart feels like it's trying to climb up my throat and out of my mouth. I crane my neck to see the clock on the dashboard so I'll know how long I've been out, but it's blocked by the seat. A dark stretch of generic highway rushes by outside the window. We could be absolutely anywhere. "Where are you taking me?" I ask.

"We're going somewhere nobody will ever find us," Betty says, as though she's describing the most delicious dessert in the world. "Our own little cabin in the woods. Once we're all alone, we'll be safe. Won't that be wonderful? Just the two of us, like it's supposed to be. We'll have such a beautiful life together, AJ."

My mind whirls in circles like Snickers chasing his tail. The last few weeks have taught me what it's like to steal, but this . . . *this* is what it's like to be stolen. In all the countless stranger-danger lectures we've had at school, nobody ever taught me how to deal with something like this. Betty's not even a stranger.

"You have to take me back to Grandma Jo's house," I say. "I can't go away with you."

"But why not? We love each other, AJ. You said you loved me like family. And your grandmother doesn't appreciate you one bit. It's like we do with the birds—snatch you from the bad owner, whisk you to a better life!"

"But I already have a really good life with my parents. They're going to be home in two days, and I need to go back and live with them. I'm really happy there, I promise, and I'm sure they'll let me hang out with you whenever I want." I obviously have no intention of ever hanging out with Betty again, but I figure she'll be more likely to do what I want if she feels like I'm on her side.

"That's not enough," Betty says, her voice suddenly scary and fierce. "*Nobody* loves you like I do. You're *my* perfect girl, and I need you with me *all the time!*" She bangs both gloved hands on the steering wheel, and the car swerves a little.

"Betty, this will never work," I say, and even though I'm trying hard to sound confident, I'm totally freaking out now, and my voice comes out shaky and unsure. "Grandma Jo and Edna and Cookie know I'm with you. They'll figure out you took me, and they'll go straight to the police. Wouldn't it be easier to take me back now, before you've done anything really terrible? Otherwise, you're going to be in *huge* trouble. They'll be able to track you down in a second by your license plate or your cell phone or your credit cards." I have no idea how any of those things work, but I'm pretty sure I've seen cops do them on the legal dramas my mom watches.

Betty shakes her head, and for a second I think I've outwitted her. But then I hear her laughing quietly. "My dear, I may be old, but I'm not stupid. I don't have a cell phone or any credit cards, and this isn't my car."

A cold finger of fear creeps down my spine. "I . . . what? Whose car is it?"

"After decades of heists, you don't think I know how to steal a car? The people who own this one won't be back in the country until Christmas. By then, it'll be in a junkyard somewhere. And as for Jo and Cookie and Edna? Bless their hearts, but they're amateurs. They'll never find me. You think I didn't learn anything from last time?"

Last time? Betty has done this *before*?

All the comments the other ladies have made about Betty whirl through my head: *She can't be trusted. She's wild. She's unpredictable. She has a faulty moral compass.* They must've thought she'd reformed—I know they would never put me in danger on purpose. But she fooled them with her sweet, repentant old lady act, just like she fooled me. Betty's crazy streak was lurking under the surface all this time, waiting for the right moment to show itself.

I'm in full-on panic mode now, and it doesn't feel like there's nearly enough oxygen in the car. Even though the air-conditioning is on, drops of sweat bead across my forehead and crawl between my shoulder blades, and the blanket Betty put over me isn't helping. I rack my brain for another way to convince her to let me go, but my thoughts are an incoherent whirl, landing on one useless, unrelated topic after another.

"I've waited years for this," Betty continues. She seems agitated now, and I can feel the car starting to wander back and forth between lanes. On top of everything else, I'm terrified she's going to crash into something and kill us both. "All this time I've been the inside girl, helping Jo and Cookie and Edna steal the things *they* wanted, and it's been years and years since I asked for anything for myself. I skipped my turn to pick the target every time because I was saving up for something really big, something really wonderful. And now I finally get what I wanted. I get my grandchild. I *deserve* this."

Do something, the panicked voice in my head screams. *You have to do something.*

And then, out of nowhere, I hear my dad's voice. *If an anaconda attacks you, AJ, you can't struggle or you're dead meat. You have to let it think it's won and bide your time. And then, when the moment is right . . . bam! That's when you strike.*

Betty is my anaconda. Flailing and screaming isn't going to get me anywhere. I need to let her think she's in control until the right moment arrives to whip up my machete hand and cut her crazy plans right in half.

I take a deep breath and try to calm down. "A cabin in the woods *does* actually sound kind of nice," I say. "Tell me more about it."

Betty starts talking about a fireplace and a woodpile and a nearby stream, and her driving starts to even out. I don't know if she's describing a real place or one that exists only in her deranged mind, but it doesn't matter as long as it's keeping her busy and calm. The shoulder I'm lying on feels like it's being wrenched out of its socket, so I brace my taped feet against the door and wriggle onto my back so I can relax and focus and make an escape plan. I'm lying on top of something lumpy, and I try to shift it aside with my hip, but it won't budge no matter how I squirm. It's almost like it's attached to me or something.

My lock-picking kit! For the first time, I feel the tiniest ray of hope.

"That sounds beautiful," I say to Betty. "Tell me more about the house. What does it look like inside?"

As she slips further into her daydream, I arch my upper body as much as I can, and I'm able to worm the tip of a finger under the closure of my lock-pick pouch. I fake a bunch of sneezes to cover the noise of the Velcro pulling apart, and Betty pauses. "Are you okay, dear?"

"I'm fine," I say. I try not to move too much under the blanket as I struggle to pull out a pick. It turns out to be one of the blunt ones, so I drop it on the seat behind me and strain for another. "What were you saying about the bathtub?"

The second pick I grab is one of the sharp, hooked ones, like what a hygienist uses to scrape your teeth. I turn back onto my side so I'll have more room to maneuver and start trying to poke it through the tape. The way I have to contort makes my shoulders and wrists ache, but the pick does its job, and it takes me only a few minutes to make a small hole. Betty's still talking, and I don't think she's noticed a thing. When I feel the tape start to give, hope expands in my chest like a helium balloon. I can do this. I'm going to get out of here.

After what is probably less than ten minutes but feels like hours, Betty says, "Doesn't that sound wonderful, dear?"

I've been so focused on the tape that I haven't been listening at all, but I say, "Yes, it really does . . . *Grandma Betty.*"

The words have exactly the distracting effect I'd intended, and Betty lets out a happy sigh as the final strands of duct tape snap. "Oh, AJ," she says, her voice choked and teary. "We're going to be so happy together. This is everything I've ever wanted."

"Me too," I say as I pull my cramped wrists apart and rotate my hands behind my back. "You're right about Grandma Jo. She never appreciated me the way you do." I feel around in my shorts pockets for my phone before I remember Grandma Jo confiscated it days ago. The only thing in any of my pockets is a stiff, thick piece of paper folded into quarters: Brianna's birthday party invitation. Great. Like *that's* going to do me any good.

Concentrate on getting your feet free, I tell myself. *You'll think of another plan.*

Careful to stay under the blanket, I roll onto my back, bend my knees, and start picking at the tape on my ankles. It goes much faster now that I have full use of my hands, and before long, I'm totally free. For a moment, all I feel is pure joy, but then I realize I have no idea what to do next. I can't exactly throw myself out of this speeding car and onto the highway. I hook the toe of my sneaker around the door handle and tug, figuring Betty will have to pull over if the open-door alarm goes off, but nothing happens—she must have the child locks on. I could lean over the front seat, grab the wheel, and crash the car into the median, but without a seat belt, I'd probably fly through the windshield. I'm not going to get very far with broken arms and legs.

I need to play into Betty's weaknesses somehow and make her stop the car. But what *are* Betty's weaknesses? If the last hour has taught me anything, it's that I don't really know her at all.

And then something so obvious occurs to me that I almost groan out loud.

I am Betty's weakness.

It takes me a few minutes to come up with a solid plan. I practice each motion over and over in my head until I'm sure I can do them without hesitating, the way I sometimes review soccer plays before I fall asleep. I'm going to get only one chance at this, so I have to get it right.

When I'm sure I'm completely ready, I snake a hand out from under my blanket, pop one of the tennis balls off the leg of Betty's walker, and wedge it deep between the seat cushions, remembering what she told me about how hard it is to walk when it's uneven. Then I start to cough violently, the way I used to when I was little and wanted to convince my mom I was too sick to go to school.

Betty breaks off in the middle of a sentence. "Are you *sure* you're all right, dear?"

I wheeze like something's caught in my throat. "Water," I choke between coughs. "Help!"

"Yes, yes, of course." Betty sounds incredibly alarmed, and I hear the turn signal flip on. "You're okay, AJ. Don't worry. Grandma's here to help you." My throat is starting to hurt, but I keep up the fake coughing until I feel the car pull onto the shoulder and roll to a stop.

Perfect.

Betty grabs a water bottle from her cup holder and opens the driver's-side door. The minute I see her struggle into a standing position, I sit up and scramble into the passenger's seat. My head swims and black dots dance at the corners of my vision—the drugs Betty gave me are probably still in my system—but I manage to grab the keys out of the ignition.

"What the—" Betty starts to say as she notices what I'm doing. She lunges for me, claws at my shoulder, and tries to catch hold of my Coke-stained shirt, but her cotton gloves make it impossible for her to get a good grip.

I twist violently and wrench the fabric out of her hands, then snatch her glasses right off her face. She cries out and tries to catch my wrist, but I grab her enormous handbag from the passenger's seat and use it as a shield, and she rears up and bumps her head on the doorframe. Something tumbles onto the driver's seat, and I seize it automatically—the more potential weapons I can take from her, the better. Then I throw open the passenger's door, and in seconds I'm out on the asphalt on my own two feet, glorious open highway stretching away from me in every direction.

Betty holds onto the hood of the car and makes her way toward me as quickly as she can. "Get back here!" she screeches. Her voice sounds incredibly strange all of a sudden, and when I look down at what I'm clutching in my sweaty, shaking fingers, I see why.

Oh my God, *I'm holding Betty's dentures in my hand.*

My stomach lurches with disgust, and I shriek and throw them as hard as I can. They land in the middle of the highway, where an SUV runs over them and scatters individual false teeth all over the road. I throw the glasses next and wait until I see a car drive over them and snap them right in two. And then I run.

When I look back over my shoulder, Betty's trying to

follow me, leaning on the median for support and moving faster than I would've expected. She must be running on adrenaline, like those mothers you see on TV who suddenly have super strength for the minute it takes to lift cars off their babies. "You ungrateful little—" she pants.

I don't hear what Betty calls me over the sound of the semi that rushes by on my right, so close that the wind it creates hits me like a wall and almost knocks me over. I scrape my shin as I scramble over the concrete median, and blood trickles down my leg. But I put it out of my mind; I can deal with that later, when I'm safe. The pain actually makes my mind feel sharper.

There's a glowing green gas station sign on the other side of the highway, no more than half a mile away, and I set my sights on it. At the best of times, I could run that distance in three minutes flat, and even semidrugged, I should be able to make it in less than ten. I'm sure I'll find someone there who can help me.

It's amazing how many cars are on the highway this late at night—there's a pretty steady stream of traffic in all three lanes. But the speeding cars feel far less dangerous than the woman behind me, who's now screaming, "*Annemarie, I love you! Don't leave me!*" When I glance back, she has her walker out and is plowing toward me as its uneven legs totter and tip. Her blue-tinted hair whips around in the cars' slipstream, there's a deranged fire in her eyes, and one of her bony hands is outstretched toward me like a zombie claw.

The moment there's a break in the cars, I rush out onto the highway and sprint for the barrier on the other side. I'm a little woozy, and my adrenaline barely carries me across before a blue van speeds by behind me, tossing a few stray pieces of gravel into the backs of my legs. It lets out a loud honk as it passes. "Thank you," I whisper to the traffic gods as I press my hands against the cool concrete barrier.

When I turn around to check on Betty, she's still on the other side, standing under a streetlight. She looks so helpless and frail that a small part of me actually feels bad for her. But a much larger part wants to get as far away from her as possible.

I climb over the barrier and fly toward the gas station as if my life depends on it.

20

I start yelling for help when I'm a block or so away from the gas station, hoping someone filling up their tank will hear me and rush to my rescue. But nobody comes, and when I finally arrive, panting and sweaty, I realize the station is closed for the night. There's not a single car at the pumps, and the little convenience store is dark and empty. I push on the glass door with all my strength, just to make sure, but it's definitely locked. A sign in the window informs me that it'll open again at six in the morning.

Good thing a locked door has no power to keep me out. I've been preparing for this exact moment all month.

I've got seven lock picks left, and one of them is the squiggly tipped one used for raking the pins. My hands tremble as I fumble the pick and the tension wrench out of my pouch, but I hear Edna's voice in my head telling me I'm a hollow reed, that I should look inside the lock with my third eye and politely ask it to open. "Please," I whisper into the little silver keyhole. "I really, really need to get inside and use the phone." I feel completely ridiculous, but there's nobody here to see me, and I'm desperate.

And maybe there really is something to it, because for the first time ever, the pins seem *eager* to pop into place. After I rake them a couple times, four of the five bounce neatly up into the cylinder. Number five is trickier, but in less than three minutes, I get that one, too—a personal record. I wish I could tell Edna. The wrench turns in my hand, and I'm through the door and inside the cool, quiet store, which smells like gasoline and coffee. I can't turn the overhead fluorescents on without giving away my location, but everything glows softly in the light of the humming drink coolers along one wall. I slide the dead bolt into place, and it makes me feel a little safer.

Then again, Betty can probably pick locks too.

The clock above the counter reads 1:18 a.m., only a little more than an hour from when Betty and I started driving, and I'm relieved that we can't be that far out of town. I know from watching movies that there are sometimes silent alarm buttons in gas stations, but I can't find anything like that behind the counter, so I grab the grimy beige handset instead. There are oily orange smudges all over the receiver, as if the clerk had been talking on the phone while eating Cheetos.

I'm about to dial 911, but then I think about the story I'll have to tell them when someone answers. *My grandmother's crazy old-lady friend who can't even walk drugged me with a Slurpee and tied me up with duct tape and tried to take me to a secret cabin in the woods, but I escaped and ran across the highway and picked a lock on a convenience store.* Nobody's going to believe that. If I were a 911 operator, I wouldn't believe it either.

My heart pounds as I glance outside the door, half expecting to see Betty out there. Taking her keys and glasses would've slowed her down for sure, but I'm willing to bet she knows how to hot-wire a car, and any good criminal would keep a spare pair of glasses in her purse. It's only a matter of time before she peels into this Citgo station and finds me.

I can't call my grandmother, since she doesn't have a cell phone, and I don't know Cookie's or Edna's numbers. The only numbers I do know are my parents' and Ben's— all useless—and Maddie's cell number, which seems like my best bet. She won't be able to help me herself, but if she wakes up her parents, I'm sure they'll come get me. I hate to ask Maddie for help, considering how our last conversation went, but I know she'll see that what's happening right now is much more important than our fight. Plus, I can't think of any other options.

I swallow my pride and dial.

But Maddie's phone just rings and rings and rings. I call her five times before I realize she must've put it on silent before she went to sleep. Every time her voice mail message starts playing and I hear her happy, giggly voice telling me to leave a message, it feels like I've been kicked in the stomach. What if I've lost her for good and *Go call your new BFF Brianna if you want someone to listen to you* is the last thing she ever says to me?

Wait a minute. *Brianna.*

The invitation is still there in my pocket, folded into a tight square and embossed with her address and phone number. She can actually get in touch with my grandmother, who's probably sitting right outside her house in her big black van.

I pick up the phone again and dial. If this doesn't work, I honestly don't know what I'm going to do. I guess I'll have to hide behind this convenience store counter all night and try to get the clerk to help me in the morning.

Five hours seems like a ridiculously long time to wait.

The phone rings six times and goes to voice mail. I'm sure Brianna's sleeping too, but I slam down the phone, pick it up, and dial again. On my fourth call Brianna finally answers. "*What?*" she snaps, croaky and hoarse and super annoyed.

I don't think I've ever been so happy to hear someone's voice. "Brianna!" I shout. "It's AJ." When she doesn't say anything, I say, "AJ Johansen?"

"Yeah, I know who you are. What do you want? What *time* is it?"

"Listen, I know it's late, but I need you to do me a really, really big favor. I'm in trouble, and I really need to talk to my grandmother, and I need you to get her for me."

"Wait, what? Why are you calling *me*? Don't you *live* with your grandmother?"

"Yeah, but I'm not with her right now. She's actually . . . um . . . this is going to sound strange, but I think she might be sitting in your driveway in a van, a big black one. Do you think you could keep me on the line and take your phone out to her?"

Brianna's silent for a minute, and I picture her struggling to wake up. "Is this some kind of joke?" she finally says.

"*No,*" I say, and my voice comes out desperate and pleading. "Come on, please? This is really, *really* important."

"Why would your grandmother be in my driveway?"

"It doesn't matter," I say. "Brianna, I'm hiding in a gas station from someone who tried to kidnap me, and I need help. I need to talk to my grandmother. Can you please get her? *Please?*"

"Someone *kidnapped* you?" I hear the rustle of blankets.

"Yes! Can you help me?"

"I should probably get my dad," she says. "I'm not going out there alone in the middle of the night. Hang on a second, okay?"

"That's fine," I say. My grandmother will have trouble explaining why she's on the Westlakes' property at one in the morning, but that's not my problem. I told her not to go.

I hear Brianna's voice say, "Dad? Dad?" but then all I hear is a lot of mumbling—she must have her hand over the microphone. After a couple of horrible, tense minutes, she finally comes back and says, "Are you still there?"

"Yeah."

"My dad and I are going outside, okay?" She sounds scared, but against all odds, she's actually taking me seriously and doing her best to help. I never thought Brianna had it in her.

"Thank you so much," I say.

There are more muffled sounds, and then Brianna says, "I see the van. Oh, they see us, too—wait, they're backing up. I think they're leaving. AJ, *what* is even happening right now?"

"*Run!*" I shout. "Please, catch her. Just you, not your dad. Hold up the phone and yell that I'm on the other end and that I need help!"

She does, and I hear the sound of screeching tires and my grandmother's incredulous voice. "*Annemarie's* on the phone? Where is she? Why did she call *you*?"

"She says—"

"Give me that." I hear a small scuffle, and then my grandmother's on the line. "Annemarie, where are you? What have you done to Betty? I warned you that you were *not* to interfere with—"

"Grandma Jo," I say, cutting her off, "I really, really need your help."

She must hear how serious my voice is, because she stops yelling. "Tell me what happened," she says.

I spill out the whole story, and she listens without interrupting. When I'm finished, she says, "Oh heavens, not *again*. I knew we shouldn't have let Betty have so much contact with you. That woman has no self-control." I hear an exasperated sigh. "Where are you now, Annemarie?"

"I don't know," I say. "A Citgo station on the highway, but I was unconscious while Betty was driving, and nothing looks familiar."

"You've disabled Betty?"

"I took her keys and smashed her glasses, but I'm not sure how long that's going to stop her. She might have extra glasses, and she probably knows how to hot-wire a car, right?"

"No matter," Grandma Jo says. "Our headsets have GPS; we can track her."

"She threw her headset out the window before she drugged me," I tell her.

"Of course she did." Grandma Jo sighs. "Look around behind the counter, Annemarie. Do you see anything with an address on it? An inspection certificate or something?"

I don't know what an inspection certificate looks like, but there are a few shelves behind the counter, so I start digging through them. There's a stained University of Illinois hoodie, a single Converse sneaker, a couple pencils with teeth marks in them, a baseball cap, a half-melted chocolate bar covered in lint . . . and a pile of junk mail.

"I found something!" I shout, and I read off the address

to her. I've never even heard of the town I'm apparently in, and I hope it's not too far away.

"Cookie, map this on your phone," Grandma Jo says.

"Roger that." About thirty seconds pass, and then I hear Cookie say, "Got it. She's right here, see?"

"Good, that's not so far," says Grandma Jo's voice. "We're coming for you, Annemarie."

My knees go weak with relief, and I sink onto the filthy gas station floor. "Thank you, Grandma Jo. Thank you so much."

"Let's go, Cookie!"

"Roger!"

"Hang on, that's my phone, you can't—" comes Brianna's voice.

"Let go, you ungrateful child. Can't you see I need it more than you do?"

"*What* is going on here?" shouts a man's voice. "Are you trying to steal my daughter's phone? And why are you even—"

"*Drive*, Cookie!"

There's a loud screeching sound, an enormous crash, and the sound of several people screaming. "What's going on?" I yell.

"Who *are* you?" shouts Brianna's dad. "What are you

doing on my property? I'm calling the police!"

"I thought the car was in reverse," comes Cookie's mournful voice. "I'm still not used to this dang van. Now it won't even—"

"Give me my phone!" screeches Brianna.

"Annemarie, we've hit a little snag over here," Grandma Jo's voice says, totally calmly. "We've also hit the Westlakes' garage. I'll tell the police to track down Betty and pick you up. Stay hidden and don't go anywhere."

"Okay," I say. I pull my knees up to my chest, suddenly aware that I'm shivering, even in the warm night air.

"And Annemarie?"

"Yeah?"

"I'm sorry about what happened tonight. You've been very brave. I respect a girl who puts her skills to use and does what needs to be done without making a fuss."

Before I can respond, Grandma Jo hangs up.

I spend the next half hour huddled behind the counter, jumping at every sound. On an endless loop inside my head, I picture Betty throwing a brick through the glass door and barging into my safe little hiding space with her toothless mouth and uneven walker, ready to whisk me away to a place where nobody will ever find me. For every endless, uneventful minute that ticks by, I grow more nervous, more sure nobody's actually coming to help me after all. Maybe Brianna's dad had my grandmother and her friends arrested before they could notify the police. I wonder if I should call 911 myself and try to explain the situation after all.

I'm about to grab the Cheetos-dusted receiver when I hear a car door slam outside, followed by the sound of quick footsteps approaching the convenience store. My heart starts banging so hard I'm pretty sure people can hear it five miles away, but then a male voice calls, "Miss AJ? Are you in there?"

It doesn't seem possible that *Stanley* is here right now—maybe I'm so stressed out that I'm hallucinating. But when I peek over the counter, there he is on the other side of the glass door. "It's just me," he says. "Can you let me in?"

I run to the door and undo the dead bolt, and then he's inside, wrapping his arms around me in an enormous bear hug. He's wearing a worn green T-shirt, and the fabric feels soft against my cheek. Since that time Stanley hugged me at the soccer field, I've imagined him doing it again a zillion times. But in my made-up scenarios, it was never in an empty convenience store in the middle of the night, and I was never crying, something I suddenly seem to be doing.

"I came as soon as your grandmother called," he says. "Are you okay?"

"I think so," I say.

Stanley lets go of me and looks me up and down. "AJ, you're bleeding."

It's only then that I even remember my scraped leg. The bleeding has mostly stopped, but there are thin streams of dried blood snaking all the way down my shin, like the veins of a leaf. "It's fine," I say. "It doesn't even hurt. Can we go home?"

"We have to wait here for the police, kiddo," Stanley says. "They're on their way here, and they're on Betty's tail."

"How did you get here so fast? Where's Grandma Jo?"

"She and her friends are at the police station. Something to do with trespassing and destroying someone's garage? I don't really know. My parents' house is ten minutes from here, so your grandma asked me to come help out. She thought you might want to see a friendly face."

I nod hard. "I did. I'm really glad you're here."

"I should call the cops and tell them I'm with you. One second, okay?"

I nod, and Stanley makes the call. When he's finished, I ask, "Did they find her?"

"Not yet," he says. "But your grandmother said you took her keys and her glasses, so she probably hasn't gotten very far. That was really quick thinking." He wraps an arm around my shoulders and gives me a little squeeze, and something like happiness blooms in my chest.

"Thanks," I say.

"Do you want to tell me what happened?"

I'm sure I'm going to have to tell the police everything, and the thought of repeating the whole story an extra time feels exhausting, so I shake my head. "Not really, if that's okay."

"No problem. Hey, I know what we can do instead."

Those drugs Betty gave me must've done something seriously weird to my brain, because for a split second, I think Stanley's going to dip me back and kiss me like in one of Amy's sappy movies. But instead he says, "Go sit back down behind the counter, okay? You're probably safest where nobody can see you. I'll be there in a second. I promise I'm not leaving the store."

I nod and huddle down in my spot by the Cheetos phone. When Stanley joins me a minute later, he's holding a pint of mint chocolate chip ice cream from the convenience store freezer and two plastic spoons. He reaches for his wallet and counts four dollars onto the counter next to the cash register, and I want to hug him for being so careful not to steal.

"Your favorite, right?" he asks as he settles back down beside me.

I nod. "Thank you," I say, and I don't just mean for the ice cream.

"Of course," he says, and I feel like he gets it.

We sit there behind the counter in silence, our arms pressed together from shoulder to elbow, and spoon ice cream into our mouths. Even before the police arrive and shatter the quiet with their sirens, I start to feel safe again.

21

The rest of the evening is a blur. A police car and an ambulance arrive at the gas station, and even though I say I'm not hurt, a couple of paramedics rush me to the hospital anyway. Stanley sits in the back of the ambulance with me and holds my hand, and it's so distracting that I barely remember anything else about the ride. In the emergency room, the doctors bandage my knee, examine me from head to toe, and do a blood test to try to figure out what Betty used to knock me out. When they find out my parents are in South America and my grandmother has been arrested, they ask if there's someone else who can come get me, and I tell them to call Maddie's parents. I can't wait to see Maddie's face when she finds out what happened to me tonight.

By the time the doctors give me a clean bill of health, I'm completely exhausted. But instead of letting me sleep, a pale, skinny police officer with freckles sprinkled across his nose takes me into a little room and makes a video recording of me telling the whole story of the kidnapping. He keeps asking the same questions over and over and over: Why was I with Betty in the car? Where did she say she was taking me? How did I manage to pick the lock on the convenience store door? It's hard to answer his questions without getting my grandmother, Cookie, and Edna in trouble. I'm not sure if you can be punished for *planning* to steal something, but I feel like it's safest to pretend I don't know anything about a heist. Instead, I tell him Brianna's family owns one of Edna's paintings and that she wanted to see its new home, just from the outside. I say I learned to pick locks by watching videos on the Internet and that I'd been practicing in my grandmother's house earlier that day, which is why I had my picks with me. The officer looks skeptical, but he doesn't push me. Sometimes it pays to be twelve.

"That's all we need from you tonight, Annemarie," he finally says when I've told the story about five times. "You've been very brave."

"Did you find Betty?" I ask.

He nods. "She's in custody. You did an excellent job immobilizing her."

"What will happen to her now?" I ask. I wish I didn't care, that I could think of Betty as purely evil, but part of me can't help feeling bad for her. Like I told Grandma Jo a few days ago, you can't ever really know what's going on in someone else's head.

"She'll likely go back to prison," he says. "Kidnapping is a serious offense, especially since she transported you across state lines."

"Wait," I say. "*Back* to prison?"

"She served three years for kidnapping a seven-year-old girl in 1991," says the officer, and I remember all the comments Edna and Cookie made about what Betty was up to that year. The trial they all followed so closely must've been hers. Man, my head is spinning.

"We'll need to speak with your parents as soon as they get home," the officer continues. He slides a business card across the table. "Please don't hesitate to call me if you remember any other details about tonight, no matter how small they seem."

I make my way back out into the waiting room, so tired I'm basically asleep on my feet, and find Maddie's mom waiting for me in the ugly orange chair next to Stanley's.

Her sandy hair is a tangled mess, and she's wearing a gray hoodie over the ratty old American Cancer Society shirt she sleeps in. I guess she was so eager to come get me that she didn't even bother to change. It's exactly how my own mom would act, and I have to swallow hard around the lump that rises in my throat.

When she sees me, Mrs. Kolhein springs to her feet like a jack-in-the-box and pulls me into a tight hug. "AJ, honey," she whispers into my hair. "Are you all right? I can't believe what you've been through tonight."

I bury my face in her shoulder and breathe in the familiar smell of Maddie's detergent. "I'm okay," I say. "Just really tired."

"She's a tough girl," says Stanley's voice, and I suddenly realize he's right next to us. I picture him telling Talia about all of this tomorrow, emphasizing how brave and cool I am, and I smile up at him, suddenly shy.

"How'd it go with the cops?" he asks.

"All right, I think? I don't really know." I turn back to Mrs. Kolhein. "Is Maddie here?"

"No, honey, she's sleeping. It's four in the morning. But you two will have plenty of time to talk tomorrow—I've worked everything out with the police so you can stay with us until your parents get home. Is that all right with you?"

A few hours ago I was sure things were over forever between Maddie and me, but now all I want to do is climb into the second twin bed in her room and fall asleep to the sound of her breathing. Next to everything else that's happened, our fight seems so petty and stupid.

"Yes, that's perfect," I say. "Let's go home."

The doctors at the hospital give Mrs. Kolhein medicine to help me sleep, which is totally ridiculous—I'm out cold the second I'm buckled into the car. When we get to their house, Maddie's mom has to half carry me up the stairs. I don't even manage to change into pajamas before I fall facedown into bed.

My night is filled with dreams of running from various things: a swarm of wasps, a taxidermy bear that has come back to life, all four of the grannies dressed in swan feathers and threatening me with giant lock picks. Sometimes my feet feel so heavy I can barely move them. Sometimes I can't open my eyes all the way, so I can't see where I'm going. Sometimes my wrists and ankles are tied. I can feel wings and claws and fingers grazing the back of my neck, and I know that if I slow down even for a minute, they're going to—

I wake up with a gasp. My legs are tangled in the sheets,

the comforter's on the floor, and my arms are trapped under me. Every single one of my muscles hurts, but I can't tell if it's from being tied up or from thrashing in my sleep. My heart starts to slow down as I look at Maddie's cheery butter-yellow walls glowing in the sunlight that streams through the windows. Then I notice my friend standing by the foot of my bed, staring at me with wide eyes.

"Mom sent me up here to check on you, and you were, like, wrestling with the mattress in your sleep," she says. "I didn't know what to do. Are you okay?"

I sit up and push my tangled hair out of my face. "Yeah. I was having a nightmare."

"Okay. Good. I mean, not good. But good that you're okay."

"Yeah."

The two of us stare at each other for a few endless seconds. Maddie's only about five feet from me, but she feels incredibly far away. When I can't take the silence any longer, I blurt out, "Maddie, listen, I don't want—"

At the exact same time, she says, "My mom told me what happened, and I'm so—"

We both burst out laughing, and spiderweb cracks appear in the barrier of awkwardness between us. I feel like if I give it a couple good kicks, it'll shatter. "You first," I say.

"I just can't believe you got *kidnapped*."

"Me neither." I feel kind of removed from the whole thing, like it's something that happened to another girl I don't know very well.

"My mom said it was a friend of your grandma's?"

"She was this sweet little old lady. She always seemed super nice. Honestly, she was the least weird of my grandmother's friends. I didn't see it coming at all."

"Did you really pick a lock on a convenience store?"

"Yeah." I smile. "Want me to teach you?"

"*Obviously*. How did you even know how to do that?"

I consider repeating the story I told the police last night. But if I want things to go back to normal between Maddie and me, I have to tell her the truth. It's not up to me to protect Grandma Jo and her friends anymore.

"There's a lot of stuff I haven't told you since I went to my grandma's," I say.

"Yeah, 'cause you've been telling it all to the freaking *Bananas*." Maddie's clearly trying to be gentle with me because of what I've been through, but I can tell she's still really angry, too. She looks down at her toes, which she's burrowing into the rug so hard it's like she's trying to dig to China.

"No, Maddie, I haven't told this stuff to *anyone*. Definitely not the Bananas. It's, like, *seriously* secret." She finally looks up at me, and I lower my voice. "If I tell you what really happened, do you promise not to tell anyone? Not even Amy or your parents?"

Her eyes get bigger. "Of course."

"Close the door, okay?"

Maddie shuts the door, then climbs onto the bed next to me, and I scoot over to make room for her. I start with the night my grandmother caught me breaking into the storage room, and I plow right through the bird heist, the lock-picking lessons, the bear heist, my scouting mission at Brianna's party, my attempts to convince my grandmother's friends not to steal the painting, and the kidnapping. Maddie listens to the whole thing, her mouth hanging slightly open. I can tell she's soaking everything up, and best of all, I can tell she believes me.

When I'm finished, I expect her to ask a ton of questions, but instead she just says, "Wow. I mean . . . *wow.*"

"Yeah."

"Wow." She shoves me with her shoulder so hard I tip over. "I can't believe you didn't *tell* me any of this! I thought we told each other everything!"

"My grandmother said I had to keep it a secret or she'd make my life miserable. I was afraid she'd bugged all my stuff, so I never knew when it was safe to talk."

"Wow," Maddie says yet again. "Are you going to be traumatized for life?"

I shrug. "Actually, the whole thing was kind of fun for a while. I got to sneak around and, like, serve justice or whatever, you know? I really thought it was for a good cause at the beginning. Even when it got complicated, part of me didn't really want it to end."

"Well, it's over now, anyway."

"Yeah."

Maddie shifts around and crosses her legs. "Do you think your grandma's going to get in trouble?"

"I don't know. I mean, she's already in trouble for driving into Brianna's garage, but I tried to keep her out of the whole thing when I talked to the policeman last night. I'm not sure he believed my lame story, though. It looks pretty suspicious that she was at Brianna's house in the middle of the night."

Maddie toys with the edge of the sheet. "So . . . you're really not friends with her?"

"With Brianna? *No*, Maddie, I swear. I only started talking to her 'cause you told me to, remember? You said I should make her jealous and put her in her place."

"That's what I thought you were doing at first, but

then it seemed like you started to mean it," Maddie says. "It seemed like you'd actually started caring about . . . that stuff. Money and expensive clothes and things. And then, when you went to her party even though you said you weren't going to, I just thought . . . I don't know, it kind of seemed like you were too good for me now or something." She abandons the sheet and starts picking at a tiny hole in the cuff of her pajama pants.

"I don't care about any of that. And that party was totally ridiculous. You should've seen the way the Bananas were drooling over the makeup ladies, like they were movie stars or something. All I could think about the whole time was how I'd rather be eating Zappetto's and playing *Mega Ninja Explosion* with you. I can't wait to move back home and have everything go back to normal."

"I bet you'll miss *Stanley*, though." Maddie makes a stupid goo-goo-eyed expression.

My cheeks grow warmer as I think about the way I cried all over his shirt last night. "Maybe a little," I admit. "But it's not like he feels the same way about me. Anyway, he has a girlfriend."

"Hey, that kind of thing never stops Brianna. That's what she *says*, anyway." Maddie rolls her eyes. "What a liar. She's such a spoiled little brat."

I've just gotten my best friend back, and I don't want to do anything to ruin it, but I feel like I should get absolutely everything out in the open. "I actually feel kind of bad for her," I say.

Maddie snorts. "For Brianna? *Why?* She gets everything she wants!"

"She doesn't, though. She has nice stuff, but her parents are horrible. Have you ever seen them at a soccer game, even once? And her mom skipped her birthday party because she wanted to go to the gym."

"*What?* For real?"

"Yeah. Brianna was super upset."

Maddie's quiet for a second. "Okay, I guess I feel a little sorry for her," she finally says. "But I still basically hate her."

"Girls?" Mrs. Kolhein calls upstairs. "I made pancakes. You hungry?"

I hadn't realized I was until that moment, but my stomach growls loudly in response, and Maddie and I both laugh. "Be right down," I call back.

Maddie clambers off the bed. "So, you're going to stay with us until your parents get home?"

"I think so . . . if that's okay with you?"

She looks at me like I'm crazy. "Of course it's okay

with me. Hey, do you want to watch *Tentacle* later? Jordan said I could borrow it."

"Yeah, sure. Is Amy coming too?"

"She wouldn't like it—too much screaming and not enough kissing, remember?"

I laugh. "Yeah, you're probably right."

"I mean, I can invite her if you want. But I thought maybe . . ."

I look at my best friend in her wrinkled T-shirt and her stretched-out pink-and-green-striped pajama pants, her hair totally flat on one side and standing up in all different directions on the other. I'm so grateful to have her back that I feel a weird pressure in my chest, like my heart's going to explode if it gets any bigger.

"No," I say. "You're right. It should just be us."

22

Two weeks later

The day of our last soccer game before the play-offs is so hot and humid that stepping outside feels like being wrapped in a microwaved wet towel. Ordinarily, I'd walk over to the field with Maddie, but when my parents offer me a ride in the air-conditioned minivan, I gladly accept. It's only partly because of the temperature—even though I'd never admit this out loud, I kind of can't get enough of my family these days. Being home is so blissfully normal, and even though I miss Debbie's cooking, it's amazing to be back in a house filled with regular furniture and dog hair and laughter and hugs from people who love me in a totally nondisturbing way.

"This heat is nothing compared to the jungle," my dad says as he hoists a couple camping chairs and a cooler full of drinks into the trunk. "There's a reason people wear loincloths there. I'm thinking about changing into one before the game. You wouldn't be embarrassed by that, right?"

Mom comes out of the house with a Fenton's Foxes flag in one hand and Snickers's leash in the other. My dog hops into the back with me and lies down on my feet with his tongue hanging out, and even though that makes me even hotter, I let him stay. I dig my fingers into the fur around his neck and give him a good scratch, and he licks my leg to say thanks. Mom climbs into the front and starts fixing her ponytail, which is coming loose—her hair is super fine and slippery, like mine. I get a whiff of her grapefruit shampoo as she swoops it up, and I breathe it in. I hadn't even realized how much I'd missed that smell until she got home from the airport and hugged me.

"So, you guys are playing the Lumberjacks today?" she says. There's this lumber store a few towns over called Lumber Jack's, and the team they sponsor is called the Lumberjacks. Lumber Jack's Lumberjacks. So dumb.

"Yup," I say. "We're going to kick some Lumberjack butt."

"You're gonna hit them like a falling tree," my dad says, then makes this really cheesy *Timmmmm-berrrrrr!* sound. Snickers starts barking, and I roll my eyes, but I also laugh.

We're at the field in less than five minutes, and my parents settle down next to Maddie's on the sidelines. Maddie and Amy wave at me from where they're warming up across the field, and I wave back and grab my shin guards and cleats out of my bag. Now that things are okay between Maddie and me, it doesn't really bother me to see her and Amy hanging out alone anymore. It's weird how that happens.

Before I run off to join them, my dad and I do our traditional good-luck high five, which involves an elbow bump and a hip bump and sticking your tongue out and spinning around. It looks really stupid, but I don't care at all—I've missed this ritual while he's been away. I'm not even embarrassed when I see Brianna watching us from across the field. I wave at her as I jog toward my friends, and she looks around to make sure nobody's looking before she waves back. She hasn't exactly been my biggest fan since the whole incident with Grandma Jo.

Amy passes me the ball, and Maddie shoots me a big smile, showing off the new hot-pink rubber bands on her braces. "Nice teeth," I say.

"I see you brought your boyfriend to watch you play," Amy teases.

"Eww, Amy! That's my *dad*!"

She rolls her eyes. "Not *him*. I know who your dad is!" She points to the sidelines, and there, walking toward my parents with a big smile on his face, is *Stanley*. When he sees me looking, he waves, and my organs start playing a really fast game of musical chairs. When they stop moving, my stomach is the one left without a place to sit.

"Why is he—" I start to say, but then I notice some-thing much, *much* weirder. Grandma Jo is leaning on Stanley's arm, holding up her skirts with her other hand and staring down the grass like it'll be really sorry if it dares to get her dirty. She's wearing her usual black dress with the high lace collar, and she stops every so often to pat her forehead with a lace-trimmed black handker-chief. I've invited her to countless soccer games since I started playing in kindergarten, but this is the first time she's actually shown up.

"Whoa," I say. "What is *she* doing here?"

Maddie turns to see what I'm looking at. "Is that your *grandma*? I thought she hated that you play soccer."

"She does."

"She looks exactly like I pictured her," Amy says. "She must be dying in that dress."

"I'm pretty sure that dress is actually attached to her body," I say.

The three of us watch as Stanley gets Grandma Jo
settled in a folding chair with a cushion behind her back,
near my parents but not quite close enough to have a conversation. Mom and Dad wave, but I see them exchange
a Look-with-a-capital-L the moment my grandmother
turns away. Since I got kidnapped on her watch, neither
of them has been particularly friendly toward her.

Coach Adrian blows his whistle and calls us into a
huddle, and I'm forced to stop thinking about the weirdness on the sidelines and focus on my team. It's more
important than ever that I play well, now that my parents
and grandmother and Stanley are all watching.

"You guys have done great work this season," Coach
Adrian says when we're all huddled up, a mass of orange
jerseys pressed shoulder to shoulder. "I want to see some
fierce, smart playing out there today, okay? You deserve to
go to the playoffs, and if you give this game a hundred and
ten percent, I have no doubt you will. What do you say?"

"Yeah!" we all scream, and my heart speeds up like it
always does when I feel like a part of something bigger
than myself.

"Hands in the middle," Coach Adrian says, and we pile
up our hands and shout, *"Go Foxes!"* I have a quick flash of
memory of my hand piled up with Edna's and Cookie's and

Betty's and Grandma Jo's inside a dark van, but I push it away.

The game goes better than I ever could've hoped. Maddie and I play seamlessly together, always open for each other's passes, always covering each other's backs. She's constantly right where I want her to be, like we're sharing the same brain. She and Brianna score a goal each, and I score two of my own. When the clock finally runs down, we're two points ahead, and my team smashes into a screaming, cheering, sweaty, grass-stained group hug.

Everyone's families rush onto the field, and my dad picks me up and spins me around. "Two goals! I'm so proud of you, AJ. You're going to the playoffs!"

The second he lets go of me, my mom swoops me up in a hug and kisses the side of my sweaty head. "You were *spectacular*," she says. I'm a little embarrassed by this super public display of affection, but then I see Brianna heading off the field alone, like always, and I remember how lucky I am.

"Thanks, guys," I say. "Hang on a second, okay? I have to do something really quick."

My mom lets me go, and I jog after Brianna. When I call her name, she turns around, and her long hair whips out behind her. Somehow, it still doesn't have any tangles. "Yeah?"

"You played really well today," I say. "I just wanted to tell you that."

Maddie comes up beside me and drapes an arm over my shoulder—a little possessively, I think—but she gives Brianna a genuine smile. "You really did," she says. "That goal was seriously impressive."

Brianna looks surprised; I guess she's not used to the people she tortures turning around and being nice to her. But she smiles back, like what we said really means something. "Thanks," she says. "Yours too. You coming for ice cream?"

"Definitely," I say.

"AJ," someone calls from the sidelines, and when I turn around, I see Stanley waving me over. He has one of those ridiculous foam fingers on one hand—I have no idea where that came from—and with his other hand, he's shielding Grandma Jo from the sun with a black lace parasol.

"Better go talk to your *boyfriend*," Maddie snickers.

I shove her shoulder. "Shut up. I'll see you at Fenton's, okay?" As I jog toward Stanley and my grandmother, I hear Maddie making loud kissy noises behind me.

Stanley holds out his hand for a high five, and I slap his palm. "Great game," he says. "You were on fire out there."

"Thanks! And thank you so much for coming." I turn

to my grandmother. "Hi, Grandma Jo. I'm really glad you're here too."

My grandmother's sitting with her hands folded in her lap, prim and proper as always. As she looks me up and down, taking in my messy hair and dirty knees and the streaks of mud running up one entire side of my body, I start to feel nervous. We haven't seen each other at all since my parents brought me by to pick up my luggage, and since we weren't alone, we couldn't discuss anything that happened the night of the kidnapping. As usual, I can't tell from her expression whether she's pleased with me or disgusted by me.

She opens her mouth to speak, and I prepare myself for a comment about how I should play a calmer, more dignified sport, like croquet. But instead she says, "You did *very* well, Annemarie."

I'm so surprised that I can't think of anything to say for a second. "Thank you," I finally manage to choke out.

"You played with great *integrity*," she says. "You're such a *discreet* athlete. You never throw your teammates under the bus, no matter what happens. That's an admirable trait in a lady."

Her icy blue eyes bore into mine, and I suddenly realize Grandma Jo's not talking about soccer at all. She's thanking me for protecting her and Cookie and Edna when I gave my statement to the police. "I'm glad you were . . . pleased with my performance," I say.

She nods. "Very much so."

"How are your, um, *bridge games* going these days?"

"They've been suspended for the moment," she says. "The players are in agreement that perhaps the game of bridge has run its course. We're considering taking up another hobby."

I want to tell her that's wonderful, but my parents have joined us now and are listening to our conversation, and I know that would sound pretty weird. So instead I say, "Well, I guess that leaves more time for . . . umm . . . *badminton*, right?"

Her eyebrows slant down into that V shape I've come to know so well. "Badminton?"

"You know," I say. "That game with the *birdies*?"

Understanding clicks into place behind her eyes, and her mouth crooks up halfway, the closest she ever gets to smiling. "Yes, absolutely," she says. "I'll be spending lots of time with the birdies."

"You've taken up badminton, mother?" my dad says. "Did you ask the doctor if that's okay? Your foot hasn't even healed yet."

"Oh, don't fuss over me. I can't abide it." Grandma Jo swats his hand away and turns back to me. "In any case, I very much enjoyed . . . *participating* . . . in this *game* with you. You played your part with great aplomb. It was my pleasure to witness."

I give a little nod so she'll know I get it. "Thank you, Grandma Jo. That means a lot." Then I tease, "You know, if you liked watching me play soccer, maybe you could come to the skate park with me sometime."

She snorts. "Skateboarding is not a sport for respectable young ladies, AJ."

I knew that's what she would say. But what I wasn't prepared for was the way my name just came out of her mouth.

AJ. She actually called me AJ.

And when I look into Grandma Jo's eyes, there's something there that tells me things are going to be a little different between us from now on.

"Do you want to come to Fenton's and get ice cream with us?" I ask, and my parents stare at me, totally baffled.

My grandmother shakes her head. "I appreciate the invitation, but I have things to attend to." She looks up. "Stanley! It's time for our next engagement."

"Yes, ma'am," Stanley says, and as he helps Grandma Jo

out of her chair and tucks the cushion under his arm, he winks at me. "Don't be a stranger, Miss AJ," he says, and I tell him I won't.

Fenton's with the team is as raucous and celebratory as usual. Amy challenges Sabrina to an ice cream–eating contest, and they both end up rolling around on the sticky floor, clutching their foreheads and moaning about brain freeze. Maddie and I get one mint chocolate chip sundae and one caramel one and trade bites back and forth until the dishes are so clean they look like they've come straight out of the dishwasher. I'm tired and happy and sun-drenched, and I put my grandmother completely out of my mind as I celebrate with my friends.

That is, until my parents and I are back in the car, driving down the highway toward Zappetto's Pizzeria. As I'm staring out the window and idly pulling on Snickers's ears, I see something coming up on the side of the road that makes absolutely no sense. There's a small crew picking up trash with those long grabby poles, overseen by a policeman—just your typical group of people who've been assigned community service for small crimes. But some of these people aren't strangers. Under the orange safety vests, I spot a red pantsuit . . . a blowing tangle of scarves . . . and a long black dress with a high lace collar.

Despite how I tried to protect them, my grandmother and her friends still crashed through the Westlakes' garage door with their car. They still trespassed on private property and tried to steal Brianna's cell phone. And now they're paying for it by *picking up trash on the side of the highway*. I think about what Grandma Jo told me the day she first confiscated my phone: *If you break the rules, you have to deal with the consequences.* Seems like her own rule has come back to bite her in the butt.

If this had happened a couple months ago, I would've laughed and screamed and made certain my parents saw that my perfect grandmother wasn't so perfect after all. But instead I point in the opposite direction and say, "You guys, *look!*"

Both my parents peer out the driver's-side window. "What?" my mom asks. "Where? I don't see anything."

"There was this huge bird," I say. "I swear it looked like a parrot or something."

"It's possible," my dad says. "Some people have no idea how to take care of their pets."

"I can't believe I missed it," my mom says.

"Really, honey? You didn't see enough parrots in the rain forest?"

By the time they stop looking for the mysterious bird,

Grandma Jo and Edna and Cookie are far behind us, and I know my grandmother would approve of my exceedingly proper, discreet behavior.

For a second it's super weird, knowing Grandma Jo and I would see eye to eye on something. But when you look past the surface stuff—salad forks and skateboards and sewing and soccer—we actually have lots of things in common. We both work hard until we're the very best we can be. We're fiercely loyal to the people we love and try our best to guard their secrets. We're brave and resourceful, and we can think on our feet under pressure. We stand up for what we believe in, even when it's hard. And if we fail at something, we pick ourselves up, brush ourselves off, and try again.

I look out through the back window for one last glimpse of Grandma Jo in her orange vest. And I smile to myself as I realize that in my own way, I've become exactly what she hoped I'd be: the very definition of a respectable lady.

Acknowledgments

I'm incredibly grateful to the following people:

My editor, Amy Cloud: I'm so glad my geriatric thieves found a home with you. Thank you for sharing my bizarre sense of humor. Say the word and I'll kidnap Christopher Guest and hold him hostage until he makes a new movie just for you.

My superhero of an agent, Holly Root, who always encourages me when I send her e-mails that begin "So, this might be a really weird idea, but . . ." For you, I would gladly seal myself inside a wine cask, roll into Cakebread Cellars, and liberate a few cases of some fabulous vintage.

Everyone at Aladdin who worked so hard to make this book beautiful, especially my copy editor, Randie Lipkin. Better clear some room in your office for the antique printing press I'm planning to steal for you.

Angela Li, who drew me the most beautiful cover in the history of covers. I'll disable a museum security alarm and lift a painting for you any day. Da Vinci? Degas? Let me know and I'm on it.

My ingenious early readers, who make me look far cleverer than I really am: Lindsay Ribar, Michelle Schusterman, Caroline Carlson, Claire Legrand, Jennifer Malone, Kristen Kittscher, and Nicole Lisa. I've liberated a parrot for each of you and am currently teaching them to sing your favorite songs. I hope none of you are allergic. (I'd better liberate some Claritin too, just in case…)

Kristin Bailey, my exotic bird expert, who was always on hand to answer questions like "Can macaws imitate the sound of a creaking door?" And Joel Kocevar, who taught me the essentials of lock picking. I'm unfamiliar with your tastes, but perhaps you'll accept a sack of liberated gold bars? Or maybe a sack of gift cards? That would be a lot easier to carry.

Erica Kemmerling, who makes it easy to write fabulous little sisters by providing such an excellent example. I'm planning to infiltrate the pygmy puff hatchery and liberate a whole kerfluffle of puffs for you. (Yes, that's totally the right collective noun. Just trust me.)

And my mom, Susan Cherry, who raised me to believe that creativity and humor are important virtues. Thanks for not caring if I turned out to be a proper lady. For you, I've liberated the deed to a small island where it's always eighty-five degrees and sunny. Pack your bags.